ALWAYS
SOMETHING
SINGS

Book One in the Ada Reed Mystery Series

Roger Lynn Howell

coffeetown**press**

Kenmore, WA

coffeetownpress

A Coffeetown Press book published by Epicenter Press

Epicenter Press
6524 NE 181st St.
Suite 2
Kenmore, WA 98028

For more information go to:
www.Camelpress.com
www.Coffeetownpress.com
www.Epicenterpress.com
www.Rogerhowellbooks.com

Cover design by Scott Book
Design by Melissa Vail Coffman

Library of Congress Control Number: 2023936024

ISBN: 978-1-68492-117-1 (Trade Paper)
ISBN: 978-1-68492-118-8 (eBook)

Printed in the United States of America

For Helen, and with good reason. No one is tougher or kinder than my big sister, nor has anyone more surely known the country and the times I describe in this book. Heck, Helen's even worn a badge!

Acknowledgments

I WISH TO THANK THE MANY FRIENDS who persevered through several early drafts of this story, and especially Cliff, who insists with not all that much sarcasm, that he is head of my fan club. Susan, Clara, and Eleanor have been kind, patient, and supportive.

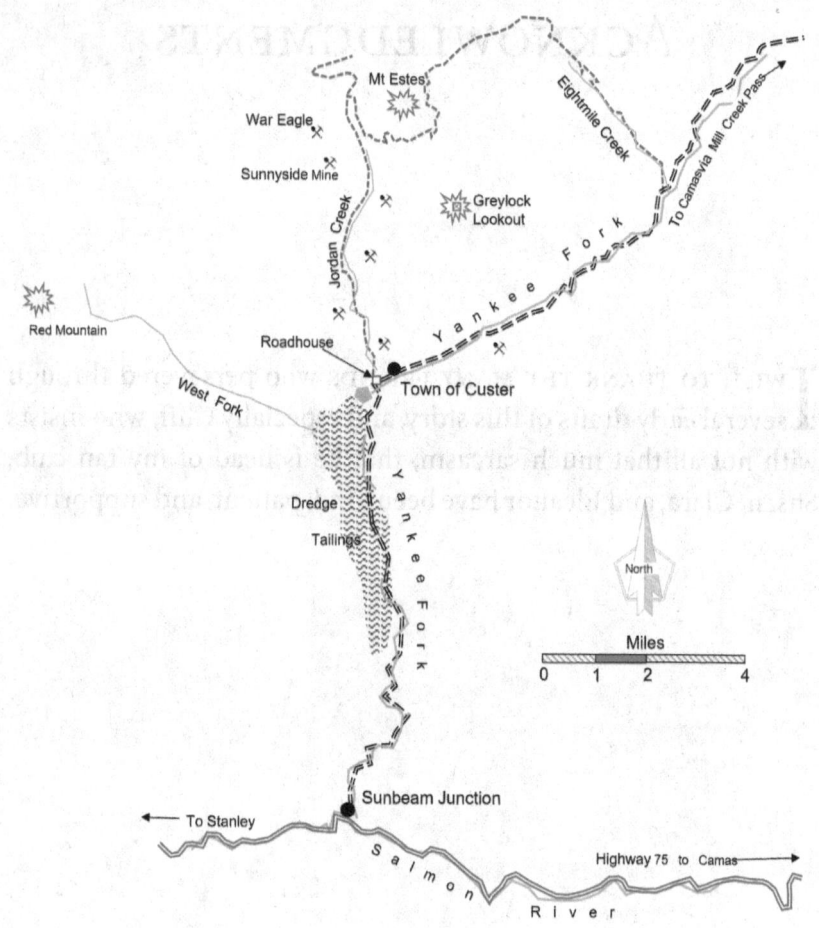

The Yankee Fork Country

CHAPTER ONE

THE YANKEE FORK SLIPPED THROUGH THE TOWN of Custer under a sharp crescent moon and lost itself in acres of willows, weirs, and earthworks. The waters reformed below town and again swirled and streamed in the moonlight before plunging through culverts into a broad, man-made pond.

A pair of smokestacks floated above the pond, disembodied by a mist that lay in the valley, and without warning black smoke erupted from one and then from both stacks. There was no sound but of birds calling from the mist, and for a few seconds more it was quiet until the rumble of diesel engines rolled through the bottoms. The sudden clamor scattered the birds and caused deer to start and turn their heads.

Less wary creatures looked up to see the smoke rise in twisting columns and felt the quickening vibration of engines through their rubber boots. It was another ten minutes before the engines warmed, and then the rubber-booted men threw switches that caused electric generators to come on. With the generators came lights from one end of the floating factory to the other, and station by station control boxes lit up, their signal bulbs flashing green, yellow, and red in the mist.

Dar Colemaker walked the screen deck from stern to bow as more machinery came on. He greeted foremen in red slickers hurrying through last cups of coffee, and workers in yellow puffing at smokes before the water started spraying. He ducked under heavy iron struts to check rocker arms and balanced along broad timbers to check for mud or gravel deposits that might gum up his operation. Colemaker carried a Zerk Gun, which he used to pump grease liberally at pivot points and axles.

The big machine components kicked in one by one: the trommel started its clanking rotation, pumps began to chug, and water sprayed over the shaker tables and rippled down the long sluice boxes. At the sound of a bell the stacker belt started up, although it and everything else were still running empty of feed, so the dredge was almost quiet. Engineers high in the pilothouse discussed the pattern they would work today, and their voices carried to the lower decks.

Colemaker ran the production deck and worked the levers at the top of the bucket line where it dropped its load of cobbles and gravel into the trommel. The trommel separated sands and gravels from the coarser material, which rolled down onto the stacker belt to be deposited out the stern. It was his fifth year on the gold dredge. It was a good job, and he'd managed to keep it even though his number had been called for the draft. He figured the boss must have spoken a few words in Boise, which resulted in him not being called into the Army. Some of his friends had gone to fight in Korea, and he'd seen how they came back. He spit a stream of tobacco down the chase of the ladder beam, four stories to the water.

But they'd nearly dredged up to the end of the claim block, and the job soon would be ending. And then Colemaker would be pulling out of town—if you could call this far back in the sticks a town. It was one hundred-fifty miles to Boise for any kind of drinking, or two hundred-fifty to Butte Montana for a piece of tail. Custer, all three hundred sorry residents, was a ghost town at best, and he would leave it to the dead and dying.

At a quarter to six he phoned up to the pilot house, then pulled the lever that engaged the wheels and belts to start the bucket line moving. The iron buckets, big as bathtubs, began a slow crawl over the cogs and rollers of the massive bucket truss. A full five minutes of empty buckets rolled by dumping only water, as each was checked for wear and for loose pinion bolts.

At a "good to go" from the men on the screens, Colemaker spoke again into the phone, and a minute later the bucket truss started a slow descent. The whole barge shuddered as buckets scraped bedrock. Winches pulled the barge forward, and as they cut into the gravel bank, all felt the bow dip under the weight of full buckets and heard the strain of the diesels as the dredge began to lift a landslide of rock and sand.

He slapped his ears to remind the crew to put on earmuffs, then turned and braced himself for the clamor and quake. Down valley they'd dug up acre on acre of gravels—five miles of riverbed—and he'd seen the occasional geological oddity brought up with the rocks. But since they'd edged up on the town, and then into the old neighborhoods themselves, the oddities were more frequent and a lot less geological. There were the ubiquitous masonry pipes, of course. Old iron rails were troublesome, and trash pits full of bottles and cans seemed to be everywhere. It was all dredged up, trommeled through, and dumped off the stacker belt. The pieces of chiseled stone spooked him a little, and he never looked carefully for what might be riding up with them.

The first full bucket reached the top of the truss, rolled over, and dumped its load into the trommel. The rush and thunder shook him to his bones. A half dozen more buckets sproled up the truss and dropped their loads, and Colemaker got a thumbs up from the boys below. Men in yellow slickers hurried to their tasks, breaking up clumps of clay in the long sluice boxes and adjusting the cants on the shaker tables.

When he turned back, it was in time to see an arm and hand flop over the iron lip of an ascending bucket halfway down the line.

One bucket dumped its rocks as he stood open-mouthed, then another. He choked on his own spit but couldn't tear his eyes from the hand on its slender forearm waving to him, it seemed, as it rose up the line. The haunted bucket topped the truss, started to roll over, and Colemaker looked into the ghost-white face of a young woman lying on her back atop a load of cobbles.

He jumped back, nearly falling from the bridge. He might even have let out a shriek, though who would have known in that cacophony. In any case, he recovered sufficiently to yank the emergency brake just as the young woman would have dropped into the trommel with the load of rocks following her down. Her legs sprawled and her head hung down; her arms flopped. But her dress caught on a bolt, which kept her from sliding off the pile. Her eyes stared right at him, though, gray and waxy. Water drained from her mouth. Colemaker fell to his knees but stopped himself from gagging, and . . . Christ, it was her! He spit out his chew and threw up after all.

THE CALL CAME IN AT 7:40 a.m., just as Ada Reed, the acting sheriff of Yellowpine County, Idaho, was stepping out her kitchen door. It was from the chief of police in Custer, Idaho, and Ada told him she'd be right there and don't touch a thing. But she sat a minute in her kitchen to catch her breath, then took another fifteen minutes to compose herself, brew a fresh pot of coffee for her thermos, and make a sandwich.

Even then, she fumbled to get the key into the switch, and she popped the clutch and killed the engine, pulling the pickup truck from the curb. This sort of thing wasn't supposed to happen; this was not part of the bargain, and she sat at the corner of 3rd and Main and fought to control her breathing. "Nothing ever happens in this county," they'd told her when she agreed to the 'acting sheriff' idea. She might see dead-drunk ranch hands on weekends, deadbeat husbands once in a while, and dead cattle on the highway. No one said anything about a dead girl.

But she pulled herself together, and once she had, the well-graded Highway 75 carried her south from the town of Camas, then west along the Salmon River toward Sunbeam Junction. The drive was long, with no traffic at all, and she was able to relax and let her mind drift. She knew the canyon highway; knew the hills and every bend and bar of the river. Ada Reed had grown up in the Salmon River country and but for a few years away at college had lived there her whole life. She passed the East Fork turnoff at half-past eight. Not far up the East Fork her childhood home sat on a full section of land, where the ground lay high, and the grass sparkled with frost nearly every morning. Her father had insisted it was a ranch, although her mother would wink and say a couple dozen cows couldn't make a ranch of a hard-scrabble farm. Ada smiled as she passed by the turnoff but held the smile only for a moment. They were both gone, her mother and father, and the fields and pastures—hers now—lay dry and neglected.

She reached Sunbeam Junction at 9:20 a.m. The highway continued west from Sunbeam, but her business took her north via the Yankee Fork Road, a dusty, washboarded county route twisting through a tight canyon. She had to focus on the rocks and chuckholes through the narrows, and that brought back the tension of the morning call. But within a quarter of an hour the canyon opened into the middle valley of the Yankee Fork, which stayed broad and flat for another five miles. The middle valley once had been lush and wild, with broad green meadows between stands of aspen and pine. Shallow streams had twined through the meadows where a child with a gold pan could dream of treasures, and where a young woman with a fly rod could shame her beau. But the streams and meadows she'd known were gone. Now row on row, acre after acre of stacked cobbles and boulders filled the floodplain. The county road wound between dredge tailings and slack-water ponds, alder thickets, and log jams. It splashed through braids of the river and rose and fell like a roller coaster.

Her arms tired wrestling the pickup truck through the turns, so she pulled over for a short coffee break along a stretch of natural stream bed. The river there had been left undamaged by the coincidence of shallow bedrock, which had required the gold dredge to detour around. She'd stopped there before and knew the place and liked the peace of it and the splashing of the water. It was 9:55 a.m., and the sun was just coming over the high ridge to the east.

The coffee was still hot in the thermos, although, rattled by the phone call, she'd forgotten to add milk. She scooted up and sat on the tailgate and poured herself a cup. Her hands shook. She lit a cigarette and blew the smoke into a light breeze, and the caffeine and nicotine made her head spin. She didn't need more coffee just then, but she did need a few more minutes to sort things out.

She'd taken the acting sheriff job just to keep the position open for her husband, Montgomery, the elected sheriff of Yellowpine County, who had been called back into the army. The Korean mess had blown up out of nowhere the previous summer. Hell, they were still getting over the second world war, just five years earlier, and no one she knew could even find Korea on a map. But Truman committed them, and the Army, caught unprepared, had needed to recall officers and technicians. Montgomery got the call-up in April, his commission as a major re-instated by the Army, and he'd caught a bus to the coast with his kit bag. He could have fought the recall, but he didn't. She could have fought with him about it, but she didn't—theirs wasn't the easiest marriage. In any case, the war, the police action, was supposed to be over, but it wasn't, and she was still wearing his badge.

When she stopped for coffee she'd left the driver's door open and the radio on even though reception down by the river was poor and came in waves. Now it came enough for her to hear *Korea*, and *setback*. She turned and tipped her head so the wind wasn't blowing across her ears: . . . *as twenty-five divisions of communist Chinese bear down on the Seoul perimeter . . .* The station faded to static, but it didn't matter; the news never changed. "The Korean situation won't last but a month or two," Montgomery and the others had assured her. "It would just be easier this way." And for three months it had been easy—even boring. But now she had a dead girl waiting for her up the road, and a head spinning with nicotine. She blew a stream of smoke and rubbed a smudge of lipstick from the cup with her thumb.

The deceased's name was Rose Braden. Ada had scribbled it into her officers' notebook when she'd got the call. She knew the girl, or at least she knew of her. Yellowpine County was five thousand square miles but not two thousand people, and it was possible to know *of* nearly all of them—especially when loose talk made the rounds, as it had recently with regards to Mrs. Braden. Rose ran the Yankee Fork Roadhouse just outside of Custer, and she was Corey Braden's wife. Everyone knew of Sergeant Corey Braden, too. The young marine had lost both his legs in Korea—at Pyongyang, she'd heard, wherever that was.

The cigarette burned her fingers. She flipped the butt down to the water. Her coffee had gone cold, so she sloshed that out over the sandy road and screwed the cup back onto the thermos. Still she did not get going but drew her feet up and sat a while longer with her arms hugging her knees. A swirl of warmer air whipped up dust and leaves and tousled her hair. It was fine and lifeless, her honey-blonde hair, and it seemed always to be in the way, and there was nothing she could do about it without a permanent wave. But she couldn't wear her hair up and her sheriff's Stetson, too, so she'd washed the permanent out and for three months had brushed hair out of her face and her coffee and everything else. She pushed the hair off her face and wiped her eyes with her sleeve, took a slow, shaky breath, and felt she would give anything just then to be on her way somewhere else doing anything else. What the hell could she have been thinking?

"What would I have to do?" She had asked—she had naively, stupidly asked. And Montgomery had made it sound so easy she would have to have been a simpleton: "Hell, babe, just show the uniform around, keep on top of the paperwork, and, well, hold a lid on things for a month or two." The County Board had needed her to step out while they deliberated. So, there she'd sat on a creaking wooden bench for nearly two hours as the whole town seemed to find business that day at the courthouse. In and out they sidled, staring, and wondering without asking why she, of all people, thought she was able to do a man's job. Or maybe did she think because she'd gone to college, maybe she was better than everyone else? She'd sat on her hands and waited as voices rose inside; laughter rose now and then; and the boardroom door cracked open for curious, amused, even disdainful glances thrown her way. In the end, the Board had gone along with the plan, but insisted on the title "Acting Sheriff," in view of her femininity, and inasmuch as she had no formal training in the law.

And now, she could not screw this up! The whole county would be watching, and they all expected her to screw up. They'd expected it from the start; she knew that. She saw the winks. She heard the oily comments and the snickering. "A woman sheriff?" some ass would say, "I hear she carries a concealed weapon." And the leering reply: "Not too damned concealed from my vantage." She wiped her nose and her eyes and pushed her hair back. She wished she could just tell them all to go to hell.

The sun finally inched down the trunks of the trees to cast her shadow over the ground, and ready as she was going to be, she jumped up and hooked the tailgate closed. Back in the driver's seat, she rolled up the window and turned off the radio, which had drifted to mostly static, then wrestled the pickup truck back onto the road and headed up the valley.

IN JUST A FEW MORE MILES the road bent around a rocky bench and the gold dredge came into view: an iron barge with a five-story factory sheathed in rusting tin. The dredge was quiet; the bucket line and stacker belt sat idle, and no smoke rose from the stacks. The crew and complement of thirty or so men stood in dungarees and yellow or red slickers smoking or leaning into shovels and mops, with a few men high on the bow gantry working with wrenches. All the men's eyes moved with her as she eased past the dredge, over the culverts, past the willows, weirs, and earthworks, and on into the town of Custer.

CHAPTER TWO

10:30 a.m. – Main Street, Custer, Idaho

CHIEF OF POLICE KELLEN MUNSON sat in the window of the Nugget Café on Main Street and watched Mrs. Reed park her cherry-topped pickup truck, hop up onto the boardwalk, and enter the café. He waved her over. It was 10:45. His official title notwithstanding, Munson was the Town of Custer's only cop and had been for some years. He liked his job, though, and his town, and he took his elected position seriously. He didn't like the notion of an appointed, "acting" sheriff, nor of the backroom deals that must have brought it about. But he liked Ada well enough from his dealings with her husband, Montgomery Reed, the sheriff of record.

From the open door, Ada smiled and nodded to Munson. She had not visited Custer since being sworn in, and now the townsfolk turned to look over their new temporary sheriff. They saw a tall, fit woman in her mid-thirties. Attractive, most would agree; her step was light, even wearing western boots, and her bearing . . . well, it was feminine. But her cheeks had seen some sun, her jaw had a strong line to it, and her gray-blue eyes were sharp. She wore a slightly large uniform of pleated, hunter-green trousers and gray, brass-buttoned duty shirt. Straight blonde hair fell to her shoulders from under a brown Stetson *Boss o' the Plains*. Folks leaned in and whispered to one another. A few raised their brows, and a few others shook their heads.

Ada stepped over to Chief Munson's table conscious of the thunking of her boots, and a little unsettled as to whether she should take off the Stetson, as seemed polite, or keep it on as some of the men had their fedoras—and as a lady would a spring cloche.

"You're timely, Ada." Munson shoveled in a forkful of eggs and hotcakes, washed it down with coffee, and added, "It's a nasty business."

She lifted the Stetson enough to push her hair back, then eased it back on. "Has anyone touched the body?" she asked. Bacon smoke drifted through the room, and the clinking of spoons and plates and the table talk that had paused for her entrance started up again.

"No one's interfered with your investigation, Ada . . . Sheriff," Munson said. "Although it'll be a short one: we already have a confession." Munson leaned toward the window and checked the sky. The sun was burning off last night's rain, and the haze made him squint. "You want a coffee first?"

"No. Let's go have a look." She couldn't stop a grimace. "Is she badly caught up in the machinery?"

"Huh-uh. We got her down and laid her on the catwalk."

Ada stopped in the middle of standing from the table and gave Munson an open-mouthed stare. "I asked you not to touch things!" A couple men at the counter turned. She lowered her voice. "Heck, who knows what we could have learned from the disposition of the body or, you know."

Munson stood and picked up the check. He was a few of years older than she, maybe just past forty; a medium-tall man with a medium waist. He wore blue denim pants as he did every day but Sundays, and a pearl-snap, western-cut shirt more brightly colored than seemed proper for his mien and manner. "Sheriff," he said quietly, "the victim was hanging precariously. She could have fallen right down into the guts of the thing." He leaned in and whispered, "She was partly exposed."

They drove Munson's truck back to the dredge because he'd already thrown an old jail cell mattress into the bed. The engineers had winched the barge over and extended the pontoon gangplank to the shore nearest the road. The two law officers eased across the gangplank, clinging to the rope and nodding to the slickered workers on deck. The workers stepped aside for them and generally pointed them up the right steps and across the right catwalks to get to Dar Colemaker's station at the top of the bucket line.

Colemaker jumped up from a tool crate where he'd kept watch and pointed out for them the deceased. Ada thanked the man and asked if she and the Chief could examine the victim in private.

"Watch the rocks in the bucket don't shift if you need to go up there," Colemaker told her. He stepped away, packing another chew into his cheek.

The victim lay on the steel grid that floored the workstation, with a sheet of black visqueen covering her from head to foot, almost. Her feet stuck out from under the plastic, showing low-heel lace-up shoes and anklet socks. Munson pulled back the tarp, and Ada teetered and had to grab hold of the metal railing. It was . . . a body.

The torso was smeared with a gray slime. "She's covered with mud," Ada managed. She'd never seen an actual body before, except lying in a casket.

"You're going to take her back to Camas, right?" Munson asked.

And much older, of course; never a young body like this. She had an odd sensation of darkness closing in around her vision. She said, "Uhm, Kellen . . ." She'd always called the chief Kellen. He'd worked on cases with Montgomery over the years, and she'd served him coffee and pie in her kitchen on more than one occasion. The first-name basis, though, seemed inappropriate today. She asked, "Uhm, Chief, aren't we in your jurisdiction? Aren't we within the limits of the Town of Custer?"

Munson tilted his head and blew a raspberry sound through his lips. He said, "Legally, this never was part of Custer proper. The Town of Bonanza—most call it the Bottoms—was incorporated separately in eighteen-seventy-some. There'd been cooperative agreements with Custer over the years, but those were cancelled when the mining company had what was left of Bonanza unincorporated in order to override the surface rights."

Ada smiled weakly and nodded. A tightness was growing in her stomach. She said, "So it's definitely within the county jurisdiction . . . not State?"

"Not State, either. We're on a county-maintained road and the nearest school section is a couple miles to the south."

"Well then, we are in the County," Ada said. "My county." She rubbed her hands together. "Okay, then."

"I'll assist you any way I can," Munson said. "Just let me know."

"Thanks, Kellen." She pushed her hair back and said as calmly as she could, "Yes, I'm going to take her back to Camas. But not until . . ." Her eyes dropped again to the body. Cold and stiff as it was, it clearly had, not long ago at all, been a living person. There was still strength in the limbs and grace in the delicate fingers. There was expression in the features, albeit a sadness and maybe a . . . disbelief—as though the victim, too, wondered how life could so suddenly end.

Ada forced in a breath and said, "But not in the heat of the day, and not until a time and means of death are established."

"We have a perpetrator, Sheriff."

She forced her eyes from the young woman. "You mean a suspect. Is he in custody?"

"No need."

"The suspect, who is it?"

"Shoot, it's Corey, her husband." Munson pulled off his hat and squinted into the almost midday sun. "He caught Rose stepping out on him, and I guess he swung a stick, and I guess she fell and drowned."

Ada stood above the girl—the woman: maybe twenty-two or twenty-three years old—and checked the viewfinder of her Kodak. "Last night?" she asked.

"That's what he says."

She checked the angle of the sun, pulled Colemaker's tool crate closer, and stood on it. "How did he get her to the pond?"

"I guess he confronted her here."

She clicked the shutter, then repositioned the crate and took another photo. It felt better if she could keep working and talking. "Well, how did he get here?"

"I guess he wheeled himself here."

"A wheelchair through the mud?"

"The rain mostly fell later in the night. It wasn't so soft yesterday."

The girl's face was not muddy, but it was an awful pallor and hard to look at. A contusion ran diagonally from ear to cheek bone. Not able to bring herself to lift and turn the girls head, Ada twisted herself almost upside-down to photograph the wound.

"Probably from the stick Corey swung," Munson offered.

She sat down on the crate and, after a few quick breaths, took out a five by seven-inch notebook to start her official case notes. She wrote:

> *3 July 1951, 11:35 a.m. Yankee Fork dredge. At scene with Chief Munson.*

Then added,

> *Deceased adult female, Caucasian, 20 to 24 yrs. Tentatively identified to be Rosalie Braden of Custer. Apparent drowning with signs of possible* ~~altercation~~ *prior assault.*

The victim's hands were the same gray white as her face. There was a little bruising of the hands, but otherwise . . . except each bore a strange design: a curved, maybe a crescent moon on the back of each hand, convex toward the knuckles. Ada laid both hands across the girl's stomach in good light, moved in as close as she could focus, and snapped the shutter of the Kodak.

As she laid the girl's hands back down, her knuckles brushed something hard under the dress. Clenching her teeth, then, she patted down the torso, waist, and upper legs while Chief Munson looked away. "Help me lift her dress, Chief, while I take a look."

"Oh, criminy, Ada, half the crew's watching!" A dozen men had stepped onto timbers and catwalks and were craning to watch. Ada yanked the visqueen back over the girl.

With a good deal of deliberation, then, she and Munson and some of the crew managed to wrap the body in the black plastic and carry it down the steps, through the manways, and across the gangplank. Munson drove the victim the half mile to the Pinyon Bar while Ada stayed behind to look over the crime scene.

The ground in front of the advancing dredge pond was rough and uneven. Nearly all of the buildings, fences, and bigger trees had been removed from what once had been a neighborhood. "The Bottoms," Kellen Munson had called it, but she knew the townspeople more often referred to it as "Chinatown." Lilac hedges, raspberries, and clusters of hollyhocks still outlined individual lots, and footpaths crisscrossed the cleared ground. In all the fifteen-acre neighborhood only a few houses remained standing. Most were at the peripheries, but one sat squarely in the path of the dredge. It was a neat cottage of forest green shiplap siding enclosed by a white picket fence. At the front gate, an old woman stood staring back as Ada spied her across the ruined field. The old woman wore pants and a gray jacket; a long braid of white hair looped over her shoulder. Ada waved, but the woman turned and shuffled back to the house.

Focused on the woman's labored movements, Ada almost missed the tracks at her feet. Grooves in the soil here and there were definitely made by narrow wheels, and pairs of grooves were spaced about right for a wheelchair. The marks were shallower than one might expect, but of course, there'd been a rain in the night which might have altered them. She photographed what she could.

There were no barricades around the dredge pond although the ground was soft and some of the paths terminated at water's edge. The pond was certainly the right place for a killing, though. It was well screened from the businesses of Custer, almost half a mile away, and any car coming from town or from the valley would have long been seen. But for the old woman's house, just a single set of windows overlooked the site: upstairs windows at the Yankee Fork Roadhouse, a few hundred yards away. The curtains of one of those windows shifted, and a face pulled back into the shadows.

ADA REED STOPPED AT HER TRUCK for her service jacket, then met Chief Munson at the back door of the Pinyon Club. She and he worked the black plastic package through the door of the walk-in cooler, where the bar keeper had already stacked beer and soft drinks aside. The body was floppy, and it occurred to her that a lot of bones must have been broken when she was scooped up with the load of boulders. It made Ada want to throw up. A wooden door had been laid across two beer kegs, and they heaved the body up onto it. She stepped back outside and watched the clouds boil overhead for a full minute before returning.

The victim, Rose Braden, was sludge-covered from the back shoulders down to the mid thighs, as though the arms and head and feet had floated while the middle sank into the muddy bottom. There were some black smudges on the shoulders and elsewhere on the dress: grease stains, she supposed.

Munson lit a lantern because the beer cooler had just a single forty-watt bulb. The room was a little less funeral with the extra light, but it was still deathly cold, and it smelled of stale beer, which did not help Ada's stomach. She wiped her hands on a towel and silently, consciously avoiding the girl's lifeless eyes, began to pat down the torso. "She's wearing something under her dress. Something hard." Her breath billowed in the lantern light. "Give me a hand with the clothing."

"Hell, I ain't reaching under a girls dress, even if she is dead."

"Well, I'm not thrilled about it either."

"It's more natural if you do it." Munson stepped to the far end of the cooler and sat on a beer keg.

There was nothing natural about this, nothing at all. The dress was slimy and clung to the cold flesh as she tugged it up around the girl's legs and under the hips. She exposed a pair of white cotton underpants and a bare torso to halfway up the rib cage. The skin everywhere was white, like a China doll's.

The hard items she'd felt were parts of a heavy metal belt looped around the girl's waist with the longer end dangling down between her legs. Ada turned slightly so Munson wouldn't see her grimace. "I don't have a flash. I won't get much of a photo in here," she said.

The belt was made up of metal discs, each about three inches across and a quarter-inch thick. Each was drilled with two holes and hooked one to another with pieces of copper wire. She rolled Rose Braden's body onto its side, again sickened by the unnatural give, and freed the long end of the belt from between the girl's cold thighs. There was no fastener, but it was hooked with a simple loop of the discs, which she undid. She pulled the whole belt from around and under the torso, leaving green stains on the girl's skin and underpants where the discs had lain. "What's this look like?" she asked.

Munson dared a couple steps closer and leaned in. "Looks like copper, I guess. What's the design?"

The discs—they had to be medallions of some sort—were cast or stamped with a circle filled with a backward 'S'. She flipped half a dozen around. "It's an oriental symbol." She flipped a few more. "They're all the same. I think this is what sank her to the bottom."

Munson leaned in and took the belt held out to him. There were about twenty medallions in all. The whole belt weighed ten to twelve pounds. He nodded. "That'd be enough to do it."

"How much is copper worth?"

"Up to forty cents a pound these days, what with the war and all."

"So, the whole thing is worth four to five dollars?"

"I guess so." He laid the belt on the bench without looking at the half-naked body and returned to his beer keg.

Ada sketched a medallion in her field book, noting the diameter, thickness, and design, then turned back to the girl. Rose Braden's face was pretty, verging on beautiful, with dark brows and long lashes. Her lips, though pale, were full and there were laugh lines at the corners. No worry lines yet. But the welt on the right side of the face reached from cheekbone to ear, breaking the skin in spots and leaving a deep bruise and a scrape and bits of scab. "Where's the stick?" Ada asked.

"Stick?"

"Presumed murder weapon."

"We can ask Corey, I guess."

The girl's fingernails were painted but trimmed medium short. Some of the nails were chipped and broken, and there was a little dirt under them—not unreasonably for a farm girl, but more than one might expect on someone who worked indoors. The backs of the hands were marked with the darned crescent moon design. With the lantern held closer, they weren't tattoos but might have been burns, maybe. They showed up red. What didn't against the white skin? She sketched a hand and the crescent mark in her field book.

Despite all the broken bones, there was no bruising anywhere but where she'd been struck on the face. The bones must have been broken by the dredge, then, and not by the killer. Ada made a note—a shaky one, because she'd begun to shiver badly.

The lips were a pale pink color, but no lipstick rubbed off with a tissue. She didn't know what lips were supposed to look like on a drowning victim. There was no eye makeup, either, and no jewelry, not even a wedding ring. She added a note about the makeup and the clothes the girl wore.

"What makes you think she was out messing around? Who was she seeing?"

Munson had seemed focused on the beverage inventory, but he answered straight away, "I don't want to speak ill of the girl. Shoot, she's laying right there."

Ada looked up and waited. He wagged his head. "I didn't have a view of her bedroom, and I rarely went into the Roadhouse but on official business, of which there was a reasonable amount. It's just what folks said about her. Corey said so himself."

She unbuttoned the dead girl's upper dress and, holding her breath, felt and looked underneath. Rose wore a brassiere. There were no marks around the neck or breasts. "He talked that way about his own wife—that she was unfaithful?" she asked.

"Yeah."

She looked up again from her examination. "Openly?" She'd known of adulterous women in the valley, or at least had heard the whispers, but that sort of thing was always kept hush-hush.

"More or less openly. And this is a known fact, she would get herself dressed up nice and drive out of town and be gone all night long. She wouldn't come slinking home till noon the next day. That happened a lot when Corey'd just left for the war."

"Where did she go? Who was she seeing?" She had to ask, of course. She hoped she didn't sound in any way intrigued.

Munson stood from his beer keg seat and crossed his arms. "Who was she seeing? I don't know. There have been a few names spoken. I guess I can ask around."

"Yes, please do."

He said, "And heck, last fall even before Braden came home all crippled, folks knew she was seeing Lonnie Barr. His best friend, the little prick—excuse my language, the little bum—and they were out picnicking all the while Corey was gone." Munson stepped closer. "That much I can tell you firsthand. I saw her and him riding off in his truck together more than one morning, not getting back to town till late afternoon." He glanced at the body on the table. She was a tall girl, and slender; well put together in a youthful way. He said, "Young men don't spend the whole day in the hills

with a pretty young woman and there's nothing going to happen."
His eyes found their way to Rose's waist, and to her underpants. He
scowled and stepped back to the other side of the cooler.

Ada tugged the dress back to cover the girl's hips and legs. "So,
she may have been careless with the company she kept. What else
can you tell me about her?"

"She was strange, Ada. She did strange things. Anyone in town
will tell you. She spent time with the old Chinese woman, Mrs.
Li. She'd be out there all night a lot of times, doing whatever kind
of Oriental rites they do. Dick Rooney—he lives on the hill above
the Bottoms, you should talk to him—he tells me fire and smoke
comes from back behind the old woman's house some nights.
Sparks rising up into the sky. Gosh darn, I'd see Rose coming back
from there on my morning rounds—this is even since Corey's been
back—and she wouldn't open the roadhouse till late.

Ada put away her notebook and covered the girl's body with the
visqueen. "I guess next, let's see what the witness has to say. Can we
lock this cooler?"

"You mean the perpetrator? And no, Fred needs to get in and
out. He's got a going business."

"I mean the suspect. I guess she'll be okay here. Fred won't get
curious, will he?"

Munson froze with his hand on the doorknob. "I hope you
don't mean what that sounds like."

"For heaven's sakes, I mean he won't be looking at details of
evidence and blabbing it around town." She wiped her hands on
the towel again, then washed them with soap in the women's room
while Munson waited.

Chapter three

THE YANKEE FORK ROADHOUSE stood on a rocky bench at the intersection of the county road and the narrow mine road twisting down Jordan Creek Canyon. It was a substantial structure for the country, solidly built back in the days of plenty. Four gabled windows on the second level looked out over a broad, covered porch running the length of the building, and four more would look out onto the back garden. But the inn hadn't slept guests in years, and the clapboard siding, once a proud cardinal red, now barely blushed under years of sun and dust.

Ada and Munson climbed the worn steps and pushed through double doors, pausing once the doors swung closed to let their eyes and their lungs adjust. The tavern occupied a large room meant for both dining and drinking, with an oaken bar at one end and a stone fireplace opposite. The lawmen moved a few steps in, hacking into their fists from the tobacco smoke. A handful of customers stood at the bar, a half dozen more sat at tables, and two old gentlemen had a game of cribbage going by the unlit fireplace. Red velvet curtains were drawn everywhere, but panes of sunlight knifed between them here and there cutting the thick atmosphere and shining on boots, and bottles, and wary faces.

Behind the bar a boney, heavily bearded man held two bottles and was pouring liquor from one. Ada stepped up and nodded to the bartender. "Are you new here?" she asked.

"I ain't really here, to speak of," he said. "I'm just fixing a drink."

Munson said, "Bob Blackmon. He's a customer, sort of. You got permission to be back there, Bobby?"

"I gave him permission." The two turned as a pair of doors swung closed and a man's head and shoulders glided into the room behind tables of drinkers. He said, "Someone's got to keep the customers happy." The chair-bound man weaved to an empty table by a curtained window. Ada and Munson joined him there.

Corey Braden, the victim's husband, could not have been more than twenty-four years old, but his face looked forty. His eyes were sunken, and his complexion ruddy. It was not from sun, Ada judged, but from whiskey. His sandy hair had long grown out of its military cut, and lay uncombed on his head. But he was broad-shouldered and might have been six feet tall . . . if he'd had legs. Where the legs should have been, two stumps terminated a little closer to the knees than to the hips.

Ada took off her hat and held it in her hands. "Sergeant Braden? I'm Sheriff Ada Reed from Camas."

Braden swung a chair out from the table and wheeled himself into the gap. "I've had dealings with your old man," he said. "You're wearing his pants now?"

"Just his badge. While he's away."

"Away in Korea. Good luck with that." He waved three fingers over his head and called for "Whiskers" to bring him and his guests some beer.

Ada pulled out a chair and sat. Munson stood until Ada pushed a chair out with her foot and nodded to it. To Braden she said, "I'm very sorry for your loss."

"Which?" he asked. The bartender brought over three beers, and Braden asked him to fetch a shot as well. He nodded to the others to drink up.

Ada let the beer sit. She said, "Sergeant Braden, I'm sorry for the loss of your wife, and I'm grateful for your sacrifice for our country."

"Drink up, Mrs. Reed." Braden took the shot of whiskey from the bartender's hand and downed it. He caught his breath and said, "I was drafted by my country, and I killed my cheatin' wife."

The tavern quieted for a moment until Munson said, "Tell her, Corey, what you told me about what happened."

Braden shooed the bartender away with his head, took a breath, and downed half the mug of beer. "I was sober last night," he said. "Mostly. I was upstairs in my room . . . Are you writing a book?"

"Just a few notes." She finished a quick description of the young man: square jaw, two-day beard; eyes, though bloodshot, a surprising blue. She put down her pen and asked, "Your wife helped you up the stairs?"

"I don't need no help. Anyway, she'd been gone damn near the whole day, so we weren't open for business. I seen her from the window get home after dark, and I confronted her downstairs. She was all upset over something. I mean, *she* was upset? What about me?"

He'd been jerking the chair side to side, but he stopped and stared straight ahead. "Anyway, she had her tit in a wringer over something." He turned and stretched down to lock a wheel, and the move showed a lithe, muscled torso under the tee shirt—a David almost, from the waist up and but for the recent effects of drink and infirmity.

He said, "She ran out back to where she sleeps, but I knew she wouldn't be staying in. She'd been gone all the previous night, too."

"Had you been arguing?"

"No. I mean, we should have been, if she'd cared enough even to argue." He threw one arm over the back of his chair and leaned back to study the ceiling. After a moment he said, "But she would just stare at me and be like, 'I'm sorry Corey,' and 'I love you Corey, whatever else you think.' That shit. Like she was feeling sorry for me; like she needed a good clubbing, which is what she got." He turned toward the bar and raised himself a few inches from the seat. "Blackmon!" he called, "Just bring the bottle for shit sakes."

The whiskered Mr. Blackmon brought a half-full bottle of Jim Beam and another beer. Braden stared a moment at the bottle but didn't pour. Ada said, "So later last night she went out? Was that normal?"

"Sometimes she would go on foot and sometimes I'd hear the Chevy start up and she'd drive away. Hell, sometimes I'd hear men's voices, and not always just one man. I don't know what she was thinking, that I got my ears shot off too? I would hear her leave and I'd hear her return."

"From where?"

"From wherever she was screwing around, don't you suppose?" He poured two fingers of whiskey but didn't drink. "I don't know. Sometimes I'd see the Chevy parked at the China-woman's house."

"From the upstairs window? The second gable?"

Braden nodded. "I didn't need no window, though. And I didn't need to hear people tell me things. I found all the evidence I needed."

Ada was writing as fast as she could. She looked up to ask, "What evidence, of what?"

"Undeniable evidence of her screwing around." He downed the whiskey.

Munson was watching the exchange hunched in his seat with his elbow on the table. Seeming to give in, he took a swallow from the beer in front of him, then wiped his mouth and leaned back in his chair without meeting Ada's eyes. "What about last night?" he asked. "What else happened last night?"

Braden nodded. "I must have fell asleep because I didn't see her go out. But midnight or later—I didn't check; the moon woke me."

"It was a waxing crescent moon; didn't cloud up till later," Munson explained.

"The crescent moon woke me, and I seen her slinking around in the Bottoms, waiting to meet someone. So that was enough for me. I got my ass down the stairs and headed right down the county road. Took that stick over there with me."

A four-foot shillelagh leaned against the wall near the bar. Ada stared at the club and shuddered, squeezed her eyes shut, and barely breathed. "Had you been drinking?"

"Hell yeah! But I wasn't drunk."

"Did you hit your wife a lot?"

The boy's grin left him in an instant. "What the hell does that mean?"

Stale beer, close bodies, and nicotine haze seemed suddenly too thick, and the idea of the truncheon laid across the girl's face turned Ada's stomach. She needed like anything to get out and get a breath of air. With her fist to her mouth, she jumped up, but then turned and jerked open the drapes nearest their table. She sat again and asked, "It was your intention at that time to kill your wife?"

"No." Braden flinched from the sudden light, and he appeared as annoyed as surprised by her question. "I mean, yeah. It was my intention to beat the hell out of her."

"With that club?"

"If I could catch her." He waved to the bartender not to draw him another beer. "I intercepted her out by the pond. We argued, but what was she going to say? She backtalked me on top of her screwing around, so I took up that stick and I belted her. She fell in the pond, and I didn't let her back up. I kept her down with the stick till she drowned."

Ada's pen stopped mid-sentence. "You got close enough to the water to hold her down? The bank didn't look so firm to me."

He shrugged. "It held. If it hadn't, I'd have had to been dredged up too." He shrugged again.

"With whom was she . . . keeping company?"

"Does it matter?"

"Doesn't it to you?"

"Not a bit. The issue was between me and her. She stepped out on me. Neither one of us needs to worry about *whom*. It only matters that I put a stop to it." His shirt was wrinkled as though he'd slept in it. He'd let himself go, become a drunk, but still he sat erect in the harsh light, head-up and square-shouldered.

"Sergeant," she asked, "you said people told you things. Who? Who tells a marine his wife is stepping out on him?"

He scowled but didn't meet her eyes. "His friends, that's who!"

She put the pen to the page, looked up, and waited. "What friends?"

"The guys. Barry at the hardware, Dee Mansfield. Hell, even Munson's said so, isn't that right, Kel?"

Ada looked across the table open mouthed at the police chief, who shrugged and pulled his hand away from the beer mug. She asked, "Mr. Mansfield, too? He came in here and talked to you about that sort of thing?" It didn't seem likely to her. Dee Mansfield was a big man in Custer County—well-connected throughout Idaho. He owned the Yankee Fork gold dredge.

"Me and Dee are friends. He respects me and doesn't pull any punches." Braden dropped his eyes but kept his jaw firm. A few of the customers plus the volunteer bartender were leaning in, listening.

"Do you want to talk somewhere else?" Ada asked him.

"No, this'll do."

She leaned forward with one elbow on the table, rubbed her forehead, and let out a slow breath. Even with the sunlight streaming in, she wished she could be somewhere else right then, talking about anything else. "So . . ." she began. She knew it was going to sound hard. "So, you come home. There was no parade and no marching band, was there? But all your friends, they were here for you. They took the trouble to come by and let you know things were even worse than you thought."

He pushed back from the table and spun his chair around. "My friends stuck with me, bitch!"

"Okay." She looked up and tapped the pen on her notebook. The word 'bitch,' spat at her like that, was meant to shock and unsettle her, she knew. But she'd been called an awful lot worse than that. She said, "Okay. Who's living upstairs, can I look?"

"Just me." He spun his chair around again.

"You can get up and down the stairs?"

"I'm an amputee, not a jellyfish. Everything works above the knees."

"Can I look up there?"

"Above my knees?" He put his hands to his belt buckle and grinned.

And now he was sneering at her. She couldn't stop her cheeks from warming, and she turned for a second back to her notebook. But she'd been disrespected a lot worse than that, too; she'd known it in spades. She fought a grin as it occurred to her she might be better inured to the situation than was the young Marine. She said, "Can I look around upstairs?"

"Why?"

"Because you're the prime suspect in a murder investigation." Not sure what she would do if he refused, she stood, squared the brim of her hat, and said, "Let's go, Sergeant."

He looked her up and down but then backed his chair from the table and led the two law officers through the swinging doors to a staircase. Grabbing hold of the newel post, he lifted himself out of the chair and onto the first step. He blew out his breath a couple times, then crab walked backward, hand by hand, to the top of the flight. Ada and Munson followed on foot. At the landing he grabbed a post and a rail and swung himself up into a second wheelchair, missing the first time but pulling the chair back and completing the maneuver on the second try.

"You have a second wheelchair," Ada said.

"A birthday present from my wife. Over here would be the room of interest."

His bedroom was cluttered, but not badly. Folded clothes lay on a coffee table along one wall. The bed was unmade, but not filthily so. The air stunk of urine, though, and what was probably an un-emptied chamber pot sat half under the bed. The room was high-ceilinged, and the walls were papered with a delicate pattern of flowers: pimpernels, or primroses. The wallpaper had been scrubbed fairly recently and the drapes were clean.

There was no chair by the window, just a small table where sat a full ashtray, an empty whiskey bottle, and a stack of letters in neatly cut-open envelopes. Braden wheeled over and grabbed them up before she could make out to whom the letters were addressed. He asked her what she needed to see.

"Do you own any guns?" she asked.

Braden was staring out the window and answered without turning. "You'll find it in the closet. Thought I'd get me an elk this fall."

The closet held no clothes except the dress uniform of a Marine Corps sergeant. On the floor of the closet, though, she found a box of socks and pant legs—just the lower legs cut from men's trousers. Another box held men's shoes and boots. There were some sports gear and fishing gear, and a quart jar of a clear liquid. The fumes burned her nose when she opened the jar, making her jerk back. "Grain alcohol?" she asked.

"Corn. Medicinal."

She re-sealed the jar, set it back in the closet, and pulled out a Winchester rifle. An unspent bullet ejected onto the floor when she cocked the lever.

For a full minute she leaned with her hand on the jamb of the closet door. The men were watching and waiting, but it just wasn't a straightforward situation. She had somehow expected it all to be more clear-cut. Nevertheless, she sighed and said, "Corey Braden, you're under arrest for the murder of Rosalie Braden. Do we need to cuff you, or would you prefer getting downstairs by yourself?"

THEY LET THE PRISONER ARRANGE WITH THE WHISKERED GUY to run the bar and kitchen in his absence. Ada and Chief Munson talked quietly by the swinging doors while keeping an eye on the patrons and the young man in the wheelchair. The customers were getting drunk and a little too giddy, she thought, given the circumstances. One man, though, watched Ada as she watched the crowd. Medium tall and just passed middle age, he wore a faded denim jacket, oiled canvas pants, and old worn-out western boots. He sipped from a coffee cup rather than a bottle.

She said, "Take the stick into evidence, Kel... Chief. Put him in your cell, and keep a hard watch on him."

"What do you mean?" Munson asked.

"I think Montgomery called it a hard watch. What I mean is, empty his pockets, take his belt, and don't give him a knife or matches or anything."

"Jeez, you think all that's necessary?"

"I don't know. When you get him settled, see if you can check something for me." Munson leaned toward her because she spoke softly with her head bent low. "There was a stack of letters. See if you can find out who wrote them." Ada had thrown some shirts and underwear into a valise for the prisoner, a toothbrush but not a razor, and a couple books. Braden had seemed uninterested in anything, but he'd held onto the letters and stuffed them into his shirt as they were leaving.

Munson assured her he would look after the prisoner, and she let him lead Braden out the kitchen door where there were fewer steps.

The kitchen of the roadhouse had turned out meals for a dozen guests at a time, in the days before the mines played out. It boasted a gas range, two sinks, and two ovens. The place was clean; the walls and floor were scrubbed, and the counters wiped down. In the Frigidaire, she found a box with a dozen sandwiches double wrapped in wax paper: roast beef and tuna it looked like. There was a covered pot of spaghetti and a plate of fried chicken under cheese cloth.

There were no knives among the utensils on the counter nor on the wall. She checked all the drawers and shelves, and finally found butcher knives, filet knives, a cleaver, twelve steak knives, and a bread knife in a metal tray on the upper pantry shelf.

The backyard enclosed what might once have been a pleasant orchard, although the apple and plum trees were old and in need of pruning. Still, the ground was more or less picked up and raked. The trees at the far end of the yard were dead and had been for years. A rusty-banked rivulet ran between the dead fruit trees. The muddy channel was choked with trash, which was not in keeping with the fairly well-kept house and yard. Beer cans and soup cans lay scattered in the stream bed, all covered with orange slime and muck.

When Ada returned to the parlor, little had changed in the demeanor of the patrons, the majority were still drinking, but the sober man had gone.

6:40 p.m. – Preparing the victim's remains
for transport to Clinic in Camas

ADA WALKED THE QUARTER MILE BACK to the Pinyon Bar warmed by a narrow sliver of sunshine. The afternoon in general, though, had clouded over and cooled, and she believed she would be okay, after all, transporting the girl's remains the long way back to Camas.

She met Munson again at the beer cooler, and together they spent a quarter hour wrapping the victim, as respectfully as possible, in a linen sheet. Munson had brought a green canvas tarp, which they used to carry the shrouded body to Ada's pickup truck and to lift it onto the jail cell mattress. She bought a couple blocks of ice from the ice plant and broke them up to put in with the girl's remains, then Munson folded the canvas tarp over and tied it all neatly with cord. He tied the package to the cargo hooks of the truck to keep it from rolling and sliding in the curves.

She was near tears and her hands were shaking by the time they were done. Munson saw it. "You okay? I can drive her in if you want to follow in my truck."

"No, it's just silly. I'm fine."

"First dead person, I guess?"

"Technically, yes." She had to grab the edge of the pickup and close her eyes to a flood of memories. "It's no problem," she said. "I just have to drive her . . . drive the remains to the clinic in Camas. Dr. Mink is expecting me."

Munson asked, "Do you think we even need the coroner involved? I mean, Rose Braden stepped out on her husband, and he clouted her. He did clout her, didn't he?"

"Says he did." She raised the tailgate and hooked it closed. She needed to get going, get out of town to where no one was watching, or telling her something, or waiting for a damned answer.

"And she drowned, right?"

"I'd bet on it." She took off her hat and tossed it into the cab. "You'll keep an eye on Sergeant Braden like I asked?" Her voice still shook.

"I'll watch over him. But Ada, do we even need a full investigation? I mean in light of his confession."

The sliver of sun had gone behind shifting, tumbling clouds, but sunshine still pried through here and there, painting the cracks and seams of the clouds bright gold. Munson watched the sky. Ada opened the door and climbed behind the wheel. "Yes," she answered, "I think we have to stick to procedure." It was 7:50 p.m.

Finally out of town and on her way down the Yankee Fork Road, she got no radio reception at all from one end of the frequencies to the other. Every time she glanced in the rear-view mirror the green tarp was there with the young girl tied up inside. She couldn't get the tarp out of her mind, nor the memories and the smell of the old canvas.

The radio offered nothing but static, try as she might with the dial. After just a couple of miles, she pulled the truck to the side of the gravel road, got out, and slammed the door. But she could not bring herself to check her cargo in the bed of the truck.

The sun was nearly down, just peeking through a narrow gap between dark clouds and the shoulder of Red Mountain. She leaned against the front fender, gathered her hair back, and threw up. Stumbling a few paces, she sat heavily in the gravel at the edge of the road, then dropped her head to her knees and cried until the sun blinked out over the ridge.

THE SALMON VALLEY CLINIC RECEIVED THE remains of Mrs. Rosalie Braden at a little past 10:00 p.m. But with paperwork to fill out, instructions for the autopsy, and just talking because she really needed to talk, Ada didn't get to bed until after midnight. She laid in her bed open-eyed until two in the morning, at which time she got up and poured herself a brandy. She finally managed a little sleep around three, slouched in the living room chair in the light of the lamp.

CHAPTER FOUR

*Wednesday, 4 July. Morning at Courthouse
Reviewing Yankee Fork case.*

ACTING SHERIFF ADA REED. She had gone along with the scheme because, well, because Montgomery asked her to, and she didn't say no to Montgomery. But also because what else was she going to do with him gone off to another damned war? She had sat home for the last war; sat for years. She knew when he accepted the commission how it would be. And the idea had been, the sheriff position would keep her busy and out of the house. She just hadn't expected the job to be so . . . just her, all by herself, all the time. But now even her friends, even Betty and Cheryl, seemed not to have time for her anymore. And like everyone else, they expected her to fall on her face. "We had to give the committee chair to someone else, Ada; you're so busy now," they told her with their most apologetic smiles. And then as kindly as can be, "We'll find something for you, of course, once you're done with this silly sheriff business."

She poured a steaming cup of coffee, the second of the morning, and let the kitchen door slam behind her. A path took her through pinyon pines and juniper trees heavy with berries, to a bluff overlooking the broad valley of the Salmon. She followed her footsteps from days ago, and from weeks and months ago to a high, flat rock where she could sit and . . . *be by myself*, she thought grimly.

An upcanyon breeze whispered through the pinyons, and she pushed her lifeless hair out of her face. She laid the Stetson on the rock beside her and stuffed the tie between the buttons of her last clean uniform shirt. It still didn't fit right, for all the taking in and letting out she'd done. But the smell of coffee and sage picked her up a little, and the pre-dawn air was heavy with dew so that a meadowlark's song carried sharp and clear. It was a perfectly lovely morning, but . . . She could be lying in her warm bed. She could be sleeping-in past eight, then golfing with the girls at eleven. It was the first Thursday of the month, and they'd all be there—two four-somes at least. And she could be part of it. She could be the center of it, but for the whole ill-fitting sheriff business.

And she had a disabled soldier in jail now, and his wife in the morgue, and that wasn't so funny. The eastern sky added an edge of coral as she sat, then of gold, and in just a few minutes the rim of the far Lemhi Range caught fire. The glow brought more birds to a chorus, and her coffee grew lukewarm as she listened and tried to think how to deal with the mess she'd gotten herself into. When at last the coffee was too cold to drink, she sloshed it out and, having come up with no particularly good ideas, headed down to start her day.

THE YELLOWPINE COUNTY SHERIFF'S OFFICE WAS situated in the courthouse, down the hallway to the left after you passed around the wide staircase in the main foyer: the third door on your left. There was room in the office for three desks, but there were only two, and only one being used. There were steel file cabinets in a row, a hat rack, and an oak table laid with a linen tablecloth where Ada kept coffee supplies and cups. The office had its own wash-room—a special perk in the turn-of-the-century building, and Harry Truman looked down with a magnified gaze from the moss-green wall above Ada's desk. The room had once been painted a harmless pear green, as still could be seen behind the file cabinets. But over the decades the exposed walls had hardened and cracked to the unfortunate moss color. In patches where sunlight streamed in from the streetside window, the moss green had further gone to a faded olive drab.

Ada would have preferred something from the seafoam palette. In any case, she needed to finish some portion of yesterday's paperwork, but she'd been interrupted almost continuously through the morning. Everyone in the county, it seemed, had heard something of the murder—the beating, the drowning, the strangulation—up the Yankee Fork, and everyone had ideas as to who, and why, and how come now and not a long time ago. In and out the old boys had ambled, shaking their heads and rubbing their chins at the tragedy, and hiding as well as they could any unease attending the realization that Sheriff Reed really had shipped off to war, and that his wife—albeit a good-looking gal—really was wearing his badge.

There were still four gentlemen hanging around her office at mid-morning. A pot of coffee, the fourth of the day, was perking, and the men had their cups out waiting for it. "Help yourself," she said to a denim-clad and leather-booted rancher—one of the Bastida brothers she'd learned as her arm was being shaken. "The sugar is in the cupboard; milk's gone bad." Ada had drunk four cups of coffee herself through the course of the morning because it was only polite not to ask her visitors to drink and speculate alone, and now she wanted to use her private washroom. But with the gentlemen crowded around as they were, it wasn't something she could do.

One of her visitors, by the name of Jack Nestor, sat on the edge of the empty desk and with tomahawk motions was making a point about Sergeant Braden's shell shock and therefore his reduced accountability. Nestor sold feed and implements at the co-op, and Ada was certain he'd never studied law or psychology.

Her travel voucher and coroner request forms lay on her desk, but she still hadn't filled out a line when Ephraim Applegate, the mayor of Camas, stuck his head through the door. "Morning Ada. Nasty business up there," he said.

She jumped up. "Doesn't get nastier, Mayor, and it isn't solving itself. I've got to . . ."

"Hell of a deal, isn't it?" Jack Nestor shook his head.

". . . get back out there," she said.

"What for?" Applegate asked from the open doorway. "I thought there was a confession."

The denim-clad rancher cleared his throat. "There are still some evidentiary details to work out." Ada started to interject but the rancher turned and ensured the whole room, "It'll wrap up soon enough."

Jack Nestor clucked his tongue and emphasized that it was just a hell of a deal.

Ada sidled toward the door, sidestepping Applegate as he made his way into the room. The mayor unbuttoned his suit coat and turned away to hitch up his trousers. He said, "I don't see what evidence or details have to do with a clear-cut case of a confession."

Holding the door and leaning for a second, she calculated her route down the hallway to the public restrooms. She said, "Sergeant Braden could surveil the whole scene from his upstairs window, Mr. Mayor. And it's a long hard push in a wheelchair all the way down through the Bottoms."

Applegate eased himself into the sheriff's chair and said, "Maybe so, Ada. But I wonder if we—if your county," he nodded to the men in attendance—"If Yellowpine really needed to pay for a coroner's report."

"I saw a marksman's medal pinned to Braden's uniform, and there was a loaded rifle right there if all he wanted was his wife dead." She walked back to the coffee table. "Why did he choose to push a quarter mile through the mud on the unlikely chance he could catch her?"

"That's how crimes of passion will sometimes play out," someone said. She didn't turn to see who the speaker was, but set a cup of coffee in front of the mayor and rolled her eyes so only he could see.

The mayor blew on his coffee and said, "I wonder if you boys could give me and Sheriff Ada a few minutes to discuss some other official business."

The men drained their cups and cleared out, to her relief, and the mayor waited for the door to close before telling her, "There're things going on here in the valley that need your attention too. Luke and Stephanie Braun, they've been at it again. Stephanie is at the clinic."

"I saw her last night when I checked in with Dr. Mink." She gathered up half a dozen cups and carried them to the washroom sink.

Ephraim Applegate started to speak but considered his words for a moment longer. He didn't like the idea of an "acting" sheriff, either, nor of a woman in the job. And he especially hated it being his niece, Ada. It had been a lot of goddamned back-room bull manure, although he would never express it in those terms to a lady. "Ada, honey," he said, "they all thought Montgomery would be gone just a few weeks when the Board asked you to step in as acting sheriff." He screwed up his lips. "It's been over three months now."

She stood in the doorway of the washroom, leaning her head on the doorjamb. "I know how long to the day, Uncle Eph." It was eighty-three days. Eighty-three, she thought, since she'd driven her husband to the bus station—both of them unsmiling; no words passing between them. Her uncle and her Aunt Corrine had been on her about it for eighty-two days; the newspaper had started sniping by the second week, and the County Board not more than a week after that.

"Corrine is beside herself; she won't give me a minute's rest. Now think about it before you say no; we could have Dave Wickers take over for the rest of the term. It's just not something you should be burdened with for such a length of time."

"It's not such a burden, Mr. Mayor. But I'll think about it, I promise." She held her hair back and kissed him on the cheek as she passed on the way to the front door.

"Come by for supper tomorrow," the mayor called as Ada quick-stepped down the corridor. "Corrine says so. She hasn't seen you in a month!"

1:45 p.m. – Bonanza (a.k.a. The Bottoms; a.k.a. Chinatown)
Interview with Mrs. Margaret Li, a potential witness

IT WAS PAST MID-DAY WHEN ADA Reed got away from the office and up and over Mill Creek Pass, the back road down the Yankee Fork headwaters. The dew by then had burned off the canyon bottom, so the road was hot and dry. As a consequence, the window stayed down, and her hair got dirtier and more tangled as she drove. The town of Custer, when she arrived from the east, sat lifeless under blue sky and a scorching summer sun.

She eased the truck past the hardware and the ice plant, and straight down Main Street. Twelve commercial buildings lined the north side of the road, hard against the hill. The buildings were of painted wood, with a couple built of brick, and mostly one story, with a few boasting a second floor. Fully a third of them were boarded up or burned out. Only a few businesses were left on the south side, including the post office, assay lab, and the burned-out and falling-down Lucky Boy mill.

All that coffee on top of a thin slice of toast made her stomach churn, and she would have stopped for lunch but didn't want to answer to another town full of crime experts. She kept driving to the far end of town, around the sharp bend at the roadhouse, to the Bottoms—or to where that neighborhood used to be before the dredge worked its way in.

Mrs. Margaret Li's house was easy enough to find, it being one of the few structures still standing in the path of the dredge. Most everything else had been torn down or cut down, bulldozed, and burned. It was Li who had stood at her gate and watched Ada walk the pond perimeter the day before. Spotting the woman's house was easy, but getting to it turned out to be a trick. Many of the roads of the neighborhood were obstructed by deep test trenches, gravel piles, or felled trees, and some of the open roads ended without warning in one of several fingers of the pond. She eventually drove across yards, gardens, and downed fences to arrive at the remnant of road in front of Li's house. The old woman, sitting on the porch, had watched her the whole way.

Ada raked her fingers through her hair and set her hat on to hold it in place. She stuffed her tie between the buttons of her uniform shirt, straightened her cuffs, and stepped out. The shriek and thunder of a working dredge pushed back on her immediately, nearly staggering her as she came around the front of the truck. The floating factory towered over the cottage not more than a hundred feet beyond the roofline.

The gate was unlatched. At the porch, suddenly unsure whether to bow to the old woman or shake hands, she doffed her Stetson, letting the tangled yellow hair fall out. "Good afternoon," she had to yell. "There's no easy way to get here."

Mrs. Li nodded in return, and may have said, "You'll find no easy way out, either," but the woman's voice was weak and drowned out by the screech of pulleys and the clang and crash of boulders and iron. Li's face was full and round, and deeply lined; her gray hair was braided into a single que. But it was her complexion that made Ada shudder. Her face was jaundiced, far too yellow—almost a cruel caricature of an Asian face.

"I'm Sheriff Ada Reed," she said. Even in the acoustic shadow of the porch Ada could barely hear the reply. 'I expected you,' she read the woman's lips to say. "Can we talk?" Ada shouted. Li nodded and stood with Ada's help.

The house, when they entered, was clean, if a little cluttered and tired looking. The old woman filled a pot from a hand pump at the kitchen sink and set it on an electric hotplate. The window over the sink was filled edge-to-edge with the rust-streaked corrugated tin walls of the gold dredge working beyond, and the room was still very loud. Neither tried to speak as the water boiled. Ada noted an ice box, but the door was braced open with no ice inside. A few small plates and bowls stood on the open cupboards. The wood stove was still warm from a morning fire.

Li filled a ceramic pot with the hot water, added tea, and indicated to Ada she should bring the tray. She led them shuffling from the kitchen to a small parlor, where they took refuge behind a closed door.

The parlor was a little quieter, but also a little darker and mustier. The lone window was closed and curtained with old lace. Ada set the tray on a low table between facing chairs. "I would like to talk to you about Rose Braden," she said.

"Yes, I know." Mrs. Li filled two cups with tea and drizzled a little honey into hers. "I'm afraid I have no milk," she said.

"Milk is hard to keep in this weather. Were you friends with her, with Rose Braden?" A plaque hung on the wall over the woman's head: a circle filled with a backward 'S,' as on the medallions Ada had found under the victim's dress. One side of the 'S' was filled in black and the other side white. "That is the yin and yang symbol, isn't it?" Ada asked.

The old woman spoke without looking back. "It is the *Taijitu*; it shows the duality of nature. Are you a student of eastern culture?"

"Oh gosh, no. Not at all," she replied. It had been years ago, after all, and just the one college class. She took out her orange field book and drew a backward 'S' and wrote 'Tie-jee-two.' She asked, "I'm sorry, but is your name spelled L-e-e, or L-i?"

"L-i. It means plum tree. Is that a ballpoint pen?"

"It is, yes. It was a gift." She handed the pen to Mrs. Li.

Li clicked the pen a couple of times then handed it back. "You are the wife of Montgomery Reed?" she asked.

"Yes. I've been appointed Acting Sheriff of Yellowpine County while he serves in Korea."

"In Korea, yes I heard. Montgomery acted like a sheriff, too, especially toward the businessmen and the dredge owners. He did nothing at all to prevent this." She waved at the scene beyond the lace curtains, at the flattened neighborhood and torn up ground.

"I'm not sure what . . ." It was not pertinent to the case, but Mrs. Li did have a five-story dredge chewing up the ground beyond her kitchen. Ada nodded and said, "There was nothing the Sheriff's Department could do about this. The surface rights were found to be subordinate to the mineral rights." It didn't seem enough, so she added, "That wasn't Montgomery's decision, it was settled in the courts. I guess it's a gray area of the law."

"Gray is the black and white we choose to mix. And now Montgomery is off fighting again. He did not slay enough dragons in the last war?"

There was no reason to be disrespectful like that. Ada scoffed and closed her finger in the notebook. "He helped get the Japanese out of your land," she said.

"I was born in the Yankee Fork. This is my land, although a new lot of invaders come to take it from me." Li's head slumped down, and she caught her breath before she could look up again. "Should you be taking notes?" she asked.

"The girl?"

"Rose."

"I'm told you knew her well. At least, she was often seen here. Did she work for you?"

"No." Li coughed into a napkin and wiped her mouth. "She helped me, and I helped her to help herself. I'm not so strong any-more to help directly."

"Did she steal from you?"

"You'd be the first one I called."

Ada knew the remark was meant to taunt, but she couldn't understand why. Aside from her uniform, she didn't think she'd caused any affront. And the old woman, even jaundiced as she was, appeared educated and otherwise kindly. She determined not to take offence. "You were born in the Yankee Fork, but you've been away, I'm told. Where did you go for forty years?"

"I was a whore." The old woman coughed again and sat with closed eyes for a moment. "W-h-o . . ."

"Yes, thank you." And the 'whore' comment would have been to shock her. It didn't. Well, it might have, a little, but she raised the cup to her lips and asked, "Was Rose Braden seeing men? Were you helping her to meet men?"

"What are grand theft and murder when there are the carnal and salacious to hold us?"

"I'm investigating a girl's death, Mrs. Li."

Li bent her head one way and the other, stretching her neck. She sighed. "It is an awful thing, to find one interesting only in death. We should show interest in the living as they live."

"Confucius?"

"Me."

The floor beneath them began to vibrate, and then shake. Ada jumped up, but sat again when the old woman stayed seated. The spoon clattered on the saucer. Li closed her eyes and breathed deeply, rubbing her elbows and knees. "What was that?" Ada asked, when it had stopped.

"Just the bucket line scraping bedrock. They'll set me adrift one of these days."

Still shaken, Ada could not recall where she was in the list of questions she'd planned to ask. She rose and peered through the old lace curtains at the ruined ground and the encroaching water. "Rose Braden's body was found yesterday in the dredge pond behind your house. Do you know what happened, who might have killed the girl?"

Li dropped her eyes and turned away. Her hands rose to hold her head, then straightened the braid of hair to fall over her shoulder and down over her breast. "I fear I may have," she whispered.

Ada opened her mouth and closed it. She fumbled for her pen. "Would you like to explain how?"

The woman didn't answer, but took a small ceramic pipe from the end table and lit the partly charred contents with a match. A sweet-acrid smoke drifted over.

"Is that opium?" Ada asked.

Li's laugh ended in a cough. "No, it's just *dàmá.*" She inhaled and closed her eyes. "Medicine for my pain."

Ada wrote, 'dah-mah.' The parlor walls closed in even more, and the cloying smoke made her nearly gag. Thumbing back through her book, she found the notes and sketches she'd made when she first examined the victim. "What is the meaning of the crescent moon?" she asked.

"I don't know to what you refer."

"The symbols she bore. If Rose Braden was marked on her hands with a crescent moon, what would it mean in Eastern culture?"

"The moon?" The old woman drew from the pipe, and strained to speak holding her breath. "Confucius said, '*When a wise man points at the moon . . .*'" She exhaled, and the sour fumes billowed through the room. "'*. . .the fool examines the finger.*'"

"That doesn't help me." Her head had begun to throb from the smoke and the din of the dredge.

"Doesn't it? How about, *Three things cannot long be hidden: the sun, the moon, and the truth.*"

Ada waited through another deep vibration. "I think that was Buddha."

"Ah!" Li nodded and puffed the embers up again.

The vibrations and noise were dizzying, and the smoke, like burning weeds, nearly choked her. And she wasn't being taken seriously. "Why would someone wear a fifteen-pound belt around her waist?" she asked as patiently as she could.

"Perhaps, like Marley's ghost, she was burdened by greed."

"For penance? Was she being punished?"

Li coughed, and took a moment to fill her lungs. "Perhaps she could not find an albatross."

"*The Ancient Mariner*? You're awfully well-read considering your previous occupation."

"You as well, I think."

A laugh escaped before Ada could make up her mind to be offended. Li stared at the wall with the tiniest betrayal of a grin. Ada bit her lip and waited. She noticed again the *Taijitu* and asked, "So was Rose Braden also part light and part darkness?"

"Oh yes, very much. Rose was neither angel nor witch. No more than we, anyway." The old woman set the pipe down and leaned her head on the back of the chair, rubbing her elbows. "She was young but not as silly as you might expect; frightened as a bird, especially toward the end, but still full of remarkable strength and courage. You and I were like that once. Maybe you still are. Rose liked bluebirds especially, and—oh dear . . ." Her voice shrank away for a moment then came back small and sad. "She would sit and wonder at sparks flying into the night sky, or at the moon racing through the clouds. And she would cry."

Li had to sink back into the chair and catch her breath. She wiped tears from her cheeks. "Rose cried far too much for one so young. But she laughed as well, and she dreamed. You should have seen that child dream!"

Ada found herself smiling. She said, "Excuse me, but I have to ask because I don't think you fully answered my question. If she wasn't seeing men, was she seeing a man? Was Rose Braden having a love affair?"

Li's head lolled on the chair back, and her voice meandered through an answer. "If Rose loved, she loved deeply. But it can't be helped. There are some who will believe in love in spite of the evidence against it. Isn't that always the way of things?"

Ada said nothing but stuck the notebook in her pocket. Through the small window and just beyond the picket fence, a robin carried a worm to a low bush, there being no tall trees left to nest in. For a long while she sat forward with her boots crossed at the ankles and her little finger raised to sip her tea. At last, and almost to herself, she said, "*It is easy to hate and it is difficult to love. That is always the way of things.*"

Li eyed her for a moment. "It is Confucius." She found the pipe, puffed up the embers, and exhaled a long stream of smoke. She said, "I loved Rose; it wasn't so difficult. You needn't write that in your book, Ada Reed, but it hurts nothing for you to know it."

CHAPTER FIVE

THE ACTING SHERIFF RETREATED WITH DIFFICULTY from the
tangle of felled trees and trenches, backing her truck, pulling
forward unable to turn around, then backing again slowly. On the
county road finally, and at the top of the bench before entering the
miles of dredge tailings, she pulled to the side and stepped out for
a needed breath of air. The Mansfield & Midlands dredge clattered
below her, its long bucket line pulling rocks by the cubic yard into
the maw of the floating factory.

From where Ada stood, Jordan Creek Canyon, spilling into
the Yankee Fork from the north, was lit brightly with dark clouds
gathering in the distance. The walls of the canyon, once logged
bare by the miners, were dotted again with young pine and aspen.
Bonanza gold veins worked in the early days had diminished with
depth to silver and then to copper ore, and mining had slowed
over the years. Or so she'd read. All she really knew was the mining district that had sustained the whole county for generations
was dying. Over several minutes there was no mining activity to
be seen—none of the old cable lines running, no dust rising from
waste rock being dumped.

The interview with the old woman was unsettling, and Ada worried she hadn't done well. It wasn't Li's bitterness, and it wasn't the evasiveness that bothered Ada, but the woman's forthrightness. Li knew something, and not just about Rose. It was something Ada had to know too, but she wasn't sure how or whom to ask.

She climbed back into her truck, loosened her tie, and headed south toward Sunbeam and the highway. Lonnie Barr, according to Munson, had somehow, and perhaps not in the best of ways, been involved with the victim. Ada needed to question the young man.

The Sunbeam store and tavern stood at the intersection of the Yankee Fork Road and Highway 75, tucked under a stand of spruce and fir at the edge of a dirt parking lot. The main building of heavy logs sat beneath a steep shingled roof that swooped down to cover a narrow porch running the length of the building. Half a dozen board-and-batten cabins stood behind the main building, strung out close against a granite face. Dense forest rose to the north. The place had long been a rendezvous for liquor and romance, or so Ada had heard. Lonnie Barr stayed in one of the small cabins in back, according to Munson, but was more likely to be found sitting at the bar.

Motor oil, cigarettes, dusty cans of pork and beans, and bottles of warm soda comprised the Sunbeam Store offerings. There were neither customers nor clerk as Ada crossed the room. A doorway in back fashioned to look like mine timbers led into the tavern-half of the business, and when she stepped through, rancid beer and nicotine fumes hit her hard, causing her to choke and her eyes to tear.

The bartender looked as close to a dead man as she'd ever seen in a vertical pose. His skin was ash-gray and festooned over his frame; waxen eyes bulged from fleshy sockets, and a cigarette hung between purple lips under a purple nose. Ada stepped up to the bar between a couple of whiskered patrons and in a hushed voice told the bartender she was looking for a Mr. Lonnie Barr. He answered by swinging the cigarette up into a smirk.

At that instant a young man three stools away vaulted over the bar, tripping as he did and knocking a bottle from a shelf. He disappeared under a blanket that screened an opening through the backbar. The bar was just high enough that Ada chose to race around the end of it.

Squeezing past the chuckling, wheezing bartender, she dodged under the blanket and into complete darkness. She dropped to a knee, grabbed the flashlight from her belt, and swept the beam around a cluttered storage room. There were cases of whiskey bottles, full and empty, and kegs of beer stacked haphazardly. Boxes of cigarettes lined the far wall. The place stank of mold, spilled beer, and rat droppings.

She sidled around a stack of beer kegs just as a door creaked open and light burst in. She darted forward but, blinded by the momentary daylight, tripped over a mop and bucket. The door slammed shut. Half soaked in soapy, beery mop water, she slipped and lurched to the door in time to see a man bolt into the trees behind the line of cabins.

She jumped from the wooden steps and chased through the gravel lot to the edge of the woods, but the underbrush there was thick, and there was nothing to see of the escapee. She held her breath, and listened. Branches snapped twenty or thirty yards ahead. Her flashlight went back into her belt, then, and her gun came out of its holster.

Gripping the pistol tightly in both hands, she worked her way into the shadowy woods, ducking and wheeling, and sweeping the gun side to side. She sidestepped spruce boughs and pushed through shoulder-high gooseberry. Slippery logs and moss-covered rocks slowed her, and it was several minutes before she gained a small freshet, which cut steeply down a fan of boulders. With the gun high and in front of her, she ducked under a log and clambered over several others. Sunlight filtered down in shafts through the mist, lighting the way and sparkling on the water where it splashed between the rocks.

She held her breath again, letting the chattering birds and the splashing of the stream fade back. She waited for a sound out of place, something unnatural or peculiar.

A rock clattered above and to her left. She grinned. A moment later she heard the very faint snapping of a stick. The guy was a good forty yards ahead and climbing. But granite crags rose steeply in the direction he'd taken. The land there rose into steep cliffs that would glow pink in the rising sun but would stay shadowed all afternoon. There was no easy escape that way for Mr. Barr.

Again, she held her breath. No noise came from above. She stepped heavily onto crisscrossing branches, causing them to snap and pop. Within seconds frantic scrambling and slipping could be heard. She grinned, and after a minute broke a limb from a dead snag, sending a loud crack through the woods. The young man's retreat was loud and hurried.

Well, he could just stay there all night. She holstered her gun and had to shake her hands out after gripping the thing so tightly. At the stream she kneeled and washed her hands of the beery mop water, then scooped a drink to her mouth. It tasted of ferns, pine needles, and moss. The water splashed too loudly to hear any more of Barr's movements, so she turned back, letting the stream lead her to the road instead of stumbling back the way she'd come.

The bartender was still vertical but hacking heavily when she entered half an hour later through the front door. She asked, "Was that Barr? Lonnie Barr?"

He shrugged.

"He's said to have a place out back."

"I don't recall the name." He rinsed and dried a couple beer glasses while he considered the question, still coughing and clearing his throat.

She couldn't read his face for the loose way the flesh hung around the eyes and mouth. "Don't recall?" she asked. Four other men in the room looked away when she glanced at them.

"Nope," the bartender said.

It was definitely a sneer on his face, and after her run through the woods she wasn't in the mood. "How's your memory," she asked, "with regards to your inventory?" She opened her notebook and took out her pen. "Do you recall how those cases of cigarettes showed up in your back room without tax stamps? Appears no federal tobacco tax was paid, sir, and you don't look like a reservation Indian."

The bartender held his eyes on her for a moment. He took a customer's mug to the tap for a refill, shifted the cigarette to his fingers, and spit a flake of tobacco. With a look of disgust he said, "Lonnie Barr? Yeah, I believe that was him that ran. Cabin four. And no, I don't recall him being around at all on Monday night."

"Which is his car?" she asked.

The man pointed through the window toward a rusted Ford pickup—pre-war from the look of it. Ada nodded and left through the side door. She marched to cabin four and padlocked the door. At the old pickup, she raised the hood and yanked out the distributor cable, which she stowed in her own jockey box.

The bartender watched from his doorway, looking even more deathly in the fading daylight. "Spread the word," Ada told him. "Anyone who gives Barr a ride in either direction, or any other help, could be considered an accomplice post-facto in a girl's death."

She climbed back into her truck and started back toward Camas, leaving young Mr. Barr to cool his heels overnight. But the truck had sat in the sun all day and was hot, and between the long interview of Mrs. Li, the chase through the woods, and the lunch she'd forgotten to bring, she could barely push through the highway turns. A half dozen civilian cars got backed up in her rearview mirror, so with an embarrassed wave she pulled over at a wide shoulder to let them pass. The Salmon River thundered below her.

Her hands, she noticed, were shaking and she wasn't surprised, either, to find her chest had begun to ache. For God's sake, she'd pulled her gun out, back at Sunbeam, and chased him—chased the kid into the woods! She shut off the engine and sat awhile as evening shadows began their climb up the canyon walls. She had pulled out her damned gun, and she'd crashed through the brush with it, and slipped over mossy rocks with the thing in her hand. She hadn't held a gun for years—since she was seventeen and . . . Lord, what was she thinking?

"You'll have a gun, of course," Montgomery had told her, as though it were the least significant thing. "I'll have a gun? I don't want a gun!" She'd stepped around and made him look at her. "Monty, you know how I feel about guns."

She grasped her elbows and with a shudder leaned her head against the steering wheel.

MONTGOMERY HAD ASKED HIS FRIENDS TO DINNER and given her little warning, as usual. Dee Mansfield had been first to arrive and the first to broach the subject; it was his idea from the start, and she'd thought, *why, he's joking!* Dee was Montgomery's best friend. He owned the Yankee Fork gold dredge, and he carried himself with the confidence of a former marine and a prominent man. He and Montgomery hunted together, and they had a poker night once a month.

She had laughed at Mansfield's—Dee's—suggestion. She'd laughed so hard she had to put down the tray. "Sheriff?" she asked, "of Yellowpine County? You mean actually wear a badge and a hat? Be a real sheriff?"

"And pants, and a shirt and tie," Montgomery said. He loaded the grill with hamburger patties. Dee stood at the cart mixing cocktails while Larry Marsh, whom she'd never liked, talked quietly with a gentleman she didn't know.

Darkness had settled in, although it stayed warm enough and dry that April evening, and a full moon rose through the branches of the elm. She lit her new tiki torches. "I have so many things going on already. The ladies' auxiliary is shorthanded; there's the church grounds committee. Am I supposed to just let the community down?"

Dee handed her a mai-tai or some silly thing with an umbrella. "It'll just be for a month or so," he told her, "Until Mont gets back from Korea."

"You're being fatuous." She turned from one to the other. "You're teasing me!"

But Dee and Monty and pinch-faced Larry Marsh all assured her they hadn't come to the plan lightly. They'd discussed it for days, and they simply had to keep the position open for Montgomery so that a special election would not be called. "We've considered who could fill the job temporarily, who would be too political, and who would . . . interfere." Monty and Dee had exchanged glances.

Torchlight flickered, and the men's shadows danced against the garden wall. She'd sat down in the folding chair as the men went on discussing, and wondered if they were serious, and if they were, what would she do? What would Cheryl and Betty say, and the others, for heaven's sake? Well, she couldn't let herself think about it because in the end they would surely say they were joking and have a good laugh at her.

But if they weren't joking, could she even do it? Could she give orders for men to follow; arrest them if they didn't?

Ice cubes clinked in the glasses, and the grill smoked and sizzled. She waved at the smoke and got up to turn the meat, but Marsh had grabbed up the spatula and taken charge, so she stayed off to the side a while longer. Monty lit a cigarette from one of the torches and nearly burned his face. He said, "Jeff Banning is a shoo-in in any special election."

"Yes," Mansfield agreed.

"And once he's in office it would take dynamite up the ass to get him out."

"He'd be trouble."

"We've got to get the Board to approve a direct, temporary action, and there's not a man in the county they'll all agree to." They had turned her way, then, *and they were serious!*

"Now, give me that tray." Dee smiled and winked. "We don't need the next sheriff of Yellowpine County serving cocktails and canapes."

Why, she'd hardly been able to eat. The April evening did turn chilly, Mansfield and the others went home, and the coals burned slowly to ashes. She was left with just a little tidying up to do. "Monty, you know how I feel about guns."

"You don't have to use it, babe; it's just part of the getup. Don't load it if you don't want to. But listen to me now." He downed his whiskey and pointed with the glass. "Don't you ever pull that gun out, loaded or unloaded, unless you are ready to shoot the man in front of you. You never bluff with a gun."

GOD, HAD HE MEANT THAT TO make her feel better? Alone but for birds on the wires, she sat at the edge of the highway and watched shadows scale the steep canyon walls. She sat a good hour before pressing the starter and moving on.

8:15 p.m. – County Fairgrounds. Traffic control

ADA ROLLED INTO CAMAS AT DUSK and found traffic backed up on Main Street all the way to the highway. Independence Day celebrations were already starting and, darn it, she had agreed to help the town cops with traffic control. "Interoffice cooperation," it was explained. She flipped on her red light and crawled along the shoulder of Main, past the traffic que to the main parking lot. She left the light flashing.

Officer Stengel was waving his arms and shouting at the taxpayers to hold on a minute, for Christ's sake, and go the way he told them to go. "Need help?" she asked him.

"I was hoping you would be here some time ago, Madam Sheriff."

"Got a murder case taking up a lot of my time." She ducked his arm as he waved a Chevy pickup through.

"Gonna have a murder case here in a minute." He threw up his arms and shouted to prevent a Rambler from turning left, then waved it straight ahead, with a "Lordy, folks!"

"Where's Deputy Don?"

"At the north gate. Take over here, Ada . . . sheriff. I've got to get patrolling the midway."

"But I don't . . ."

"Someone has to patrol the midway. It's better I do it; they've already tapped the keg."

He didn't wait for an answer but trotted off, leaving Ada with a line of cars a quarter mile long and wondering how far from the beer garden the town cop intended to patrol. In any case, she started waving this way and that, dodging the vehicles as they rolled by and halting traffic now and then for pedestrians. A half dozen cars returning from where she'd sent them to the left let her know that lot was full, but she eventually found a rhythm swinging her arms, and got the cars all going to the right instead.

A lot of the folks whistled and yelled "Ada!" as they passed. She smiled and called back to each of them but kept the tangle of cars rolling. A few she did not hurry through, but leaned into their open windows and told them, "Evening Sherm," or "Nice hat Stacey," and answered that Montgomery was fine, thanks, and she was sure Andy, or Eddy, or Phil was fine too, and Mont wanted to assure everyone the United Nations forces had the upper hand. "And besides," she told them, "They're already talking about peace talks, and I'm betting they'll be home by Labor Day."

The sunset had faded to silver and cobalt, and music was coming from the bandshell by the time the traffic thinned to where folks could park themselves. Ada turned off her red light and continued on foot to the front gate. But instead of continuing into the grounds as she'd intended, as she had since forever, she wandered the outer boundary of the fairgrounds between a wood fence and an empty field.

The air drifting from the midway smelled of green grass crushed under polished shoes, and corn dogs and cotton candy, and it made her smile. She stood a long while with her boots up on the lower rail of the fence, leaning in as the county promenaded two by two, or by family, or in small groups of friends. She'd grown up in the valley, and she knew almost everyone strolling by. And they almost knew her, she supposed. She'd gone away to college right after high school, but then she'd come home . . . but then she'd gone away again as a new bride before coming home again for the war—the last war. And though it had been six years now, she sometimes felt her neighbors considered her an outsider in her own hometown.

A tall man in Forest Service green ambled beneath crisscrossed strings of lights. Ada stood on the fence rail and watched him for a minute. He kept his hands in his pockets and moved easily, dipping his smokey-bear hat to the ladies as he passed. It was District Ranger Ben McGann, and she nearly called out to him. Ben had been a close friend in high school—a lot more than a friend—and Ada didn't know why he'd not looked her up. He'd gotten back to town half a year ago, and had to feel a little bit like a stranger himself. But he hadn't been to see her, and she didn't know why.

The lights of the Ferris wheel flickered on, interrupting her thoughts of tall Ranger McGann. Beneath the lights the people laughed a little louder and stepped livelier. Ada jumped down from the fence and cut through the field back to her sheriff's pickup.

Her house—Montgomery's house—was in the newer, west end of town where the trees were not much higher than the rooftops and the houses had few gables and fewer porches. But it was a decent neighborhood with lawns and sidewalks, although the sidewalk had never been completed to their house, which sat at the end of the lane hard against the bluff. It was a single-story ranch style, although it didn't look like anything she'd seen on the ranch.

The kitchen smelled empty when she entered, and it was chilly inside although the day had been warm. She'd burned the last piece of firewood two days earlier but still hadn't refilled the box and felt no inclination to do it just then. Instead, she found a slice of fried ham in the Frigidaire and ate it cold with a piece of toasted bread and butter.

From the back door, music and rowdy shouts floated over from the fairgrounds, and the Ferris wheel lights glowed in the clouds overhead. Ada leaned on the door jamb and listened for a minute before closing herself in.

She sat in a bath because the water was warm and she was cold and still smelled of mop water and beer, then got into her pajamas and slippers. She put the smelly uniform in a tub to soak, put a stack of Sinatras on the record player, and carried last night's plate and glass into the kitchen.

Far back in the cupboard she found the open bottle of Christian Brothers and poured herself a brandy. "Here's to . . ." she began. But she couldn't think whom or what to toast, and her words sounded echoey against the knotty pine cabinets and linoleum floor, so she let it drop.

The living room faced south and was still warm from the day and comfortable. But the harvest wallpaper, when she turned on the lamp, made her sigh, and the floral drapes clashed with it, and it all just felt like a lot of work she was not getting to. She clicked the lamp off, slumped into the over-stuffed chair with her legs over the arm, and hummed along to "Some Enchanted Evening" until the brandy loosened her neck and warmed her enough that she could sleep.

CHAPTER SIX

Thursday, 5 July
Yankee Fork case. Expecting coroner's report today.

A DA WOKE TO MOONLIGHT THROUGH WINDOWS frosted at the edges, still slouched in the chair, cold, and achy. But she stretched, cleaned her face and her teeth, and was dressed and had a pot perking on the electric plate before the sky began to lighten.

She skipped making breakfast, as she had most mornings for three months, because it was hardly worth getting in the firewood, starting a fire in the stove, and breaking eggs for just one person. She had to be the last woman in Camas, Idaho not to have an electric range, and she sometimes resented it. But it was ungracious to complain about the wood stove, since Montgomery had bought her a beautiful new Frigidaire, after all, and she had an electric toaster, electric mixer, and the electric hot plate.

They'd moved from her farm in the East Fork where she'd had practically no modern appliances at all. That was five years ago, not long after the war—right after Montgomery had taken the job with the County. Ada hadn't had a lot to say about the move, but she'd gotten her way with Formica countertops and a porcelain sink with chrome faucets. The wood stove was not a bother really, and Monty loved the smell and crackle of the fire in the morning. He loved his eggs and hotcakes and liked that she would sit with him and fuss over his uniform as he ate.

Now she buttered her own toast, gulped her coffee, and tugged at the fit of her own trousers.

The hot plate, really, could fry up some eggs if she wanted them. But she wasn't all that hungry this morning—the coroner had asked her to stop by at eight.

YELLOWPINE COUNTY DID NOT HAVE AN ACTUAL CORONER. Dr. Dennis Mink ran the Salmon Valley Clinic, and he handled most county business for a negotiated fee. Ada knew Mink from civic events, and from the country club, of course. But she saw a different family doctor and so did not know what to expect at his clinic. It was a relief when he met her in his office and not in the examination room. His office, like the hallways and like the examination rooms of the clinic, was of cinder block painted a light and unremarkable blue. There were two large casement windows looking into a garden, and the office was clean and tidy.

She sat down with him at eight o'clock sharp and thanked him but declined the coffee offered in a small glass beaker. He called her Sheriff, she noted, and she made a point to call him Doctor.

"Well, she drowned, as presumed," Mink told her. He set his beaker on the steel-frame desk and opened his lab coat to sit. "Lungs full of water." A confirmed bachelor, Mink was somewhat small of frame and, though barely a decade Ada's senior, was graying from the temples back.

"I thought that the case." Ada nodded but kept her eyes on her notebook. "And the other wounds?" She shifted, causing the oak swivel chair to creak loudly.

"Broken leg, broken ribs, crushed hip. It's possible some of it was pre-drowning, but more likely just the rough treatment she got from the machinery. Frankly, it's lucky the body came up in one piece." He looked over his glasses to the windows, and seemed interested in a bank of morning clouds. "Otherwise, except the wound across her face, not even a lot of bruising."

Ada made a long note, then crossed her booted ankles and studied the diplomas on the wall over the doctor's head. She'd known the coroner's report would require certain discussions, of course, and it wasn't that she was stuffy or at all prudish, but . . . "What about . . ." She cleared her throat. "Her last evening?"

Doctor Mink cleared his throat as well. "She had not recently had intimate relations."

"Hadn't she? I mean, of course not. It didn't seem like . . ."

"However, she was pregnant."

"Ah, damn it to hell!" Ada creaked back and turned in her chair, crossing her arms tightly. She had till then somehow been able to hold the girl's death at arm's length—as though maybe Rose Braden had been reckless and her death inevitable. But pregnant blew away that smokescreen; pregnant made her a young mother and the death a tragedy, awful and unmitigated. "Pardon my language, Doctor." Ada blew out a long, breath. "How, uhm . . . how far along was she?"

"About twelve weeks, as close as I can estimate."

"Around Easter, then." Her cheeks burned. She focused on the diploma on the left behind Mink, which was from Midwestern University Medical School. The bookshelves on the right held mostly thick medical texts, with a few loose journals and folders. She pulled in another deep breath and asked, "And was her husband the natural . . . Was Corey Braden the, uhm . . . the biological . . ."

"The father?"

This was not a part of the job she'd imagined, and she wondered how she was going to face Dennis Mink at the next charity raffle. She cleared her throat again.

The doctor said, "Unfortunately, Sheriff, I've treated Sergeant Braden before and since his service. I really can't discuss his medical conditions."

"No, of course you can't." And that was just fine, because she certainly didn't want to discuss it either. Through the casement windows, and backlit by the morning sun, crabapple trees in a long row were in full scarlet bloom. Without turning, she said, "But we can assume his medical condition would factor into a paternity discussion?"

Mink stood. "Ada, you know I can't."

Damn it to hell, why did the girl have to be pregnant? Ada slammed the door of her pickup and hunched over the steering wheel. Of course, pregnant made it neat and easy. Sergeant Braden learned his wife was carrying another man's child—*damn it!*—and he couldn't reconcile with the dishonor. She started up the engine but let the clutch out too quickly and jerked away from the curb. Why did it have to be that kind of killing?

All the way up the Salmon River canyon she went over Braden's version of the girl's death. It was neat and easy. Except it wasn't, quite. There was something wrong about it. Still, a lover made sense now. Munson said she was messing around with Lonnie Barr, and that would certainly explain why Barr ran as he had.

At Sunbeam, she killed her engine and coasted to the front of the store. The business was deserted even though it was nearly half-past ten. A heavy river fog had settled in overnight and still hung thick, keeping the ground glistening with dew. Under the fog the clearing sat quiet but for the tumbling river a hundred yards away.

Ada eased her truck door closed and crept around the back of the main building. For several minutes she waited, hearing and seeing no one. But tracks in the dew showed a man had gotten into Barr's pickup truck then retreated the way he'd come. She returned to her own truck and brought it around to the side lot, raced the engine once, and slammed the door when she got out. From her lunch box she took a piece of coffee cake wrapped in wax paper and placed it on the hood of Barr's truck with a note:

Mr. Barr, we need to talk when you're ready. No sense starving in the meantime. —Sheriff Reed.

She slammed her door again and kicked up a little gravel as she turned and headed up the Yankee Fork Road.

11:05 a.m. – Custer jailhouse
Follow-up interrogation of Sergeant Corey Braden

THE POLICE OFFICE AND JAILHOUSE SAT at the east end of Custer, on the north side of the street catty-corner to the burned-out Lucky Boy mill. Ada didn't like to park there because the mud of the street was blackened with sticky mill ash. She parked nearer the assay office and walked the boardwalk through the business district.

Chief Munson kept a spare office, with a small desk, three chairs lined up against one wall, and a low bookshelf cluttered with papers and a few volumes of State and local statutes. The law books were for the prompt resolution of disputes. Absent resolution, two cells opened off the opposite wall.

Corey Braden waited in the far cell with his wheelchair rocked back so that his head and shoulders leaned against the stone wall. There was a single barred window above him. The lintel and posts of the window were of thick blocks of wood, and they were pocked with the names of the many guests of the town over the years. In the cell there was room for a bunk, and for a table between the bunk and the bars.

"I guess you should wait outside," Ada said to Munson, and nodded toward the door.

He cocked his head back in surprise. "I should be included in the interrogation."

She whispered, "You can't, Kellen. You're compromised."

"What the heck does that mean?" he whispered back.

"Don't take offense, but you're one of the persons who communicated to the suspect with regards to his wife's alleged infidelity.

You can't be considered an uninvolved . . . a non-vested investiga-
tive . . . you know."

The chief sighed dramatically but snatched up his hat and
stepped outside. Ada waited for the door to close, then walked
to the prisoner's cell and stood with her field book in hand. He
watched through narrowed eyes, rocking the chair slightly on its
rear wheels.

She asked, "When did you get home?"

Braden didn't look at her or show any sign of hearing her, but
after a moment spoke to the side wall of the cell, "Stateside six
months ago. Yankee Fork three months ago."

She pulled a chair over but remained standing. "A long time in
the hospital. Did you land in Seattle—Whidbey Island?"

The young man rolled his head back and forth on the wall, eyes
closed. Ada started to speak again, but he said, "No. They brought
me through San Francisco. Air cargo, you know. Re-habbed me at
the Presidio."

He turned toward her, and she thought she might never have
seen such a lost and weary gaze. It caused her to lose her words for
a moment. She dropped onto the chair, focused on her notebook,
and said, "Three months convalescence must have seemed like forever. Did anyone visit you there?"

He turned from her again and stopped rocking the chair. She
waited. He cleared his throat and said, "She came to the hospital. A
couple of times. I told her she should get back and take care of the
business, but she stayed for two weeks the second time."

"Were things bad between you at that time? Turn this way,
please."

He didn't turn toward her but started rocking again. "Naw, hell.
We yucked it up. It was a laugh riot."

She scooted her chair around square. "I'd like you to look at me,
Sergeant."

"I'd like you to get me a whiskey or unlock the damned cell so
I can get my own."

"You're a suspect in a murder investigation, Sergeant Braden. You have to do things my way."

"If I'm still just a suspect, you're a pretty slow investigator." He laughed, and it started a small ache in her chest: the cornered marine trying to be tough. But he pivoted his chair without putting down the front wheels and faced her.

"When did things get bad between you and your wife?" God, her questions sounded as empty as the look in his eyes. She turned from him, and for a short while they both stayed quiet.

The jailhouse floor and walls were of mortared stone, and the ceiling was of dark timbers; heavy iron bars fronted the cells. Someone had hung travel posters on the wall opposite the cells— for decoration, or maybe to taunt the prisoners. It was in the posters Braden seemed most interested. At last, he said, "Things never got good."

"There must have been a homecoming between you."

"Now you're the laugh riot. Did she jump into my lap, throw her arms around me? No, ma'am. Maybe she was waiting for the rest of me to get home."

"Were you?"

His jaw tensed but his eyes stayed focused beyond her. "Huh-uh. I knew what I was coming back with, and so did she. She couldn't square it. She could barely look at me let alone touch me."

"Did you want her to?"

The front wheels of his chair came down hard. "My legs got shot off. They missed my dick, if that's what you're asking." He wheeled up to the bars, just a foot from her. "Do you think I'm making it up? She was out a night or two every week, sometimes all night long. She told me it was nothing, she was visiting a sick friend, but that was bullshit. Everyone knew what she was up to."

When he advanced on her, Ada nearly jumped up. But she kept her head down and her eyes on her notes. After a moment she faced him and said, "So, everyone knew. That couldn't have sat well with you."

"What the hell was I supposed to do?" He backed away and pivoted sideways. "A man's got to take care of business." He settled down but stared at the posters for what seemed a full minute. "She got herself knocked up, but you probably know that by now, don't you?"

Ada kept her voice even. "Mm-hmm, yes. Who was the father?" she asked.

Braden jerked the wheels until his back was to her and wiped at his eyes with the back of his hand. He said, "Maybe it's poetic justice after all, you know? I did my share of screwing around. Running a roadhouse and tavern? Hell, yeah!"

Again the tough Marine—or was he now apologizing for *Rose's* behavior? Either way, Ada had to steady her voice before asking, "You had a lot of girlfriends, did you?"

"Are you kidding? I got more ass than a rented saddle." His back was to her, and he wiped his hand down his face and breathed out hard. "You think that's why she did it?"

She leaned forward, elbows on her knees for a long moment, then spoke softly. "Every marriage goes through tough stretches, even unfaithful times." She sat up and faked a smile. "But no, I don't think . . . revenge is never a reason a woman is unfaithful."

Braden didn't answer but turned and studied her more closely. "Where's your old man?" he asked.

She was staring at the travel posters, and answered without turning back. "The Seoul perimeter."

He nodded, and after a pause said, "I guess it's tough there." He pivoted his wheelchair in small arcs, side to side. He said, "When Rose wasn't gone, she'd be out in the backyard all night. She couldn't stand to be with me."

Ada turned back to him. "Maybe she was afraid of you."

"She wasn't afraid. Look at me, what could I do?"

"I know she hid the knives."

"I wasn't going to hurt her!" Tears welled in his eyes.

She started to speak but stopped and studied the boy's face until he turned away. It was true, Rose hadn't put away the knives out of fear for *herself*. "Your clothes were folded, and your room was pretty clean," she said. "There were meals. That was Rose's doing, wasn't it?"

He stopped rocking and peered back at the window over his shoulder. "She took care of me in that regard. I won't lie, Rose was good to me in those ways."

"Did you . . ."

"She just needed to keep her ass home."

"You said you found irrefutable evidence. Did you confront Rose with what you had?

He hung his head, barely moving. "No, huh-uh. No."

A loud clattering outside the barred casement window startled them both. Braden wiped his upper arms across his eyes and asked, "What is it?"

The young man couldn't see out, and Ada felt embarrassed for him. Neither could he reach to add his name to the lintel. She stood and craned to see. "I'm sorry. It's just some work going on. They're pulling away some of the corrugated siding; getting inside the old mill. That's all."

"They've been yakking all morning."

"There are a half dozen birds sitting on the phone wires."

"Those I can see myself."

He turned his chair, and without thinking she reached through the bars and touched her fingers to his shoulder. He flinched. She asked, "Does it hurt? Your legs, I mean? I've heard they can still hurt."

He didn't answer right away but turned the chair sideways to her. "Sometimes," he said, "usually not too bad."

"Were you scared in Korea?"

Again, he stared a while at the travel posters. She sat and crossed her legs. "Never mind. What did you do for Easter?"

"Easter? We went to church. Rose took me to church, and we listened to windbag Niedermeyer thank the Lord for the miracle of my delivery."

"Who's Niedermeyer?"

"Aaron's old man." He turned away again and scowled for just a second. "Our preacher-man. Then we spent the afternoon at the town picnic up Eightmile Creek. Some guys must have helped her get me into the Chevy, because I woke up at home."

"Are you churchy, or was she?"

"Neither one of us, really."

"Tell me what you know about Lonnie Barr."

He shrugged. Ada asked, "Is it possible Barr was the . . .?"

"Father?" Braden laughed. He wheeled back to the rear wall and rocked back on his wheels with his head and shoulders against the wall. "I can tell who all you been talking to by what you ask. No, ma'am. She may have been seen with Barr, but she was just using him. She wasn't interested that way in limp-dick Lonnie."

"He ran when he saw me."

"That's 'cause he's a limp dick."

"Why won't you tell me who the father was?"

He looked down, avoiding her eyes when he spoke. "Because it just isn't . . . I just don't want to, is all. It doesn't have to be advertised she was pregnant, does it?"

"It goes to motive, but I can keep it Official Eyes Only. Would you prefer that?"

He looked away and nodded and the jailhouse quieted for a minute. He asked, "He shipped out in May?"

"April. I write to him all the time, but I haven't heard much back." She turned toward the door and crossed her arms.

"Look," he said, "it doesn't mean anything's wrong because he doesn't write to you. It's hard to write sometimes. Writing things on paper makes it harder to pretend they're not real. And it isn't easy sometimes to get your head back into home and feelings, you know?"

She nodded but didn't answer. Braden set his wheels back on the floor and turned until he was facing the wall again. "What was

Montgomery like when he came home before?" he asked. "From the Europe war. How did he treat you?"

"Fine. It was fine. What do you mean?"

"It's none of my business."

"There were some rough times, of course. Getting used to each other again, I suppose." She kept her arms hugged tightly to her chest. "Some nights when I had to, you know, stay somewhere."

His head had slumped, but he nodded. "Everyone's scared over there," he said. "It doesn't matter what they tell you." He turned back to her. "I'm sorry I called you a bitch, ma'am. I know you're trying to do your job." After a minute, he said, "I'd like to rest a little, if you don't mind."

"Help me help you, Corey."

"I'm guilty, Mrs. Reed. You've got to understand that. You don't owe me nothing but a noose."

CHAPTER SEVEN

12:35 p.m. – Interviewing patrons at victim's place of business

CHIEF MUNSON WAS LEANING AGAINST THE RAIL out front of the office when Ada stepped out. He moved toward the door, but Ada suggested they give the prisoner a little time alone. The engineers and workers must have seen what they needed to see, because the street out front of the mill was empty. In the quiet they left behind, more birds lit on the wire for Braden to watch. Ada said, "I'd like to talk with some folks about the other night. There are still some loose ends to gather together if possible."

"Talk with who? Why do you need to worry about loose ends?"

She put her hat on and started down the boardwalk. "Chief, you didn't tell me Lonnie Barr was seen leaving Custer early the morning after the drowning."

"I didn't mention it because we already had a confession. We still do, right? We got our man?"

"Probably. But Rose had fixed a week's worth of meals for her husband. She wasn't just stepping out for the evening; she was going somewhere."

They walked past the barbershop, the dry goods, and the Farmers Insurance office. Conversations stopped and eyes followed them as they passed each door and window until she had to step off the walk and continue down the middle of the street. Munson tagged behind. "Ada, the kid admits to killing her. I don't like it either after all he went through. But he says he clubbed her and she drowned. And sure as heck, she's been clubbed and drowned, and we even have the stick."

All that was true, but... "Sergeant Braden is, well, he's upset for the wrong reasons. He cares about the wrong things."

"There were wheelchair tracks at the scene of the crime. You said you saw them."

"And maybe the tracks were his and maybe it happened just like he said." The sun had burned through the valley fog and now baked the oiled dirt of the road. She raised her hat and wiped her forehead with her sleeve. "Why did Lonnie Barr run from me?" she asked. "He's scared of something."

"I'd love to think it was Barr, the shiftless drunk. But we have a confession in hand."

"Why would Sergeant Braden go down there to ambush his wife when he could have waited behind the door or behind a lilac bush? Or even shot her from his window?"

They were in the street in front of the assay and post office. Munson stopped and stuffed his hands in his pockets. "Jeez, Ada, if you aren't convinced he did it, why have me lock him up?"

She stared at her boots and scrunched her lips. The last thing she wanted was for Munson to think her crazy—or silly. She said, "Because he has a loaded rifle in his bedroom, flammable liquids in the closet, and a box full of empty shoes."

"Oh," he said.

They stood in the street looking down with their hands in their pockets. Both turned at once to a scuffing on the south-side board-walk and someone clearing his throat. A thin, mantis of a man stood nearly lost in the backdrop of dead trees and grey snags lining the mill pond. The man said, "It's a shame an Army hero will hang for the sins of that harlot." He turned from them and gazed out across the blue-green slurry.

"How's that?" Ada stepped forward. "I'm Sheriff Ada Reed."

"Mrs. Montgomery Reed." The man wore a double-buttoned vest over a white shirt, pressed slacks, and a pair of shiny black western boots that raised him up to well over six feet tall.

Munson hopped up onto the boardwalk, almost like a referee separating them. "This is Reverend James Niedermeyer," he said. "Our good pastor here in Custer." He took off his hat and asked, "How are things at home, Reverend?"

Niedermeyer hoisted his elbows to rest his hands on narrow hips. "How should things be?"

"Millie wasn't at the prayer supper last night, is why I ask. That and to be polite."

"Millie was feeling poorly last night." The man turned his chin as Ada stepped onto the boardwalk, and still with arms braced on hips, asked, "Do women wear pants now? There was a time people knew to dress decent."

Ada grinned. "Not wearing pants would be a lot less decent."

Niedermeyer didn't smile. Munson stifled a grimace. Ada cleared her throat and, feeling a little bit of a flush, said, "The uniform goes with the work. You're Aaron Niedermeyer's father, then. I understand Aaron was friends with Rose and Corey Braden."

"He certainly was not! Not with a whore and a tavern keeper. Aaron is a decent . . . a God-fearing boy. He didn't even know her."

Munson said, "They went to school together, Reverend. I mean, gosh, there were only twelve in their class."

Niedermeyer flicked it away. "Well of course he knew them in that sense. I meant he was never friends with her. I'm sure he never spoke to her. Not once." He grasped the railing and stared down into the mineral solutions. "I guess she drowned. Well, God come collect her. Or more likely the devil will. What was she doing out at that hour anyway?"

"What hour?" Ada asked. She didn't like the man.

His head jerked around. "Well, how would I know what hour?"

"You mentioned it. Where is your son now?" Her questions, she knew, might seem aggressive, but she didn't care. It was an odd feeling and nearly made her grin; she didn't like the man, and she didn't feel like apologizing.

Niedermeyer said, "Aaron is away at college in California, studying engineering and Christian theology."

"When was he last in town?"

"I don't know that it matters. I don't appreciate being questioned in this way." The tall, thin minister tugged at his cuffs and looked annoyed that Ada had not stepped aside for him although it should have been obvious he was ready to go. He said, "In any case, Aaron hasn't been back since Christmas." Pulling back his chin, he looked Ada hard in the eyes. "I heard the girl walked the streets at night, is all. Past midnight, often. I assume she died in the course of plying that trade."

Ada breathed in deep and slow, and waited. Again, she felt a bit of a flush, but not from her own discomposure. She said, "Reverend Niedermeyer, Rose Braden ran a roadhouse with six empty guest rooms. If she was in 'that trade,' why would she be out walking the streets?"

Niedermeyer's expression didn't change. Ada said, "There was a time people knew to speak decently of the dead."

THE WHISKERED MR. BLACKMON was still at his station at the Yankee Fork Roadhouse, and sloshing drinks and drawing beers almost defensively. The bar was crowded with a rowdy bunch of rubber-booted miners and lug-booted timbermen with wood chips in their hair. Another dozen or so men sat at tables, also drinking. Ada pushed her way through the crowd, caught the bartender's attention, and asked if he was keeping a tally of the receipts because Corey and Rose had an inventory list, and every beer and bottle of whiskey was accountable.

"Corey never said nothing about accountable," Blackmon shouted over the hubbub.

"Did he give you explicit permission to give away his inventory?"

"Maybe not explicit." The man's jaw slackened.

She turned around shaking her head, and the drunks, finally noticing her uniform, parted for her. The place seemed different from her first visit, but not in any specific way. The red velvet drapes were still pulled shut and the air still hung thick. She hadn't noticed the copper chandeliers before, but now saw the bulbs were extra bright but more than half were burned out, so the chandeliers managed not to emit enough light, but still hurt the eyes. Ash trays needed emptying, and there was a scattering of bottles, papers, and items of clothing.

A number of patrons sat apart with their drinks, and each turned away as Ada scanned the room. She stepped over to a table where just one man sat and did not turn away. Neither did he smile or nod. A miner, by his steel-toe boots and canvas pants, the man sat quietly amid the giddy drunkenness. He'd been the sober one two days before.

Ada doffed her hat, and the man allowed a nod. She sat and introduced herself. He didn't shake her hand but said, "Where's our usual Sheriff Reed?" The man was medium tall and narrow of frame, but his shoulders were square and his forearms sinewy. He hadn't bathed, and from across the table smelled of sweat, motor oil, and pine smoke.

Her lips parted to answer him but bent slightly into a grin instead. The man seemed familiar in a way, but of course she couldn't have known him. She hadn't really sat down with a working man since she'd left the farm, although she had workers fix things at the house, of course, and she spoke often with Ed at the auto shop. But she hadn't really sat and talked with any of them. The man's hands were rough, like her father's had been, and his fingers were calloused and scarred. His face was lean almost to hollow, with a two-day stubble, but it was pale while her father's had always been tanned.

He was watching her watch him. She turned her eyes away.

"The Major's back in the Army for now. Korea." She dropped her hat on the table. "I didn't get your name."

He weighed his answer, or perhaps whether to answer. "Cuss Pearen," he said.

She opened her notebook. "Is Cuss your proper name?"

"Custer, for your records."

"Named for the mine, the town, or the general?" She tucked her hair behind her ear and half-grinned, again without looking up.

"Not a one of 'em offer a shining example of success," he answered. "Consequently, I prefer the shorter rendering."

She grinned fully and jotted the name in her book. "Cuss it is, then. Did you know Rose Braden, Cuss?"

He hesitated only a second or two. "There isn't anyone who didn't know Rose."

"Well, I didn't know her. And I've heard a lot of rough talk about her. Messing around at night. I've even heard people suggest witchcraft. Is any of that true?"

Pearen turned in his chair and crossed his leg over his knee. "Folks say stupid things when they're scared and scared things when they're stupid. And we've come to expect damn little from law enforcement in this valley."

She rested her pen and sat back in the chair, not sure how to argue with the man or even if she should. She'd never heard disapproval voiced about the job Montgomery did. But of course, she'd never asked anyone, and especially not anyone outside her circle. Now this man's comment sounded a lot like Mrs. Li's the day before. "I'm new to the force, Mr. Pearen," she said, putting pen to her notebook. "Do you have a specific complaint?"

He didn't answer.

"Well then, what can we say about Rose Braden? She was a different sort?"

"Different? Yeah. You might even say a rare sort."

"How so?"

Pearen fingered a Lucky Strike cigarette, tapping it on the table and putting it to his lips. He didn't answer but for a shrug.

"Do you know her husband? Did she get along with him?"

"No." He took the cigarette out and wagged his head. "I mean, yes I know him and no, they didn't get along so well."

"Sergeant Braden says he hit his wife and then held her down until she drowned."

He lit the cigarette and blew a stream of smoke from the corner of his mouth. "You think he could have got his chair close enough to the edge of the pond?"

"You don't think he killed her?"

"Doesn't matter what I think. I'm just a bankrupt miner."

"Still, she was hit, and she drowned."

"Braden wouldn't need to hold her down. I expect she'd have sunk on her own."

Ada's pen stopped moving, and she stared at Pearen until he pursed his lips and looked away. She made a quick note in her book, then without raising her eyes asked as calmly as she could, "What makes you think she'd have sunk on her own?"

He took the lit cigarette between his fingers, turned his head, and spit a flake of tobacco from his tongue. "What I mean is, in ice cold water like that, and fully clothed? It's not like she was the Unsinkable Molly Brown, right?" Tobacco smoke curled in a knife edge of sunlight. Pearen pursed his lips and almost turned away, but said, "She was a different sort like you said. A good sort, I don't mind telling you that much. There was plenty of times she found something in her kitchen for me, off the tab." He knocked the glowing end from the cigarette into the tray, squeezed the end between his fingers, and stuck the butt into his shirt pocket.

A stubble-headed man had been listening to the conversation, and now sidled up to the table. He was older than Pearen but just as wiry. Half a dozen others glanced away as Ada looked around. The stubbly man said, "You heard someone say witchcraft?" He chuckled. "I'll be damned. And I guess you'll call it messing around no matter what anyone says. Rose did what she did, and she knew what she knew, which was more than most on both counts."

Pearen rose from the table and said, "Shut up, Jubal." To Ada he said, "Unless I'm under arrest, I have appointments to honor." He walked into the crowd just as an argument started at the bar, where the bartender apparently had begun asking payment for drinks. A fair amount of shoving and kicking followed, and Munson hurried from the other side of the room to separate the troublemakers.

Ada asked, "Jubal?"

He sat. "Jubal Mason. I got a hole in the mountain where I throw all my money." His hand, when she shook it, was rough and knobby as a pinecone. He said, "You shouldn't take Cuss's attitude personal. He's had a lot go south on him."

"So, what did Rose Braden do and know?"

The man wagged his head one way and the other and leaned in. "She knew what Mansfield is up to, that's for damned sure. Rose kept an eye on that cheating so-and-so."

Ada barely hid a smile. The old man noticed her smirk and said, "You think the Lucky Boy mill burned by accident last winter? Dee Mansfield burned down his own damned mill. Most everyone's figured that much out."

A number of the patrons looked over or made a point of not looking over. She said. "Well, I haven't. Why in the world would the Mansfield & Midlands Company burn their own mill?"

Mason stared at his hands for a minute then hunched in close. "Burn the mill, you starve out the mines. That squeezes out the businesses; you have the place to yourself. This district isn't done paying by a long shot."

A curtain shifted and the room grew lighter. Jubal Mason sat bent and half crippled; overworked and under-fed by the way his skin hung on him. He'd worn a clean shirt and pants, though, and sat straight to hide what was probably a pretty strapped situation. He was a likeable old guy, although she didn't believe a bit of his conspiratorial bluster. He said, "Rose told me not to sell;

convinced a number of us to join together and hold on for a bit longer."

Pearen had stepped back while she was jotting down some notes. He stood over Mason and nudged him with his knee. "Shut your trap, Jubal."

3:35 p.m. - South to Sunbeam Junction to check on Mr. Lonnie Barr

A HAZY AFTERNOON SUN BURNED HER EYES as she headed out of town, but there was little traffic on the Yankee Fork Road, so the drive stayed mostly clear. Interviewing the old miners had been nerve-wracking at first, but she'd left feeling relieved, even heady. Of course, the conversations had not gone as she'd expected: mill fires and claim jumpers, for heaven's sake, and cheating capitalists. Still, she'd done well, she thought. She pulled into Sunbeam Junction around six o'clock and parked across the lot from Lonnie Barr's truck. The coffee cake and the note she'd left in the morning were gone.

The cadaverous bartender eyed her as she entered and lit a cigarette from the glowing butt of another. Four or five patrons sat slumped over beers. No one made a lot of eye contact as she questioned them one by one, and no one seemed able to offer more than a muddled, boozy reply. Nevertheless, she was satisfied that the kid had not been seen nor aided.

Back out in the parking lot, she took from her lunch box a sandwich wrapped in wax paper. She laid the sandwich on the hood of Lonnie Barr's truck, then got back into her sheriff's truck, backed away, and drove off around the bend of the highway.

Twenty minutes passed with the afternoon sun darting between rain clouds building from the south. Half a dozen crows gathered in that time in the trees and on the tavern roof, chattering and eyeing the sandwich. Before the birds could make off with the goods, however, a wraith of a man emerged from the underbrush and skulked forward between the cabins. He clutched himself around the middle as though shivering cold. His clothes appeared to be soaked, and his arms and face were red from brush lashings. He scurried across the lot and ducked along the side of the truck, reached over the hood, and grabbed the sandwich.

"I'll need to see your hands, Mr. Barr!" Ada Reed came around the corner of the tavern with her gun drawn. Lonnie Barr spun around and put one hand and half a ham sandwich into the air while the other hand went to his mouth, where he tried to stuff in the second half in a single bite.

His eyes were robin's egg blue, and they blinked as Ada approached fast, her gun pointed at his chest. The kid got the half sandwich stuffed in and raised his second hand. "Who are you?" he managed with a full mouth. "Where's Sheriff Reed?"

She cuffed his hands, still gripping the half sandwich, dragged and pushed him around the building, and backed him to the passenger side of her truck. There, she uncuffed him, sat him in the pickup, and stuck his left hand through the wing window and his right hand through the side window, cuffing them together again. In that way, Lonnie Barr rode through the winding Salmon River Canyon hunched forward with the wind blowing in his face. The open window was a good idea in and of itself, because the kid could barely sit up, his head wobbled, and his shoulders heaved like he might throw up.

"Are you drunk?" she asked, as they rounded the broad, open bend at Robinson Bar.

"Yeah."

"How the heck did you get yourself drunk?"

"I had a bottle stashed behind my seat. It got frickin cold last night!" His head bobbed her way. "It's all I had to eat."

"Lord."

"Do you suppose I could finish the ham sandwich?"

Ada scoffed, but then steered with her knee for a moment while she unwrapped the uneaten half sandwich. She reached the sandwich over to him and held it as he see-sawed his arms around the window frame to take it from her. He leaned his head on the jockey box for balance as he chewed.

Up close, Barr didn't really have a criminal look to him, although he needed a haircut and a few minutes with soap and a razor. He might have been athletic a couple years earlier, but he'd already lost the high-school lankiness and was starting to fill out around the middle. "Did you know Rose Braden?" Ada asked. She slowed the truck a bit and took the curves as smoothly as she could, not wanting to test the kid's stomach.

He swallowed. "Yeah, I knew Rose. I knew her better than almost anyone."

"She was killed Monday night. Did you know that?"

His head rolled on the jockey box, and he stared out the open window for a minute. "Of course. Why do you think I ran?"

He finished the sandwich and wiped his mouth on his arm. "What you got in the thermos?" he asked.

She sighed, but in the next straight stretch poured him a coffee.

CHAPTER EIGHT

6 July – 7:55 a.m., County courthouse and jail.
Suspect interrogation: Lonnie Barr

S HE OPENED THE VOLUME A THIRD TIME and tried again to focus on the text: *"Relatively few investigators consistently and thoroughly document the key evidentiary facts to reasonably assure that the prosecutor can obtain a conviction on the most serious applicable charges . . ."* It wasn't exactly Carson McCullers.

She closed the book on her finger when a car horn sounded on Main Street and swiveled in her oak chair to peer out the window. Foot traffic was light on the sidewalk, just a couple shop girls hurrying to work and a couple gentlemen stepping out of Dolly's Cafe. A grocery truck was unloading at the curb in front of the IGA, where round steak was on special for eighty-nine cents a pound. Ben at the Ace Hardware was cleaning the walk out front with a bucket and broom.

Newberry's had not been busy when she'd passed by on her way to the office, but it rarely was on a weekday morning. The lunch counter was empty, and Rita was standing alone at the check stand filing her nails. Rita hadn't recognized her walking by, or if she had, didn't wave back. The bakery next door was doing a brisk business, but no one there turned to greet her, either.

Up the block, however, she had spied three ladies in light summer dresses sitting in the front window of Dolly's Café sharing coffee and an animated conversation. Her heart had sunk when they turned out to be Linda, who was unmistakably pregnant again, and Cheryl and Betty whom she had seen but whose eyes she had not caught at the fairgrounds the other night. Betty had changed her hair, and Cheryl wore yet another new hat. Ada had yanked the Stetson from her own head and thought about dashing by without stopping. But the girls noticed her before she could get up a good pace, so she'd stopped and stood there at the window in her damned pleated slacks, nodded, and waved back when they all raised their brows and put on bright smiles. She turned as soon as she properly could, threw them another smile and a big wave, and hurried on to her drab-green office—where she sat now with a finger squeezed between pages of *Modern Methods of Criminal Investigation, 3rd edition.*

She opened the book, found her place, more or less, and read: *"A police arrest is justified by probable cause, which is an articulable, reasonable belief that a crime was committed, and that the arrestee was the offending . . ."*

She stuffed the book into the desk drawer and headed down to the basement, where her first arrestee dried out in a holding cell.

"HIT THE DECK, MR. BARR," Ada called as she flipped on the overhead light, "or I'll hose you down where you lay." The heavy wooden door slammed behind her.

The young man bolted up and fell off the narrow bunk. He stood, falteringly, in t-shirt and undershorts and holding the jail cell blanket in front of him. "Crap, what time is it?" he asked. He coughed a couple times and said, "I gotta use the can."

"It's almost eight, and you have a toilet right there in the cell." A seatless ceramic commode stood in the inside corner of the cell. "We're modern here in Yellowpine County. Put your pants on when you're done. I'll be back in five minutes."

She brought two cups of coffee on her return, reached through the bars to set one cup on the floor of the cell, then pulled a wooden chair up close and sat. "I have a number of questions for you Lonnie. Are you in a condition to answer?"

"My head hurts."

"Drink some coffee."

"Fine, then. I got nothing I need to hide."

A long sip of coffee let her eye the prisoner more closely. His disheveled clothes, the matting of his hair, and the scratches and scrapes on his arms showed he'd had a rough couple of nights. His face was creased from the pillow, and his eyes were blood-shot and sunken. He looked in sad condition for a kid in his early twenties. But there was a genuine sadness about him, as well. She crossed one leg over the other. "Nothing to hide?" she asked. "When was the last time you went picnicking with Rose Braden?"

"Who cares, that was last fall. She wanted a ride to Bayhorse and there was nothing else to it than that. She brought a picnic, and I filled my truck with rocks for her and hauled them back to Custer."

"Rocks?"

"Heavy rocks. She said we didn't have the right kind of rocks in the valley and Bayhorse was the only place this side of the river to find it."

"What kind of rocks?" She set her coffee on the floor and pulled out her field book.

"Grey rocks."

She put down her pen with a sigh and picked up her coffee. "Why did you run from me?" she asked.

"I thought for a second you were Sheriff Reed."

She didn't bother to explain. "Why did you run from . . . the law?"

"Rose told me to watch out, is all. She wasn't sure, but I needed to keep my head down just in case. I took that to mean watch out for Reed, you know. Anyway, I didn't realize Montgomery was off to Korea, although in retrospect I guess I must have heard that at one time."

"Still, the sheriff is here primarily to protect you."

"Sure, if your name happens to be Mansfield." He carried the coffee back to his bunk. "I should have remembered he was away."

"You picnic with Rose a lot?"

Barr shrugged and sat heavily. "Used to. We were all friends." He slurped a long drink and blinked his eyes several times. His head couldn't seem to anchor itself on his shoulders and his left knee bounced up and down. He said, "I know what Corey's saying, but he's an idiot. I never messed with his wife."

"You're a drunk, and a shiftless one from appearances. You'll do a lot better not talking down a wounded soldier to me."

"I didn't mean to talk him down, nor any disrespects to your situation now that I remember your old man's off in Korea. It's just that Corey's wrong about me and Rose. She was a friend and I helped her if I could. She needed help with some things."

"What kinds of things?"

He rocked forward, making it back to his feet but grabbing a bar to steady himself. "Help getting out of the Yankee Fork. She didn't want to die there." He clung to the bar and leaned his head on his arm. "She didn't mean it literally like that. Shit, Corey changed. Corey came back different."

Ada stood, turned her back, and took a deep breath. The kid's words bothered her, and that made her impatient with herself. She had to focus and not let her mind drift. "I imagine he did return different," she said. "What he went through is bound to change a man."

"Is there any more coffee?" he asked. "Maybe a little milk if there is any."

She let a moment pass, but then stood and took his cup through the bars. She brought him a second cup of coffee, black, and sat again with her notebook and pen. "Corey changed?" she asked.

Barr steadied himself and stared through the bars to the far side of the room. "It didn't matter what anyone said or did." His throat was still phlegmy, and he cleared it a couple of times. "Corey was going to hate Rose no matter what. He was going to hate Aaron, and Susie, and everyone else."

"Why Aaron?" She wrote the names in her book, still having to control a growing unease.

Barr stepped backward and sat heavily again on the bunk, sloshing a little coffee on his shirt. He seemed to be done, and her mind wandered again to Corey's return. After a while she heard him say, "You ever ride up the West Fork of the Yankee? Damn, but it's beautiful up there when everything smells like syringa and iron clays and pine needles in the sun."

"What's that?" She opened her notebook. "The West Fork?"

He closed his eyes and breathed in deep, rocking just slightly. "The four of us, we'd ride horseback all the way to Crimson Lake sometimes. Before the war."

"Four of you?"

"Corey and Rose—they were an item since back in high school; me and Susie Hailey. Remember Susie? Did you know her?"

"No."

"She went off to college in Boise. We'd lay our bedrolls under the stars, and I'd build a big fire and Corey would cook biscuits and stew. He had the touch for cooking. Did you know that about him? Early on at the roadhouse it was him doing all the cooking and folks would drive from Clayton and even Camas to eat there. Rose would wait tables and tend the bar. They were swell together." Barr coughed and cleared his throat. "Anyway, we'd have a fire in the night, and it was cool and clean up there, and we'd pass a jar of 'shine around. Me and Corey used to help old man Boniface work his still up in Basin Creek—good luck finding it, Sheriff Reed never did—and he'd give us a jar or two in pay.

"Damn, though. The fire would die down to red embers and the stars would just fill the sky. Rose loved the stars, and she'd wait for them and step clear of the fire to see them better. It'd be quiet, and she'd be there with the sky glowing purple, a down-canyon breeze blowing her hair around."

"Of course, you were more attentive to Susie."

"Corey was nuts about Rose; good to her. He wasn't mean back then."

"So, you were all friends once. Why'd Corey go to war, and you stay home?"

The kid cleared his throat again, got up, and hurried over to spit in the bare toilet. He leaned hard with his hand on the wall and said, "Your old man is gonna' come back, and he's going to be full of hate, too. Even if he's got all his limbs."

Ada sprang to her feet, dropping her notebook, and grabbed the bars of the cell. "I'll slap the shit out of your mouth!"

He stood straight but stumbled backward to lean with his back to the wall. "I ain't wishing you ill, Mrs. Reed, nor Montgomery either. I'm just saying, it changed Corey."

She stood, hands on hips and her face burning, then had to turn and walk a few paces to stop from trembling.

Barr sat back on the bunk, seemingly oblivious to the effect of his words. He said, "Saturday nights we'd go dancing at the Rod and Gun. Drive all the way to Stanley and back dodging old Montgomery Reed." He laughed and coughed. "Why Aaron? Niedermeyer was one of us. A decent guy—or used to be. He's gone off to college too."

She picked up her notebook and pen, sat, and tried to slow her breathing. She let a half a minute pass, then said, "Rumor has it, Rose Braden was seeing men."

"It's bullcrap; she wasn't no floozy."

"She wasn't seeing anyone?"

"She saw lots of people every day; she ran a roadhouse. That isn't why she was leaving."

"Don't smart-talk me! When I ask . . . What do you mean, why was she leaving?"

"She needed to go. One night she was sad, like, 'He found them; I so screwed up,' and the next night she was like, 'He stole everything. I'll kill the son of a bitch!'" Barr was beginning to pale, and his shoulders heaved. "I can't believe she's dead," he said.

"Where was she going?"

"I don't know. But why'd you have to lock me up? Crap, does anyone else know I'm in here?"

"Why?" she asked.

"Shit!"

"What are you afraid of?"

"I don't know!" He hurried again to the porcelain toilet and threw up.

Ada cringed and moved away but turned at the heavy wooden door. "Corey Braden says he killed his wife for screwing around."

Barr leaned heavily against the stone wall. "I don't know, it's messed up. Maybe he did kill Rose. He's fubar, man."

WELL, ANYWAY, THERE WAS NO EXCUSE for her getting upset like that.

It turned out Lonnie Barr had a file on him, albeit a thin one: under-age drinking, public lewdity—teenage stuff. Custer Pearen was another story, however. There was a long list of charges against him, and he'd spent several nights in the county jail for fighting and for threatening with a weapon. There had also been a serious altercation a few years before arising from the repossession of equipment at his mine. He'd taken pot shots at the bank's men who came to haul away a backhoe, earning himself two weeks in the county jail. Aside from that, there was a long note about requiring restraint during court proceedings. A year ago, apparently, he'd been sued by Mansfield & Midlands Company.

Ada left the files on her desk and stepped down the hall to see if Ethel knew anything about it. Ethel Grimes was the county clerk and recorder, whom Ada had discovered in her first weeks on the job. Ethel was a wealth of knowledge, if somewhat testily dispensed knowledge. Tall and solid, she'd made it into her late thirties unmarried and, most intriguing to Ada, unconcerned to be single and living alone. She had her own place and her own job, which she was good at; she had her friends, and was a leader in the Methodist Church.

Ada liked Ethel and believed it was mutual for the most part. She asked her to look up any information there might be on a particular lawsuit.

"Mansfield & Midlands v. Pearen?"

"Why, yes. How did you know that? Is there some kind of a connection?"

Ethel pushed her glasses onto her forehead and stood from her desk. "It's the only lawsuit not involving a dog bite in years. It was quite the drama last November. Tell me you remember it, Fancy Badge?"

Ada crossed her arms and shrugged. "No, not really. Mont was still in office, of course, so I didn't pay much attention to legal matters back then." She rested her elbows on the counter. "There were so many other things to attend; I was always busy with something." Ethel hid the rolling of her eyes, but Ada noticed her puckered grin. "Well, I was! Lottie Foss got herself pregnant and had to resign from the holiday decorations committee. You know that. And they all asked me to fill in even though we were compiling the Junior League cookbook right then. I chaired that, you might recall."

"Would you like to see the files, Sheriff?"

"Yes, please."

Every room and hall in the Yellowpine County Courthouse echoed, but the clerk's office was especially noisy with its creaky oak floor and blue tile walls, and especially when Ethel Grimes strode the boards with purpose. She creaked to the back of her office, disappeared down a stone stairway for a minute or two, then creaked back to the front counter with a four-inch-thick legal binder.

"What was the lawsuit about?" Ada asked.

"The defendant, old man Pearen, had 'vindictively and with harm to business and reputation' accused the Lucky Boy mill of under-reporting gold values and cheating him and other miner's out of their royalties." Ethel looked up to make sure Ada was following. "He'd been saying it for years, the old crank. Mr. Mansfield just had his fill, I guess."

Ada picked through the stack of court records. Ethel explained, "The case turned on testimony from the local assayist, a Mr. Denisovich. The big Russian gentleman testified under oath that the mill assays were essentially correct."

"So, Dee . . . Mr. Mansfield won?"

"The court awarded the plaintiff a fifteen-hundred-dollar settlement, for which—and this was the surprising part—Mansfield was willing to accept Pearen's worthless mine." She shrugged. "Mansfield probably thought it would get the old loud-mouth out of the valley permanently."

Ada flipped through a few more papers as Ethel watched. Just before she closed the file, near the end of the court transcript, she saw the name *Mrs. Rosalie Braden*. "Whoa! What's this?"

The young woman had been called by the defense to testify but was dismissed for lack of expert credentials.

CHAPTER NINE

3:25 p.m. – Yankee Fork Dredge.
~~Interrogation~~ Interview with Mr. Dee Mansfield

SHE ROLLED OUT OF TOWN LATE and was made even later by taking the long way to Custer, via Sunbeam instead of driving up and over Mill Creek Summit. She'd taken the highway route with the idea of maybe stopping at the White Cloud Ranger Station and saying hello to her old friend Ben McGann. After all, he was the newcomer to town, in a way, and maybe she was the one being rude by not stopping by to welcome him home. But at the station gate she checked the time, saw she was already late, and didn't stop. She pushed the pedal to get to Custer.

DEE MANSFIELD HAD AGREED TO SEE THEM at three o'clock. His office was on the Yankee Fork dredge, and that is where she had arranged to meet Kellen Munson. Ada was ten minutes late, and cussed herself for it. But then, Munson wasn't there yet at all, and apparently Mansfield was running late himself. Dee was an important man, and she was only upset because she didn't want to waste his time. Other than that, she had no reason to be nervous because he was also a family friend. Of course, he was Montgomery's friend, really, and Mont wasn't there today. If Ada was unsure of anything, it was whether she should be all business with him today, or use more of a familiar tone. And, of course, what to say and how much.

She waited on the tailgate of her Ford on the side of the county road above the gated pontoon bridge, watching tons of rock scroll up the bucket line and tons more disgorge out the back end of the tin-sided factory. From time to time she checked her watch, but mostly she sat in the sunshine enjoying the cool mist blowing off both ends of the operation. Just enough traffic passed her on the road that she could not have a smoke while she waited.

The barge moved on cables almost imperceptibly side to side, but ever forward. The chain of buckets gouged up massive loads of gravel and cobbles, spilling water and rocks the whole way up the inclined truss, and the empty buckets returned to the deep in a graceful festoon of iron. At the back of the barge, the stacker belt wagged back and forth like a ponderous tail dumping an endless stream of cobbles and boulders into neat, arcuate rows that looked like dinner plates drying in her rack at home.

Chief of Police Munson arrived wearing an orange and black checked western shirt with double-snapped breast pockets. They waited together on the tailgate an additional fifteen minutes.

When a couple of gentlemen in coats and ties exited the barge by way of the pontoon gangplank, the two law officers took it as their cue to come aboard. They were greeted at the gate by a security guard and led over the bridge and through a maze of iron catwalks and wooden steps and stiles. The clamor of rocks on metal and rocks on rocks was deafening. Rubber-booted and slicker-clad workmen watched them at every turn, stepping to the side casually or training their hoses away at the last second. They climbed four flights of stairs to the control room, with its hand levers and meters, and passed between white-shirted engineers to a wood-paneled and well-appointed office. Dar Colemaker opened the door for them, stepped out, and closed the door behind them.

The office floor was thickly carpeted, and when the door closed the room got surprisingly quiet. Dee Mansfield was a tall man and taller still in his fancy western boots. He offered Ada his hand with a broad smile, and held her arm with his other as they shook. "Ada, it's always a pleasure to see you, even if this is not a social visit. But tell me first, what do you hear from the Major?" He nodded to Munson. Mansfield's face was lean, sharp as a faceted stone, and not so tanned in the light of day as the boots and work shirt would give you to expect.

She hadn't presumed to talk about Montgomery, although maybe she should have. "I got a letter from Monty a week ago, Dee. The Chinese are pressing down around Seoul, but the boys' spirits are high." A half smile was the best she could do. "He asked for socks and soap."

"Yes, they are bearing up under tough conditions, I hear. Send him foot powder, too, and a tin of hand balm. If he doesn't need them, someone else does."

He raised his brows as an indication, surely, that it was time for business. She began, "The girl, Rose Braden . . ."

"Can I offer you a drink, by the way?" A credenza under the starboard windows held bottles of liquor and cut crystal glasses. Mansfield poured two drinks and added ice cubes from what must have been a miniature electric ice box.

She said, "Um, no. I still have a long drive ahead of me." Taking out her notebook and pen, she started again. "Did you know the girl?"

"No."

"But you knew her husband."

"Oh, well in that sense, of course I knew her. It's a small town, isn't it, Kellen?" He handed the police chief the second glass of whiskey with a wink. "I thought you meant did I have a friendship with her. No, I don't believe we ever spoke."

She jotted a quick note. "Did anyone on your crew know her in that way?"

"Not that I'm aware of, but I will have Mr. Colemaker ask around."

"You never saw her hanging around?"

"Not at all. Why is any of this important?"

Ada stopped writing and looked up, embarrassed to have to explain. "She died on your dredge, so I have to ask."

"Of course. Although in point of fact, she was pulled up by my dredge. Most likely she drowned in the pond."

"Your pond." She dropped her eyes.

"My pond." Mansfield's face remained pleasant, even amused. "I understand there is a confession on the table?" He glanced Munson's way. "Now, Ada, you probably think you have to tie a ribbon around the case because it's your first, and you're a woman being judged in a man's job. But look here, sometimes the simplest answer is the right answer."

"Sometimes, I guess." She almost folded her arms across her front. She asked, "Could Mrs. Braden have been on the dredge the night she died?"

"Not possible. We keep the pontoon bridge tied back from the shore, and the pulleys are locked."

Ada wrote in her book while the men waited. She turned back a couple of pages, checked her notes, and said, "The victim appeared to have grease smears on her clothes, is why I ask. I noticed a lot of black grease coating the posts and railings coming up your stairs."

"Yes, we choose between grease and rust in an operation like ours. But Ada, I think if you opened the hood of your pickup, you'd find the same kind of grease in there."

Behind Mansfield and through a bulkhead doorway, a bunk and a wardrobe comprised private sleeping quarters. The bed had been made up, but hardly Marine-Corp-neat, and the clothes hanging in the wardrobe were just wrong. Dress slacks shared hangers with checked shirts, and khakis with dress shirts. The shoes were piled in the bottom of the wardrobe. She would have expected fastidious. "No maid service on a gold dredge?" she asked.

Mansfield laughed, stepped across the room, and closed the bulkhead door.

"Do you sleep here at night?" Ada asked, then immediately stuck her face in her book, hoping no one else read any suggestiveness into the question. She smiled calmly and asked, "Were you on board the night Rose Braden died?"

"I haven't slept here for a month or more. We're winding down operations, as you know; less reason to work late."

"Winding down because you're running out of placer ground?"

"That's right. We're at the end of our claim block. Am I a suspect, Ada?" he grinned broadly.

"No, of course not, Mr . . . Dee." She cleared her throat and said, "I'm interviewing possible witnesses at this time. There are some evidentiary . . . Well, some details that don't tie together in Sergeant Braden's account. I'm having trouble believing the young man's story, at least the bigger part of it." A high drafting table in the center of the office was covered with maps and papers. Ada leaned against it and noted a topographic map with claim blocks outlined and annotated in colored pencil. A few of the properties were circled. She turned the map right-side up. "Are the circled mines . . . ?"

Mansfield sighed, stepped over, and rolled up the maps, explaining that his previous visitors had been curious about land boundaries. "I have a hard time accepting Sergeant Braden's guilt, too," he said. "We're both marines, you know, and I hate to see him go down like this. I understand you found his wheelchair tracks by the pond?"

"Tracks possibly—well, most likely—consistent with a wheelchair. There are a number of persons of interest, and I do have another Barr . . . another suspect behind at this time. That is, behind bars at this time." She shuffled her feet and closed and then opened again the notebook.

Mansfield nodded and pursed his lips before saying, "Listen Ada, and I mean this from my heart. We asked you to hold the job open for Mont—I fought for it, as you know."

"I know you did. Thank you."

"Yes, out of respect for you and Mont both. But maybe we were asking too much. Not just of you, but of any lady. Hell, you shouldn't be wearing boots and pants like this. A shirt and tie, for crying out loud, on such a beautiful woman?"

His smile wasn't far enough from a leer. She crossed her arms and stared at the floor. "I'll let . . ." She wanted to say, "*I'll let you go on talking that way while I check out some license violations I noticed coming in,*" but she exhaled, and instead said, "I'll be sure to let Monty know how attractive you find his wife."

"Ada!" Mansfield grinned, then dropped his head and stuck his hands in his pockets. "Sheriff, that is. Acting Sheriff Reed. A dead girl on my deck and an open case of murder does not sit well with potential investors. So how can I help you wrap up this investigation? I'm at your service."

Ada walked to the port side of the office, trying to breathe through a flush of embarrassment. What was she thinking, for God's sake, to admonish Dee Mansfield like that? And in front of Kellen! The last time she'd run into Dee, a couple weeks earlier on the steps of the courthouse, she'd misconstrued things too. He'd been oddly possessive of her, reminding her somehow of Rhett Butler in the parlor with Scarlett. "Have a drink with me, Ada. I have an hour," he'd said and winked at her. It was probably nothing, but she'd nearly choked, thinking he couldn't possibly have meant it like that. "Frankly, Sir, I don't . . ." she'd begun, and laughed. But her laugh had sounded simpering, and she realized she'd left it hanging as though she was saying she didn't have a whole hour, and it all unsettled her to where she felt herself blush. And so, she'd stuttered when she explained, "I'm afraid I . . . I haven't the time. Expense receipts and, you know, travel vouchers and stuff." He'd laughed, tipped his hat, and walked on.

The port window looked down on Mrs. Li's small green cottage, and the old woman was in her yard hanging a few pieces of linen. Her back fence was nearly all slumped away. Ada knew the men were waiting, but she just needed another moment. She turned, smiled brightly, and asked, "Mansfield & Midlands owned the Lucky Boy mill as well as the dredge?"

"Midlands had the mill and some idle mining properties up on the hill. I had the dredge. We merged. Well, in fact I bought them."

"Was the mill insured when it burned?"

"I believe the mill fire case was closed months ago. Aren't you here looking into something quite different?"

"I'm sorry. Yes, except it came up in some of my other interviews."

Mansfield swirled his drink and puckered his lips. "Yes, it was insured, and so the fire turned out to be a lucky spate of bad luck, inasmuch as the business had been declining rapidly."

"Is that because of the lawsuit? The miners started trucking their ore somewhere else?"

He leaned with the heels of his hands against the drafting table, still holding his Scotch, dropped his head, and after a long moment said, "The miner-gentlemen's ores are not worth the trucking cost let alone the milling cost. That was shown in court, Ada." His voice rose slightly. "The damned district is played out."

Chief Munson, who hadn't figured out what to do with the whiskey he'd been handed, cleared his throat and asked almost under his breath if maybe they should get back to the case at hand. "Maybe we should do just that!" Mansfield barked.

Ada jumped at Mansfield's sudden vehemence. She wanted to ask, *"Why, if the district is all played out, then why did you agree to accept the Sunnyside Mine in payment from Pearen?"* Instead, she said, "I'm sorry, Dee. I'm being a pill, I know. But I just have some loose notes and I'm trying to make heads or tails of some of it."

"How can I help us back to the unfortunate case in hand?"

Ada glanced at Munson, who'd found a small table to set the drink on. She said, "Some folks say Rose Braden was talking people out of selling to you."

"I can guess who's spreading that nonsense." There was silence but for rocks banging iron. Ada bit her lip, waiting. Mansfield set his drink down firmly and took a moment before turning with a serious look. "Ada, I am loath to interfere; the sheriff is the sheriff, that's how it has to work. But it worries me you're giving too much credence to the grumblings and ravings of one Custer Pearen. Am I right?" He tilted toward her inquiringly.

I spoke with Cuss, uhm, Mr. Pearen at the roadhouse the other day, yes. Along with some other witnesses."

"Pearen is a crank and a con artist, and you need to watch him. I hear he's catching a lot of his neighbors up in some kind of investment scam." Mansfield turned to gaze out the port windows, to the mine-pocked hills above town. "As for the implication he no doubt pressed on you, I am buying, it's true, but no arms are being twisted. And in fact," He gave a quiet laugh. "You know, mining is a tough business. I've given a few old codgers— decent hard-working fellows—a chance to make a little something after a lifetime of disappointment. I don't apologize for it. It costs me little enough."

TWENTY MINUTES LATER, CHIEF MUNSON sat rocked back on a bench in front of the jailhouse with his hat pushed back, balancing with his boot braced on the middle rail. A *Field and Stream* lay open in his lap, but his eyes were taking a break from the fine print. He hadn't expected Ada to come bounding across the graveled Main Street, and he nearly upset himself dropping down and twisting away to spit out his chew. Ada did not hop up on the boardwalk but stayed in the street with her arms draped over the top railing. "That went well," she said.

"I guess."

With the Mansfield meeting over, her steps felt lighter, and the air fresher. The sun shined up and down Main Street, and a dozen or so magpies chattered loudly atop the false front of the Feed & Seed. She raised her Stetson and pushed back her hair. "It's a nice afternoon."

Munson nodded. "The time of year for it. Would you call them a murder of magpies?"

She laughed, but glanced up to where he was looking. "It's supposed to be a murder of crows."

"Same for magpies?"

She shook her head. "I believe it's a parliament of magpies."

Now he grinned. "Why a parliament?"

"Maybe it's the tuxedos they wear." Over her shoulder, the rusted hulk of the burned-out Lucky Boy mill took up nearly a full block, still looming over the smaller buildings in town. The blackened skin clattered in a light breeze. Ada turned and studied the structure, leaning back now on the railing. Except for the miners it directly affected, no one said much about the mill fire. The town just seemed to accept the loss of business and the eyesore into their midst. And maybe that was the way in a dying town. Even Mansfield seemed to brush it off.

Munson saw her eyeing the mill. "It could have been arson," he said, "or it could have been a hobo cooking dinner."

"You've had three fires in the last half year. Did you investigate any of them?"

He stopped grinning. "I do my job, darn it! What are you saying?"

"I'm not saying anything, Kellen."

"This isn't exactly the sheriff's purview. You're in charge of the homicide."

"Purview?" She turned away again, so he didn't see her roll her eyes. "I'm not second-guessing you Chief. I'm only asking in case there's a connection."

Munson had gotten to his feet, and he shoved his hands in his pockets. She fought not to laugh. "What about the old stables?" she asked.

"Abandoned, no owner. No insurance claim, so we didn't look too closely at that one."

"When you say we?"

"Me mostly, because it's my town. But Montgomery helped me with some of it."

"Montgomery did?" She stopped grinning, too. "I know no charges were filed, but did you have any theories on who might have set this fire, if it was set?"

"Are you talking about the rumors? There's always rumors."

"You're right." She checked the angle of the sun, still feeling a bounce. "Kel, where is the Pirate's Gold mine from here?"

"Huh? That mine has been shut down for thirty years or more. Why would you . . .?" He sighed. "I think we need to focus the investigation."

"It was one of the properties Mansfield had circled on the map in his office. I just thought I would check it out. It's a nice afternoon."

"Ada . . ." It was his turn to look away and make a face. "It's about a half mile up Jordan Creek on the left. A jeep trail forks off the main road that'll take you right to the portal. There ain't much you're going to see."

"Thanks. Want to go?"

He blew a raspberry, pushed his hat back, and fought a scowl. "I've got rounds, Sheriff."

4:55 p.m. – Looking into annotated properties up Jordan Creek: Pirate's Gold Mine.

THE JEEP TRAIL TOOK OFF JUST where Munson said it would. Ada bounced the truck through Jordan Creek then eased it up the steep, winding course, over rocky ledges and between pine and fir trees grown up so closely they brushed and scraped the side panels. The trail ended on a flat-topped mine dump just big enough to turn around on.

A cabin stood back a ways in the brush, toward a sound of splashing water. The cabin was in bad shape, with the roof fallen in and brush growing out of glassless windows. The mine dump was littered with barrels, rusted screens, and timbers. A trickle of effluent from the portal snaked across the dump, staining orange the rocks and debris it touched. There was evidence possibly of teens carrying on way up there, with beer cans left behind in the general disorder of the place. A wooden barricade closing off the mine portal had long ago fallen or been pulled down, and the portal itself yawned black against the bleached and iron-stained rocks of the hillside.

Ada retrieved the flashlight from her truck and checked the mine opening. A cool breeze carried from deep in the mountain smells of clays and rust and rotted wood. Inside the entrance, the floor was damp and the clay soft and heavily trampled. But the footprints became fewer as she sidled farther in, until they were mostly those of a young person, an adolescent from the size of the prints. The small prints led deeper in.

It seemed hardly a healthy place for kids to play. Ada followed the tracks a short way and bent down to look more closely. They were not made by a young person's shoe after all. The print was too narrow and pointy, and the heels were slanted in and elevated just a little. They were the prints of a woman's work shoe: a Lady Lane lace-up Oxford if she knew a thing about shoes!

Curious now, she followed the woman's tracks. They led her forward between crumbling rock walls and beneath a spalling roof held up in places by rotting timbers. At nearly a hundred yards in, the tunnel turned, and it got black and silent as a tomb. Her flashlight barely lit the way, throwing a skittish circle of light on damp wallrocks and roof beams, and into yawning crosscuts. She was stopped by a fall of rock and sluff, which pooled water behind it. There the woman's prints stopped also, fussed around a good deal, and turned back the way they'd come.

As she followed the tracks back out, watching more closely now, it was apparent the woman had not been alone; her tracks were accompanied—or more accurately, over-printed—by a man's large western boot. Everywhere she checked on the way out, the man's boot overlaid the woman's, as though he had followed behind her.

Ada was shivering by the time she got out to daylight, so she found a squared timber on the edge of the dump and sat in the late-afternoon sun to write a few notes. The woman's footprints were unexpected and interesting and, she believed, might have been made by Rose Braden. It was not a certainty by any means, but really not an unreasonable stretch, either. There were not that many women in the Yankee Fork, after all, and fewer still who were active enough or would have the curiosity and gumption to poke around in an abandoned mine. It was possible.

But how long ago had the footprints been left? There were no good prints on the surface, but of course, it had rained in the last weeks.

She got up to look around a little more, but ducked low when she heard a rustling in the brush. A rock clacked on the hillside. Her pickup truck—and her gun, damn it—were twenty yards in the direction of the noise. She gripped the flashlight and took a crab step, then another toward the truck. A movement in the corner of her eye caused her to swing around.

It was an orange and black tartan movement. "Kellen?" she called.

"Ada, are you okay?"

"Yeah, I'm fine. What are you doing?"

Munson stepped out of the brush waving at deer flies with his hat. "Just looking out, is all. Old mines can be dangerous places."

ADA FOLLOWED MUNSON DOWN THE JEEP TRAIL and the Jordan Creek Road into Custer, where they parted ways. All up the road to the pass and down the other side, and then for a good part of the evening, she worried vaguely there was something else about the footprints she'd seen. Something wasn't right about them.

CHAPTER TEN

Saturday, 7 July
Morning at the sheriff's office, Catching up on other things today

A FLEET OF CATTLE TRUCKS WERE LOADING down at the pens, half a mile or more away on the far side of the highway, and clouds of swallows swooped around them. The birds made little more than shadows in the faint light before dawn. Ada sat on her rock and sipped from her coffee, which was already beginning to cool. The cattlemen were pushing the stock through wooden chutes, and their distant hawing and whistling carried on a soft breeze. It made her smile. Her father used to holler a cattle-call a mile up a canyon. Neighbors would joke about it.

Cattle lowed in the valley. Ada took another sip of coffee, cradling the cup in her hands to keep it warm for a few minutes longer. As a young girl, she used to ride with her father on the tractor as he seeded the fields, and on the wheel rake bringing in hay under the Autumn sun. He wore a farmer's dungarees and a rancher's Stetson every day but for weddings and funerals. A tree-trunk of a man, he knew right from wrong and never failed to stand up if the town, or a neighbor, or just a teary-eyed girl needed help. Like Ada. Or maybe like Rose Braden.

Rose had needed help. She still needed help. Now Ada's chest felt hollow and achy, because it was she who had to stand up for the girl. She had no idea if she was doing it right—if she was doing any good at all.

Below her, headlights swept the highway and wheels whined in the chill of the morning; a pickup truck and then another rolled up the valley toward the city of Salmon. Voices carried from across the highway: the cattlemen at work. The sound was clear, but the words themselves were unintelligible across the distance. That was the thing about distance, she supposed. And it was just that distance between herself and Rose Braden that kept her from hearing what the girl was trying to say. *Would Rose's voice have been soft?* Ada wondered. *Would it have been low-pitched?* She knew what the girl looked like from head to foot, the poor thing, but had no way, really, of knowing what her voice sounded like.

She sloshed out her cold coffee on the walk back. By 7:45 she had a load of laundry washed, wrung out, and hung on the line, and by 8:10 the coffee pot was perking in the sheriff's office.

8:20 a.m. – Paperwork, probably all day

LEANING FORWARD WITH HER FOREHEAD RESTING in her hand, Ada mouthed the words a second time to no greater effect. At the sound of the door, she stuffed *Modern Methods, 3rd edition* into the desk drawer.

It was her Uncle Ephraim come for a cup of her coffee, as had become his morning routine. Today he was accompanied by two Idaho State law enforcement officers: a sergeant, Ada judged, and a young trooper. Their blue uniforms were neatly pressed, and their boots were shined. They both sported flat-top haircuts that bristled when they removed their flat-brimmed trooper hats.

Mayor Applegate said, "Morning, Ada. I told Ken the only place to find a pot of good fresh coffee on a Saturday is in Sheriff Reed's office. Didn't I say that Ken?" He nodded an introduction: "Sergeant Ken Blevins, Idaho District Six."

The sergeant, a tall, solid man, stepped forward and shook her hand. "Pleased to meet you, Sheriff. I should have come by sooner to congratulate you on your appointment." The young trooper hung back, studying the map on the wall.

Ada had a ton of paperwork to get to but rustled up a smile for the gentlemen. "I've a pot just started, Mr. Mayor. I didn't expect so much company on a weekend." She nudged the desk drawer closed with her knee, stepped to the coffee break table, and opened a new box of sugar cubes.

As the coffee perked and then settled, Applegate kept up a chatter of news and rumors from down the river. They were already fighting over water in the Lemhi Valley, he said. The recent rains hadn't helped them over that way. And the City of Salmon was going to have to replace half their sewer lines, they thought, what with the Health Department's new regulations.

Ada found herself pinned back by the coffee pot like a hostess, but she didn't feel comfortable squeezing over to her desk with the two big men crowding around. She saw no easy way out, so she stood halfway with her hands in her pockets. The young trooper remained by the map as though he wasn't sure where he was or where he was supposed to be, either, while Blevins eyed her uniform more closely than was necessary. "There's a lot of political pressure to wrap things up in the Yankee Fork," she heard the mayor say.

Blevins laughed. "There always is." He shook his head in no uncertain way. "No one likes that sort of thing hanging over a community."

Ada said, "The investigation isn't complete. Corey's—Sergeant Braden's confession . . . He's lying about unimportant things."

Sergeant Blevins sniffed the air, apparently at the coffee aroma. But the act in conjunction with his Smokey Bear hat almost made her laugh. He said, "My first murder case was not so different than yours, Ada. You don't mind if I call you Ada, do you? They're all different of course, but it seemed to me at the time to be a complete conundrum." He sat, lit a cigarette, and rocked himself back in his chair with his foot on the edge of her desk. "The fact is," the state cop went on, "I just had to learn to trust my own evidence. I came to see crimes of passion—and make no mistake, Yankee Fork was a passionate killing—they're never as intricate as an Agatha Christie novel. They're generally spur of the moment things; ill-planned and poorly-covered up."

She stood by the corner of her desk as Blevins talked on, wearing as much of a smile as she could hold on to. She backed away at his first pause and took down four cups, filling one with coffee. She doctored it with a little milk before returning to her desk and sitting.

Mayor Applegate raised his brows for a long moment, but eventually found a cup, the sugar cubes, and a spoon all on his own. Blevins took his coffee hot and black, he said, and looked as though he'd ordinarily extend that information into an off-color joke. But he, too, got up and fetched himself a cup.

To Ada's "Trooper?" the young man said, "No thank you, ma'am."

Applegate wanted to know why Ada shouldn't consider enlisting some help on the case. "The Brady girl's killing," he said, "was a sordid affair." There were some unsavory undertones he just wished Ada didn't have to slog through. "Like a sewer, like a damned rat-infested sewer, and a lady shouldn't have to soil herself on such . . ."

"Braden. Rose Braden."

Blevins said there were resources the State crime lab could bring to bear that could resolve any remaining questions. "Scientific methods; solid experience; professionalism."

She sat forward, listening and smiling. She may even have crossed her ankles, although they were out of sight under the desk. Her uncle's intentions, once they dawned on her, put her off a little, but she wasn't about to show it. Her eyes did widen a bit, and her lips parted at the mention of 'professionalism.' The mayor glanced at his coffee cup, and Blevins said, "That is some good coffee." She turned from one to the other and said, "Help yourselves, gentlemen. It's a big pot."

Blevins got up and poured a second cup, then sat on the edge of the desk and leaned toward her. She jumped up and moved around to the open office.

He twisted around but stayed seated. "It sounds to me like the kid hit his wife. He probably didn't mean to kill her, but he was angry, betrayed, and ashamed. He lashed out."

The lost young trooper had taken a couple steps back from the map and now faced the group with his hands on his hips. "Well hell," the boy said, "who can't understand that? Any man would be capable of homicide if his woman was adulterizing on him."

She wasn't sure, at first, she'd heard him right. "Are you joking?" she asked. His face was barely shaved. She turned back to Sergeant Blevins, open mouthed.

"Richard didn't mean it like that," the sergeant said. He stayed on the edge of the desk and crossed his arms. The clock ticked.

The young trooper stepped to the reading stand where a shaft of sunlight found him and shined like a halo on his bristly head. He said, "You can't know what that sort of thing means to a man, if she was whoring around like that."

Ada stood a moment with her eyes closed and her mouth ajar and, oddly, bent into a smile. Rose Braden's voice might well have been low-pitched, she thought, or it could have been high. But it would not have been soft when she told this pissant to go to hell. She took two steps toward the kid. "When you say Mrs. Braden was whoring around, was she actually engaged in prostitution for money or just having extramarital sexual relations?"

Applegate gasped. "Oh, for God's sake, Ada!"

The kid's face reddened. "Heck, I heard she stepped out, is all."

She noticed her fists had clenched, so she stuffed them into her pockets, but the smile stayed where it was. "That's all? Hearsay and drunken rumors are enough for you to find a woman's killing understandable?" She spun around and addressed the sergeant, who by then had stood from the desk. "This is the kind of professionalism you want to bring to the case?"

Blevins set down his cup. "We look at statements and evidence, and we look at it without getting emotional."

"Emotional?" The smile disappeared. They faced each other, hands on hips.

Blevins said, "The suspect says he had motivation to kill his wife, and witnesses agree he had motivation." He flipped the fingers of his left hand to count the points he was making. "There are wheelchair tracks down by the pond."

"That part I can't explain yet."

"He says he hit her with a stick, and you have the stick. It matches the wound on the victim's head.

"Consistent with. It's consistent with a backhand blow from left to right."

"And she drowned." He reached his pinky.

"She did drown, yes."

"Case closed. What's your hold up *Acting* Sheriff?"

Ada strode to her desk, requiring him to step aside. "The blow to the face broke the skin," she said.

"Braden's a Marine. He's got some shoulders on him."

She took several glossy photographs from the desk drawer and laid them across the desk, then nodded for Blevins to look. Mayor Applegate leaned in as well. "The wound on her face, Sergeant; it had already scabbed over. The blow would have had to occur several hours, at least, before she went into the water."

The men took turns holding the photos and variously scrunching and pursing their lips. Applegate asked, "Well, why would he say he knocked her into the pond?"

"I suspect, Mayor, for *emotional* reasons."

The clock ticked for what seemed another minute, until Blevins asked, "Who, uhm . . . How did she end up in the pond, then?"

"I don't know yet. But I think her husband knows. I think he might have seen the whole thing from his upstairs window."

Ada had to say three times she had paperwork to catch up on before Applegate and Sergeant Blevins got the message. When they had gone, she sat for half an hour with her feet on the edge of the desk and *Modern Methods of Criminal Investigation* pressed to her forehead. Could she be wrong and everyone else right? Could Corey Braden be as guilty as he insisted? In the end it still didn't add up to him. It was more than just the timing of the facial wound. One could reason around that. There was more, but she just couldn't put her hands on it.

CHAPTER ELEVEN

IT HAD FROSTED HEAVILY DURING THE NIGHT, and as a result a thin layer of chimney smoke hung between the valley floor and the moon in its first quarter. Chief Kellen Munson started his Saturday morning at the wood pile, and stood there long, axe in hand, observing the gossamer veil rising and falling almost organically in slow undulations, like a lover moving . . .

He kicked the kitchen door closed, dropped an armload of firewood into the wood box, then proceeded with his morning preparations. Dodging from the stove to the icebox, back to the stove, and to the radio, he got a fire started and fine-tuned the radio as it drifted in and out of a station. He'd put on a good bright shirt, anticipating a gray morning, and had shaved and combed his hair over the thin spot on top. He thick-sliced a can of spam and laid the slices in the frying pan, brushed his teeth in the kitchen sink, then poured and drank half a glass of milk as the spam fried up crisp. He laid the spam slices between buttered toast, making two sandwiches, and double wrapped one of them in wax paper.

His movements were practiced and smooth, and from outside looking in through frosted panes one might have thought Munson was waltzing to a Radio City Music Hall production rather than listening to the weekend edition of the National Farm Report. He buckled on his revolver, donned a denim jacket, and stuffed the wrapped spam sandwich in the jacket pocket. He ate the other sandwich while completing his morning rounds.

At the jailhouse Munson put on a pot of coffee, banging pots and slamming cupboard doors to help his prisoner shed the morning slumbers. He served Braden the second spam sandwich and a cup of coffee, then read from a Field & Stream until Braden called for him, at which time he opened the cell door and let the prisoner help himself in the toilet room.

At a quarter to noon Munson opened the door of his office to slosh out the last of the morning coffee and spied Ada Reed behind the wheel of her pickup truck, bent over her notebook. "You're getting to be a regular customer," he told her.

"Yeah, I'm getting to hate that road." She blinked a couple times, gave the chief a half smile, and put her pen back in the pocket of her duty shirt. "I won't be a bother to you today, Chief. I really just want to look around the roadhouse again."

"It's no bother. Do you want to drive?"

"Gosh no. I just drove an hour and a half." She reached into the jockey box for her badge. "How's the prisoner doing?"

"He's quiet. Doesn't ask for much. I didn't tell him you doubt his story."

"He knows. But you're not on board with me, are you?"

Munson leaned his hands on the door of the truck, speaking to her through the window. "You don't believe Corey because the welt on his wife's face came earlier than he said. But Ada, that isn't a heck of a lot to put up against a straight confession plus wheelchair tracks at the scene of the crime. I mean, maybe he hit her earlier and then again down by the pond."

She shooed him back so she could open the truck door. "Maybe." She stepped out of the pickup and stretched, throwing her arms back over her head and arching her back one way and the other. Munson turned a quarter turn and cleared his throat.

Ada said, "Corey isn't feeling good about life, and he probably doesn't think he has much left but his pride. He believes—he's been convinced—his wife's behavior dishonored him. It's possible he wants to take credit for her death because it would, you know, give him back his honor in other people's eyes."

Munson worked a piece of spam from between his teeth with his tongue. "Even if it puts a rope around his neck?" he asked.

"Even if that."

"He knows a lot about it. He's got all the details pretty much right." Munson took out a can of snuff and packed it down, but in deference to the lady sheriff stuck it back in his hip pocket. "You say he's been convinced she dishonored him. What makes you think she didn't?"

"I'm not saying she was a choir girl, either." She donned her hat and turned to the west, toward the roadhouse. "I have no idea what kind of ritual she was part of with those marks on her hands. And Chief, you have to keep this quiet: she was pregnant."

"Oh, jeez. And it wasn't Corey's?"

"It's not likely given his . . . from a physical standpoint."

"Oh, jeez!"

They walked down the street with the morning sun at their backs. Munson was a man of average height, but Ada's shadow was a little longer than his. Of course, she was in her boots, but still she caught herself hanging back half a step to bring her shadow down to his level. She'd done it her whole life. She quick-stepped to catch up again.

Munson said, "Okay, well let's just suppose, then, Corey didn't do it. She had a boyfriend, and . . ."

"You might keep your voice down."

He glanced at the open shop doors and said more quietly. "That makes sense, then. She was out seeing her boyfriend. They argued. Maybe he wasn't excited about paternal responsibilities. We find the father of the baby, we find the killer."

"I don't think so."

He stopped and took a deep breath. "Now what, Ada?"

"Rose Braden was wearing a plain house dress, no makeup, her hair down, and shoes on her feet you could wear through a rail-yard. That's not how a woman steps out to see her lover."

"It's not?"

She threw him a sideways glance. "So I'm told, Kel."

They moved to the south side of the street, away from the businesses and nearer the mill pond, which today stank of sulfur. Munson said, "Ada, what you say about the clothes Rose Braden was wearing—well, it also doesn't make any sense she wore a heavy metal belt under her dress. I mean, that's not how you go anywhere. You'd keep such a thing in a suitcase or a bag, wouldn't you?"

She nodded, holding a finger to her nose for the sulfur fumes. "If the belt was worth no more than four or five dollars, it makes no sense at all." Munson's question was a good one. Why would Rose wear such an unwieldy thing?—assuming she was the one who put it there. But if a killer had used the medallion belt to sink his victim, he'd have wrapped it around her on the outside, not hidden it under her clothes. Was there another meaning to it?

Munson said, "The medallions had an Asian symbol. Was it part of whatever kind of cult ritual?"

"The old woman, Mrs. Li, told me it was an albatross."

"What's an albatross?"

"A big bird. Or an encumbrance of one's own making."

Munson wanted to go with her to the roadhouse, but Ada insisted he'd already helped her more than was expected. Besides, he had his mid-day rounds to complete. In the end, although the chief still complained, Ada went alone to see what she might find in the victim's apartment.

The trucks and cars that had crowded the parking lot the previous day were gone, the front door was locked, and no cussing or laughter came from the dark interior. Munson had, at least, put an end to the party. She skirted the side of the building, picking her way through a tangle of lilac and honeysuckle bushes to the sad back yard with its neglected fruit trees and trash-cluttered stream.

A sagging barbed-wire fence bordered the property on the upstream side, and beyond that, raw, scarred hills rose steeply on either side of a deep, barren gulch. A score of mines with their loading chutes and dumps of wasterock could be seen climbing the slopes on either side of the gulch, and each trickled a brightly colored liquor into the lifeless slough. The waters made their way down to flow past her feet. At this upstream end of the property there was no trash in the channel, but piles of grey rock strewn over the stream bed. The slimy effluent caked the rocks orange.

She hadn't checked the carriage house on the day she'd questioned Braden; there had been too much to see to with regards to the deceased. She found the door to be locked. For ten minutes she searched under bricks, on top of beams, and in discarded cans. She found no key, but still needing to look inside, she jimmied the latch with her pocketknife. She wondered, briefly as she pulled open the door, if the other ladies of the country club knew how to jimmy a lock.

Once her eyes adjusted, the lower level looked to be used for nothing more than to store trash. Boxes and barrels of empty cans filled the space. A narrow stairway led up to a second floor, and there she found Rose's private lodgings.

The place was small but cheerful; lived in. The walls were painted a springtime yellow, and green floral curtains hung at the two windows. The room was sparsely furnished, but tidy. The bed was made up, and the pillows were covered with the same floral print as the curtains.

A teapot, a cup and saucer, spoon, and a jar of jam sat on the counter as though a tableau—all neat and clean. But in the cupboards she found baking powder put away with the canned soup, along with a canister of sugar. Jars of honey and mustard were stuck up with canisters of oatmeal and flour. The unsorted shelves seemed inconsistent with the neatness of the place.

A color photograph held to the small refrigerator by an Old Faithful magnet showed a cookout by a willowed, rocky stream—summer by the foliage and the young people's attire, probably taken two years earlier. Corey Braden stood tall and fit in the photo, his head shaggy with pre-military hair. Lonnie Barr sat by the fire pit holding a case of beer. There were several others she wasn't sure of; maybe Lettie Niece's daughter from Stanley; perhaps one of the Rustin boys. Rose had to have taken the picture.

The drawers of a small dresser held women's clothes, all folded neatly. But dresses and pants, blouses and underwear, though folded, seemed to fill the drawers without regularity. It was a lot like the disorganized cupboards; as though someone had—of course!—taken everything out and then put it back wrong. If so, an effort had been made to cover up that the place had been searched.

A desk and small bookshelf took up a good part of the living space. Atop the desk, a rosewood writing box held pens, stamps, and a silver letter opener. There were a bundle of envelopes and another of stationery, but she found no correspondence. In fact, there were no other papers of any sort. In the flat drawer of the desk she found trinkets, but just a few. She pulled out a plastic heart on a chain, a pen tied with ribbons, a pink rabbit's foot keychain. There was a Hallmark Valentine's card covered with bees and flowers, addressed to *My Honey* and signed *Your Darcy*. No date. And there were canceled event tickets: a lecture at the junior college in Boise on the influence of war in French romantic literature; Boise Symphony Orchestra tickets, one in September 1950—just two months after Corey joined up, and the second a month later; a play, *The Glass Menagerie*, at the Egyptian Theater. She found a schedule of theater productions, but it was for the season just ended. The cancelled tickets stopped about when Corey returned stateside.

The girl had not sat at home knitting, and that thought made Ada smile. And the trips to the city?—well, Rose would have dressed up for them, as Munson had described, and they had to have kept her out overnight, hadn't they? And, of course, the town would have noticed all that, and gossiped about it, and would all have agreed to despise Rose for it.

A book lay atop the bookshelf, left either by Rose or by the burglar. Most likely it was Rose, since it was Charlotte Brontë. Ada took it down and let it fall open to a pressed flower marker and underlined words: *I am no bird; and no net ensnares me.* She touched the book to her forehead. She'd been sixteen when she read *Jane Eyre.* She didn't remember those words; they'd meant nothing to her back then. Not yet. But Rose had found them and underlined them.

She read on: *I am a free human being with an independent will, which I now exert to leave you.*

"And did you exert that will?" Ada whispered. "Were you leaving?"

There were other books, dog-eared and book-marked: the poems of Robert Frost; a volume of Walt Whitman's collected works; Dale Carnegie's *How to Win Friends and Influence People.* On a loose leaf inside the Whitman, Ada found at last some writing—probably Rose's, as the hand was girlish, with full, open loops and bouncing humps. She'd written:

> *From all I have, the junk and jetsam, dreams and rust,*
> *I'll forge a chain of pirate's gold*
> *and a love to stir this mortal dust.*

She stuck the sheet of paper back into the Whitman. "My gosh, you were young, you poor thing," she said. She smiled, but felt a small ache, as well, and a gladness that whoever else had searched the room had not found the poem.

Ada had read nearly all the books on Rose's shelf by the time she was sixteen and was already turning out her own purple poetry— or like Rose, was trying to. She put down the Whitman, stood from the desk, and stretched one way and the other. There hadn't been much to be poetic about at sixteen. Had there been for Rose? For Ada it was a few hot, gawky dances under the gym lights; a pink chiffon dinner at the Cattlemen's Club. She'd smiled and winked at the farm boys in their clean, pressed shirts and whispered secrets about the town boys with their slick hair and polished shoes. But at seventeen . . . The childish intrigues were behind Ada by seventeen. She wouldn't bother with makeup or try on a party dress; she hardly washed her hair unless her mother forced her to. A net had ensnared her at seventeen and there was nothing to be done.

From the small east window, Ada looked out on Rose's lifeless orchard and her junk-strewn stream. *The junk and jetsam, dreams and rust.* "But you were barely more than a schoolgirl," she said aloud—then wondered for which of them she'd meant the words.

5:00 p.m. – Sunbeam Junction:
Exercising search warrant at Lonnie Barr's domicile.

THE PICKUP TRUCK BUMPED AND RATTLED all down the Yankee Fork Road, and the low afternoon sun blazed through rooster tails of dust. The carriage house had caught her unprepared and had troubled her more than she could explain. She'd left there hurriedly, clomping down the narrow stairway and scratching her arms coming through the lilacs and honeysuckles. She'd hurried from the echoes there; hurried from a girl's life exposed, from the handwriting with the pretty bouncing loops, and from the silly love poems and rabbits' feet.

Dusty as the road had gotten, Ada rolled down her window and let her hair blow loose in the wind. It had sounded awful, hollow—her boots clomping down the stairs. She'd come close to knowing something about the girl, and she'd hurried from that as well. The thing of it was . . .

A log truck pulled up close behind her, and she pulled the pickup to the side of the road to let it roll by. But she didn't get her window up in time and the pickup cab filled with dust from the truck's wheels. She opened both doors to let the dust clear out and stood awhile, leaning against the tailgate, cursing herself in the heat and the haze.

The thing of it was, in spite of a dozen years difference in age, there really was not so much distance between herself and Rose Braden. The poems she'd laughed at, she had written too. She had pinned travel posters to her walls and walked over broad hills of wildflowers. She'd had her lovers and her dark times and bruises. And yet, she was alive, and Rose Braden was dead.

It was the damnedest thing, and Ada stood in the sun long after the dust had cleared. They'd both dared to dream. Who doesn't dream? Had Rose dared to stop dreaming? Was that the difference?

THE GRANITE CLIFFS ABOVE SUNBEAM were throwing shadows across the whole of the parking lot when Ada pulled in. The tall pines to the north were waving in a strong canyon breeze. She parked in front of Lonnie Barr's cabin, removed her padlock from the door, and entered the room. It was a small space with a bed, a table, and two chairs. A Zane Gray novel lay open and face down on the nightstand. The walls were tongue-and-groove knotty pine, and a wagon wheel light fixture hung from the ceiling. A kitchen cove included a sink and mini stove, and behind them, a tiny bathroom and small closet. There were no clothes strewn about, and the bed was pulled together for the most part. A pair of cowboy boots, muddy at the soles, lay in the closet.

She found a suitcase in the closet as well, felt it was full, and tossed it onto the bed. It was not locked. Inside were summer blouses and a couple flowery skirts, neatly pressed but again folded with a little less care than a woman would have taken. There were sandals and slippers, toiletries, and hair curlers.

The acting sheriff closed and locked the door to the room and picked slowly through the packed items. Rose had been on her way after all; she was leaving. The blouses and skirts suggested casual fun, but not too casual—nothing a belt or ribbon couldn't dress up.

There were a pair of new, open-toed heels wrapped in paper bags. She refolded the clothes carefully.

In the pocket of the suitcase were a Greyhound schedule, forty dollars cash, a map of the San Francisco Bay Area, and brochures from the California Visitors Bureau. Rose had had one foot out of town. What happened? What net ensnared the girl in the end?

Ada dried her eyes, closed the suitcase, and continued her search of the room. The cupboards under the counter held a couple of glasses, half a bottle of whiskey, coffee grounds, a pot, and some spoons and forks. It was all arranged neatly; more neatly than she could credit the hapless Mr. Barr. This room, too, had been searched. Her lock had to have been picked, and within the last thirty-six hours.

The day still held a little sunlight although the shadows stretched the length of the parking lot and crossed the dusty county road. She opened Lonnie Barr's truck door with a coat hanger, and in the cab found candy wrappers, Seven-Up pop bottles, and Cracker Jack boxes carpeting the floor and half-filling the space behind the seat. In the crease between seat cushions, she found a single copper medallion with a yin-yang symbol. Either the truck had not been searched carefully, or the searcher was unaware of the medallion belt, it occurred to Ada. Or he was aware, and the medallion had been planted there for her to find. Carefully tucked into the springs under the driver's seat, however, where she could barely fit her slender arm, she found a five by seven-inch book: a journal, half filled with notes and drawings.

Chapter twelve

LONNIE BARR WAS PUSHED INTO HER OFFICE, and the door slammed behind him. Ada nodded to the suitcase lying open on the spare desk. "Do you wear women's clothes, then?" she asked.

"It was Rose's." He stepped up to the desk and with cuffed hands picked a flowered blouse from among the garments. "She wore this to the Flag Day picnic last month, with a yellow skirt. Were you there?"

"No. You and she were going away together. You left out that part yesterday."

He put the blouse down and backed a couple steps to where he could lean against the row of file cabinets. "Not like you think. I was giving her a lift out of town. That's all."

Ada remained standing behind her own desk with her hands in her pockets. "Did you fight? Something must have gone wrong between you."

"Huh-uh. It isn't like you think." The boy looked as though he'd found a shower and a razor somehow, and his clothes were clean and pressed—Ethel's work, no doubt. He said, "Rose called me that Sunday."

"The phone booth outside the bar?"

"Uh-huh. We had a ring code. I'd just gotten off shift, down from the lookout. Rose was keeping her voice low. She said she had to leave here, and she was pretty upset about shit, although she didn't use that word."

"Was she scared?"

"No. Maybe. Mostly she was sad. She brought the suitcase to my place that night, but she said she couldn't go yet; she had something else she had to take care of. We sat out on the porch because there was no one at the bar or in the parking lot, it being Sunday, and I got us a couple beers from my ice box. She kept saying, 'Damn it, damn it!' and stuff, and she cried a little. It got late and she stayed there in her car all night. She slept there. I gave her a blanket."

Ada had come straight home from Sunbeam the previous evening, and she'd made herself a nice early dinner. But then she'd spent half the night fixing a leak under the bathroom sink. She was tired, and now Barr wasn't sounding any more guilty than he had before. She said, "So, you saw her Sunday night late. Was her face banged up at all?"

"Huh-uh. She called again Monday night, and a guy at the bar came and got me. This time she was angry. I drove real late to Custer and waited by Mrs. Li's place. That's where we were going to meet, but she never showed."

"What else did she have to take care of?"

"I don't know for sure. She said something like, 'keep the engine running,' but then she laughed."

Ada took the copper disc from her pocket. "Mr. Barr," she demanded, "did you get this medallion from Rose Braden?"

"Where did you get that?"

She laid the medallion on her desk, sat, and crossed her legs. "I found it in your truck. Are you claiming it's not yours?"

"No. I just didn't think I had any left. I must have forgot when I was drunk."

"What do you mean any left? Where did you get this?"

"Well, Rose gave it to me, like you said. That's how she paid me. There's a guy in Salmon who'll give me fifteen dollars for it."

"Fifteen dollars? For just one?" Ada snatched up the medallion again and examined it more closely. "Why would anyone pay that much?"

"He extracts the gold out of it."

"Gold? Wait, how she paid you for what?" She stood, then sat again.

"I got her stuff she needed. I got chemicals and charcoal and stuff, special ceramic things. I know a guy in Ketchum who can get his hands on reefer."

Ada was taking notes as fast as she could write, but looked up and asked, "Reefer?"

"Cannabis."

"I know what it is. Did Rose take cannabis?"

"Smoke it? Beats me; she never smoked any in front of me." He stepped forward and leaned with his cuffed hands on the back of the oaken guest chair. "Are you going to book me for the reefer?" he asked.

She was sitting open-mouthed, her pen at a standstill. "I'll look it up."

"It's illegal."

"I said I'll look it up. How long had this been going on?"

"Since last fall. It started then and just kept going."

She made a few more notes. "Where did the medallions come from; where did she get them?"

"Beats me. The way she talked, like, 'These are from the War Eagle,' or 'These are from the Gold Coin Mine,' it sounded like she got them from the miners."

"Why were you helping her?"

"Why wouldn't I?" He looked at the floor and smiled. "I mean, Rose helped me a lot too. At least she cared one way or the other if I was alive. She gave me books and told me to keep a journal, to write down all my thoughts. And she told me I should apply for the forest service job because I was a loner, and she could tell because she was one too." Barr sat down on the edge of the chair so he could lean his elbows on Ada's desk still cuffed at the wrists. "Rose told me once, the loneliest place on earth can be in the middle of a crowded room."

Ada looked up from her notebook and smiled. "She said that?"

"Yeah. She said you can't tell just by where someone is. It's how far they are from where people think they are that makes them alone."

"Rose really said that?" She closed her eyes and barely breathed. The girl could not possibly have said that! She could not have felt that way or known those things.

"What do you think? Mrs. Reed?"

"Hmm?"

"Rose said I should get out of the Yankee Fork and maybe go to school for electronics or something; radios and TV and stuff. She said I was good at it, and I should do something with it."

"It would be better than living behind a bar, selling reefer."

"That's just what Rose said."

Ada put down the notebook and stood. "Do you have any more cannabis now?"

"In my room. In a jar in the closet, in the bucket under the mop. Are you going to press charges?"

She moved a box of Kleenex closer to him because he'd begun to sniffle. "Not for that; I don't think so. Not yet, anyway." She reached across the desk and turned his hands. "Are your cuffs too tight?"

"Naw, they're okay. Mrs. Reed, Rose said something about letters. She told me to be careful and keep my eyes open, like she was worried I might be indicated."

"Implicated?"

"Probably. She said she had to let things cool off for a bit. I told her I would drive her wherever she wanted." He blew his nose into a Kleenex and looked away. "She was going to have a baby, you know."

Ada nearly dropped her pen. "You knew?" The boy was near tears when she looked back. "Was it your child, Lonnie?"

"Mine? No, hell!" He did start to sob, then. "I told Rose I didn't care; I'd raise that kid like my own." Tears streaked his face.

Ada sat again and leaned her elbows on the desk, studying the young man. The tears were unexpected, and her first thought was he was somehow drinking again. But his hands didn't shake nor his knee bounce; his blue eyes were clear, though a little red from crying. He wasn't a half-bad looking kid, cleaned up. She unlocked the cuffs. "What else happened that night, Lonnie; what went wrong?"

He rubbed his wrists and wiped his eyes on his upper arms. "Nothing else that I saw. I waited. Goddamn me, I must have fell asleep because it was almost daylight, and I drove back to Sunbeam."

"Did you see anything or hear anything?"

"I can't close my eyes, but I see her in the water, reaching up, sinking into the dark." He hunched forward and laid his head on his arm. "If you want to throw away the key, it's fine with me."

10:20 a.m. – Prisoner returned to cell.

SHE KEPT THE DOOR CLOSED AND the lights off because, weekend or not, folks seemed to find her office, and she was too far behind on too many things to be chatting and gossiping over coffee. Requisition forms and travel vouchers took up the rest of her morning, but the Yankee Fork case took up most of her thoughts and kept her nerves on edge. Margaret Li kept poking her strange face into everything. The old woman knew something. Cuss Pearen was a problem too. He knew too much. Poor Lonnie Barr knew too little and, naturally, Dee Mansfield knew everything.

No one bothered her until midafternoon when a call came in about an altercation at the middle weir on Warm Springs Creek, north of Lone Pine. Someone's brother and someone else's field hand were going at it, the voice on the phone said, about irrigation schedules.

"Men won't kill each other but for gold, women, or water," Montgomery used to say. She grabbed her hat and jacket, and at the last minute went back for the revolver, which she rolled in its holster and belt and stuck in the jockey box.

Forty minutes later, she turned off the rutted Lone Pine Road onto a two track between wire fences that took her a couple hundred feet to the concrete weir. She parked under a Russian olive.

2:30 p.m. – Report of trouble up Lone Pine Road. However, highline weir #4 appears deserted.

But for the rush of water over the weir and the chatter of magpies in the Russian olive, the place lay empty and still. There were no tracks—foot or tire—to indicate a confrontation; nothing seemed out of place. The gate wheel at the weir was padlocked, and there was no sign of it having been forced or jimmied.

As she started back to her truck the dirt in front of her made a 'pfft!' and sprayed up a foot or so. A second later she heard a loud crack reverberate off the hill behind her, and a flurry of magpies took wing. It made no sense, and she stood, turning slowly, seeing just hills and sage and trees around her. A sharp buzz passed over her head followed by another loud crack, and that, finally, caused her to dive into the dirt, losing her hat and scuffing her face. She wriggled on her belly and elbows to her pickup, and keeping low, reached inside for her service revolver in the jockey box.

She fumbled to load the gun, but another buzz just overhead and another rifle crack caused her to drop the bullets onto the ground. She dove again and covered her head with her arms. Her ears echoed with the sound of the shot, and she struggled to draw in a breath. All got dark and slow, just as it had seventeen years before.

Then it had been a perfect day for hunting, cold but clear. The underbrush stood out bright red under a new dusting of snow, and campfire smoke spread overhead so close you could reach up and touch it. Pine Creek steamed in the pre-dawn. One elk was hanging, and in the night they'd spied the main herd. They would be on it as the sun topped the eastern ridge.

They climbed on foot, she, her father, uncle, and cousin, through aspens standing bare and ghostly against a pink sky. The snow deepened as they climbed and sweat beaded on her temples. Her breath fogged ahead of her.

It was her own gun. It had fallen from its holster as she clambered over a log. There was a loud bang, and with it a sharp pain that dropped her. The bullet burned inside. The perfect day slowed, and the pink and gold of dawn faded to gray, and then all went quiet until it just fell away into darkness and cold.

They thought she'd been killed. Her father carried her back to camp where they packed her in snow and wrapped her up in a green canvas tarp. She was skidded out to the road on a pine-pole sledge behind the bay gelding.

And that was it. She was quite certain, too, she'd been killed—except for the sunlight barely dappling the green tarp, the musty smell of old canvas, and the big bay's hooves on the frozen ground. And the silence of the others but for her father softly crying; and her trying to cry if only she could. And the numbing cold.

ADA MANAGED TO FIND MOST OF THE BULLETS, wipe them clean, and load them into her pistol. But she stayed down in the dirt under the open door of her truck for another ten minutes. When her breathing was almost normal and the muscles of her jaw slackened a bit, she sat up, forced herself to stand, and forced herself to walk fifteen feet to retrieve her hat. Breathing hard again and nearly in tears, she walked slowly back to her truck, climbed in, and started the engine.

She circled around and drove back between the wire fences to the Lone Pine Road. There was nothing to see but a stand of trees a few hundred feet to the east, the direction of the shots, she believed, and low hills beyond that. A short distance back toward the highway, another dirt road turned off to her right and appeared to wind back behind the stand of trees. Part way in, a rifle crack made her cry out and hit the brakes.

SHE WAS FOUND TO BE ALIVE, they said, but just barely, when they got her to the funeral home in Camas. The doctor was called. He shook his head but packed her in ice again and drove her himself to the hospital in Salmon. The attending physician told them the seventeen-year-old would not live through the night.

ANOTHER SHOT RESOUNDED, and this time she was able to determine that it was fired away rather than toward her. She pulled forward, parked, and belted on her gun. One hundred feet farther up the road a clearing opened into a broad, shallow gravel pit. A young man shouldered a rifle, took aim at a line of cans some forty yards across the pit, and fired. He shot toward the east, though, away from the creek and the weir.

As he chambered another round Ada called, "Hello." The boy turned. "How long have you been here?" she asked him.

"A few minutes; just sighting in my rifle."

She continued toward him, looking around, gaging her directions. "Do you always shoot in that direction? Ever shoot that way, toward the west?" Her own voice sounded shaky, but she believed the kid would not notice, nor see her hands still trembling.

"Only an idiot would shoot that way," the boy said. "There's a road over there." He might have been eighteen, but barely.

"See anyone else when you got here?"

"Huh-uh. There was a Studebaker pickup on the road, though, going toward the highway." He eyed her uniform as she walked up and asked, "Is the sheriff still over in Korea?"

"He is. But peace talks, you know. They've started."

The kid nodded and went back to his target practice. Ada climbed the low hill on the west side of the gravel pit, and from under dry, stunted pines looked down on the Russian olive and the weir. The fresh prints of a work boot clustered in the dirt between a couple pine trees, and she found a .30-30 casing still smelling sharply of powder smoke.

The weir was one hundred-fifty, maybe two hundred yards away. It was an easy shot. She sat in the dirt and leaned against a pine, not minding the sap and the twigs. The weir and the ground where she'd parked were clearly visible. Hell, back when she hunted, she could have made that shot easy. Even with iron sights.

The kid was gone when she got back to her truck, and the sun was setting blood red over the hills. Not a single car passed her on the Lone Pine Road, and only a few headlights rolled by once she made the highway. She wiped her eyes from time to time but didn't have a damned handkerchief and had to clean her nose on her sleeve.

SHE LAY IN THAT HOSPITAL BED for two weeks without moving, then stayed four more weeks learning to go to the bathroom by herself. Her mother visited, and Uncle Eph and Aunt Corrine, but her father could never bring himself.

"The scar won't be visible to anyone but your husband someday," the doctor told her with a professional smile. "I'm confident you'll make a full . . . a fine recovery, Ada. And, well, you can lead a full and happy life."

And she had, so far. Unless full and happy meant taking part, not just watching, as the ladies of the valley brought home baby after baby.

CHAPTER THIRTEEN

9 July – Monday, 7:45 a.m.
At residence. ~~Not going in today~~. Late start.

MONDAY MORNINGS ETHEL WOULD HAVE PAPERS for her to sign and Officer Stengel would need to go over . . . whatever. But the last few rains had come in and nearly ruined the ceiling in the bedroom. So, to hell with paperwork and to hell with Stengel, and to hell with the case, too. Ada donned a pair of coveralls instead of her uniform, got out the ladder, and rustled up some tools.

Once up the ladder, she found all the shingles to be old and brittle, with moss curling the bottom edges and pushing open the seams. The whole roof needed replacing, but that would be a little beyond her scope today. The air was crisp and the sun, just rising, jabbed at her eyes between the branches of the elm. Camas was coming to life below her, with screen doors slamming and horns honking. She set to work tacking down the loose shingles, sitting tall for the whole town to get a look.

The shooting had been meant to scare her; any fool could see that. Hell, with a .30-30 she could have made that shot standing in a wind. And it was just as obvious, as she layered in new shingles, nailing them down and overlapping them row on row, that it had been about the Yankee Fork case. No one takes pot shots over traffic violations.

Well, to hell with him, whoever it was, if he thought she was going to be scared. She weaved in the last new shingles and dabbed a little black roofing putty over the top row of nails. It made an ugly smudge on her red roof, but it was done.

The black smudge wouldn't be there long, in any case. Montgomery would be home soon, and he would want to replace the whole roof. He would just tear it off and start anew. Peace talks had already started, or at least they were talking about starting peace talks, and Mont would be home in no time. And that would be a good thing, by and large.

She inched her way down the roof on her rear. At the eve she reached with her foot and found the first rung of the ladder. She found the next rung with her other foot, and the next, and just like that she was out of sight of anyone who might be watching. Montgomery would be home, and she would have a chance to get the kitchen and laundry room back into shape. And folks wouldn't look away anymore or screw up their lips but would smile and nod when she stepped with shiny new heels into Newberry's for lunch.

The soffit and fascia were starting to flake, and the whole place could use a fresh coat of paint, house and garage both. But she would let Mont take care of that, too. The big jobs seemed to calm him last time. He would want to move the television back into the living room, of course, and the bed back under the window. And that would be fine; she would let him have his way. It wouldn't be like the last time.

She stepped off the ladder into tall grass—it needed cutting—and pulled the ladder vertical, letting it fall slowly toward her, walking it out with her hands until she could take hold of the two rungs that balanced it over her head. She carried it to the shed and hung it on its spikes. The shed door needed fixing too: a loose hinge just took some re-nailing while she had the hammer out.

A quick bath reminded her to check the water heater because Mont didn't need that aggravation too. In the closet she found a blue floral tea dress and tried it on just for the hell of it. She'd almost forgotten what clever stitching could do for her waistline, and she turned and flounced the skirt several times in the mirror. She looked darned good. But the thing of it was . . .

She pulled the dress off over her head and tossed it onto the bed. The damned thing was, Montgomery wasn't almost home, and she was still the sworn-in sheriff—even wearing a pretty dress and even if no one else thought so. And she still had a dead girl, and no suspects, and no leads. She had no suspects, that is, but for Corey Braden who admitted to the killing, and no motive but Corey Braden's, and no evidence but the evidence pointing to him. And she now had someone who wanted to scare her into believing it.

It was all a little beyond her scope today. Nevertheless, she stepped into her pleated pants, pulled on her boots, and touched up her face.

8:45 a.m. – Road trip to Idaho City. (Working undercover.)

Ada started out for the office but changed her mind and did a U-turn on Main Street. Fifteen dollars for a copper medallion? The discs had to contain gold to be worth that much. And the whole belt?—it would be worth, heck, three hundred dollars!

She left the sheriff's truck on the curb in front of her house and, after gathering a few things inside, backed her Buick out of the garage. She gassed up at the Frontier station instead of at the motor pool, keeping the receipt for her expense account, then followed the highway around to Sunbeam.

But she did not turn right and up the Yankee Fork this time. The assay office in Custer wouldn't do. The assayist there had already been involved in the Pearen lawsuit and in dealings with the mines and mill. She would have to get an outside opinion, and for that she would have to drive four hours further, to Idaho City.

Straight on from Sunbeam, the highway wound through a steep canyon with the roaring Salmon River on her left and forested cliffs and sage-covered hills on her right. A half hour beyond Sunbeam, Ada eased onto the broad gravel bar at Mormon Bend for a coffee break under tall cottonwoods and ponderosa pines.

She got out and stretched, leaned against the smooth back fender of the car, and took her time pouring a coffee from her thermos. The morning sun shined down the canyon, warming her, and she would have stayed a good while in the sun, but her hands shook too much to drink the coffee. The air was calm, but the river behind the willows was loud and dizzying. She caught herself scanning the hills across the road for shooters and checking the brush for stalkers. After just a couple minutes, she crushed out her smoke, climbed back behind the wheel, and continued west.

A few more miles and a dozen more bends brought her to the Sawtooth Valley, where snow-capped peaks loomed over the tiny village of Stanley. A right turn at Stanley, then, began the long, slow climb up Valley Creek and the slow drop into the headwater canyons of the Payette River. Two hours from Mormon Bend she gassed her car in Lowman and entered the switchback climb up to Beaver Creek Summit. Then, just beyond the pass, she turned onto a lonely-looking forest road and at the nearest clearing shut off the engine and let the Buick cool.

Under towering firs, Ada kicked off her boots and stepped out of her trousers. She took off her duty shirt and stood a moment in shafts of late morning sun, hugging her shoulders against the cool mountain air. Her hand dropped to the scar, as it always did. Montgomery had never asked her about it, and wasn't that just like him? She never told him, either, what the doctors had told her. From a box in the back seat, she brought out the blue floral tea dress, twirling it again in the dappled sunlight. She pulled the dress on over her head and struggled but got it zipped in back.

She'd bought the dress in Pocatello almost two years earlier. It had a sweetheart neck and cap sleeves and she'd fallen in love with it in the window of Falk's. Mont had thought it too spendy and yelled at her for it. She talked back, so he'd slapped her to the floor. The dress still fit, and maybe had even loosened a bit.

She cupped her hands over her face for a moment and caught her breath. She probably would have told Mont what the scar meant if he'd bothered to ask. But that's just how it was between them, and all had been okay until he'd insisted they see a doctor about their childlessness. The son of a bitch!

But she never wore the tea dress for him again, not even on the day he left for Korea. A pair of black pumps and a patent leather belt completed the ensemble. She brushed and pinned up her hair and dabbed on a little lipstick, checked her reflection in the car window, then headed on down the pass.

COMING INTO IDAHO CITY, the highway cut through familiar half-moon stacks of dredge tailings. She didn't know who operated the Mores Creek dredge, but this was not Mansfield & Midlands country. She turned right onto the oiled Main Street and then right again onto Walulla, staying a good distance from the Boise County courthouse where she might be recognized despite her disguise. She parked her Buick behind the hardware and crossed the street to Baughman's Assay and Supply.

The office was cleaner and more modern than the assay in Custer. The old man behind the counter—Baughman she supposed—wore steel-rimmed glasses, an old, rumpled suit, and a bowtie. From her purse Ada brought out a vial containing metal shavings. Copper, Baughman thought at first, but definitely alloyed with something. "We were just curious, my husband and I," she explained. "The candlesticks have been in the family for years, and I was always told they had a little gold mixed in."

"Did you want to know all the constituents, or just how much gold, if any?"

"What's the difference in price?" she asked.

"Three-fifty for a full suite; two dollars just for gold."

"Let's just do gold then." She took two bills from her purse. "Can I telephone you for the results? It's something of a drive."

She'd been too upset to make any kind of breakfast that morning, and she really needed something before starting the long drive back to Camas. The Diamond Club on Main Street served wonderful food and a famous rhubarb pie, but she'd actually been to the Diamond with Montgomery within the last couple of years. A small but clean-looking cafe stood catty-corner from the assay office, so she crossed to there instead. Curious stares greeted her when she entered. She passed an open table by the window and chose instead a table back near the kitchen.

The waitress looked at her funny as she studied the menu and asked if someone would be joining her. "No," Ada told her, "I'm travelling alone today." A lock of hair fell across her face. She brushed it back, cleared her throat, and asked for the grilled tuna and a Coke, please. Every one of the six patrons in the café plus the cook managed to turn and look her over as she waited, until she had to go to the ladies' room to check for herself what might be wrong.

Halfway through her sandwich, two men in Bell Telephone coveralls came in and sat at a table near hers. She didn't mean to eavesdrop, but she heard 'Yellowpine County,' and 'sheriff,' and her stomach tightened. "I hear she doesn't wear a holster," one man told the other. "She tucks a gun in her brassiere in case she has to draw down fast." Both men laughed.

"Whoa, is that a thirty-eight you pulled out, sheriff? the other said. "I surrender!" They had a real good laugh at that.

Ada left the tuna sandwich half eaten and a dollar bill under the saltshaker. She boiled with anger all the way up and over Beaver Creek summit and stayed angry as the pimple-faced attendant filled up the Buick in Lowman. But the daylight softened, and the air cooled climbing up the winding Payette canyon, and she was laughing aloud by the time she started down the Valley Creek grade.

5:30 pm, Weapon skills training (target practice).

THE SUN WAS STILL A FULL HAND ABOVE the Sawtooth peaks when Ada pulled the Buick into a roadside gravel pit. It was crude, what the phone company jerks had said, but a little too true. And the shooting the day before was a little too real, as well. She took her revolver and ammunition from the jockey box and set them on the front fender.

A couple of cans lay on a mound of dirt at the edge of the gravel pit, and she walked over and re-set them. But coming back to the car, her pretty pumps filled with gravel. So, she slipped back into her cowboy boots and, with the sun softening behind wispy clouds, took target practice in a blue flowered tea dress and tooled-leather boots, her hair pinned up like Doris Day's.

The first crack of the pistol brought a sharp pang and a flood of memories, causing her almost to put the gun away. But she blew a long breath, cocked the hammer, and aimed and fired again.

A pistol is hardly a hunting rifle, and the cans were perfectly safe from forty feet. She moved closer, reloaded, and took another six shots without hitting a target. She was shooting angrily when wheels grinding in the gravel and the slam of a truck door took her by surprise. The sudden intrusion unnerved her until she remembered, with some irony, that she was armed.

"Don't shoot, I surrender" a man's voice called from behind a mound of road gravel. A tall, slim man in Forest Service green peeked, and then stepped from behind the mound.

Ada eyed the man and then eyed him closely, a grin growing on her face. "You son of a bitch!" she said before he'd taken five steps. It was Ben McGann, the old friend whom she'd seen at the fairgrounds, and who had not bothered to call on her when he got to town.

"I beg your pardon?" He shifted his feet and pushed back his hat. Then he, too, smiled. "Ada Ulbright? It is you! What in heaven's name are you doing all dolled up in a gravel pit?"

"Dolled up? That's what you want to ask me, darn you, after all this time?"

He took off his ranger hat and offered a guilty shrug. "It has been a long time. I guess I should have come by when I got to town, but..."

"Hell, yes you should have come by."

He was taller than she, but not a heavy man. Lean and hard, he'd always reminded her of a fence post weathering in the sun— though pleasant-looking in a Jimmy Stewart, Hollywood kind of way. He'd grown up on a farm not two miles from her father's place, and they'd . . . gotten to know each other in high school. She eyed him sideways and bit her lip to stop the grin, which was starting to hurt. "And it's Ada *Reed* now," she said.

"I know that, too. No offence meant." He spread his arms and let them drop. "You've changed your hair," he said at last.

"You know, I'm holding a gun on you."

"I already surrendered to you once."

"I remember." She gave in to the grin, and he came right up to her then, but seemed unsure what to do or how properly to greet her. So, they stood grinning, he with a flat-brimmed ranger hat in hand, and she with a Smith & Wesson .38 caliber Police Special in hers.

He said, "I should have come by. I saw you the other night at the fairgrounds."

"Why didn't you say Hi?"

"You waved me right by. I tried to stop but you waved me to the left and the next car to the right, and you looked pretty determined behind that badge, so I just kept driving. The left lot was full, by the way."

"I know. Shut up."

He looked her over again. "Different uniform today," he said.

She rolled her eyes and scoffed.

McGann picked his words carefully. "I heard you're, uhm, helping out . . . at the sheriff's office?"

"I am, yes. I am helping at the sheriff's office. Temporarily." And that was truthful. There was no need to stand there in a pretty blue dress and go into detail.

They talked for a good part of an hour without regard to the daylight stealing away. She had looked for him right after graduation, but he'd vanished. He was sorry, but he'd gone to Oregon where his uncle had work for him. Then the war, of course, and he'd taken the job in Poulson afterwards, and just stayed the course. "You know how that goes," he said.

"Uh-huh. I heard you married what's her fancy pants: Martha Ganz."

He nodded. "I came back to Camas after . . . she left." He cleared his throat. "I'm here now."

"So it seems." Ada turned back to the tin can targets and took a couple shots. The crack of her gun scattered a tree full of jays and echoed off the forest wall, but the bullets didn't even raise dust.

He scrunched his lips. "You shooting blanks?"

"No!"

"You're aiming a little high, I think. Try using two hands."

She gripped the revolver with both hands and fired a couple more shots to no greater effect. McGann tossed his hat down and stepped behind her. Muttering, "I'm just gonna . . . let's just hold it like . . . this, I think," he stretched his arms around her shoulders and held her hands and the gun in his hands.

"Is this necessary?"-

"Just focus on the target, forget the gun. The gun is part of you."

She didn't care for a gun to be part of her, but the mountain breeze had gotten cool, so she let him help her to aim. She pulled back the hammer with her thumb and squeezed the trigger. The jolt knocked her back into him. She straightened herself and reloaded the gun.

"I took the job in Poulson right after we married, and we were there through the war years," he said. "And then we just stayed on—you know how it goes, day by day."

"I do know, yes." They were quiet for a minute. Ada asked, "Did you teach her to shoot?"

"Martha? Thank God, no. So, what's your story, Ada Reed?"

She stared at her boots and shook her head so slightly you'd barely notice. "Day by day. You know how it goes."

She turned back to the target, and McGann stepped in again to help. Their shots inched closer, though they never really hit what they were aiming at. "It takes practice like anything," he told her. "We'll get there."

The sun slid behind the peaks, and golden rays fanned across the sky. They practiced until they were out of bullets, then Ada changed her shoes again and they stopped at the Rod and Gun Club in Stanley for a steak and a glass of wine. She got home after midnight with the northern lights making a rare show over the rim of the valley.

CHAPTER FOURTEEN

10 July – 7:50 a.m., Releasing Mr. Barr today, then suspect interview in Custer. One week since Rose Braden's body was recovered.

WHEN SHE GOT TO WORK TUESDAY morning, Ada walked straight down to the holding cells, made sure Lonnie Barr got a good breakfast, then released him on his own recognizance.

Apparently, Barr had no one to call for a ride, as he was still hanging around when she returned from the recorder's office at ten o'clock. Ada was heading out anyway, so she ended up buying him a Coca Cola and driving him back to Sunbeam. At the last minute she remembered the boy's journal, found it still in her jockey box, and returned it to him. It just never occurred to her, until much later, that she might ought to have looked through it.

12:15 p.m. – Custer jailhouse. Reviewing case again with Sergeant Blevins of the State Patrol

BLEVINS AGAIN. THE STATE TROOPER STEPPED out of the Custer jailhouse as Ada was pinning on her badge. She tried to sidestep him, but Munson was on his heels with a pot of coffee, effectively trapping her on the boardwalk. She took the cup Munson offered, but only nodded to Blevins' "Good morning, Sheriff."

Munson swept a bench clean with his hat and he and Blevins sat. Munson said, "I thought we could meet out here. It's better if we talk out of earshot." He jerked his head in the direction of the jail.

Ada leaned and then sat on the railing, hooking her boot around the lower rail for balance. "Talk about what?" To Blevins she said, "Are you still saying I'm not up to the job?"

Blevins said, "Not at all, Sheriff, and I'm sorry it came out like that last time. I wanted to see if we could step back and get on a better footing."

"Talk about the Braden case," Munson said. "Maybe run back through the evidence."

She sipped her coffee, eyeing them both.

"We looked for you yesterday; no one had seen you. The truck was in front of your house all day, but no one answered the door."

"I took the Buick. I had to do some undercover work."

Blevins turned to face down the street, so she didn't see his smirk. He said, "As far as this dredge pond case goes, it looks like we have the Marine sergeant's tracks down by the water. And we have the stick that struck the girl, and we have a belief she was cheating on her husband that night."

"There's no evidence she was cheating that night, and in fact . . ."

"Actually, it doesn't matter if she was or wasn't." He waited through Ada's look of annoyance. "The boy thought it true, and that by itself is motive. So that right there is means, motive, and opportunity."

She turned from the Chief and the State cop at the sound of a truck rumbling by on the street behind her. A load of cattle was being taken to summer pasture up around the pass. The smell of the animals hung in the air, and Ada watched the truck until it disappeared around the first bend. Munson was saying something—agreeing with Blevins. But they were just mouthing more of the same nonsense. Corey Braden was the easy answer. The poor kid was eager to put a rope around his own neck and the whole county was ready to help him do it. They didn't see it wasn't just Corey's answers that weren't right. Rose wasn't right; she wasn't the right girl to get herself killed for cheating. Rose's life meant more than that.

She answered without turning back, "Braden's blow was made a long time before she went into the water."

"Exactly!" Blevins said. "It is possible the young man's confession is not true in a literal sense."

Her back and arms ached from the long drive from Camas, and all the arguing made her weary. Munson said, "Listen to this, Ada." He nodded for Blevins to go on, then crossed his arms and sat back. A warm, piney breeze whirled down the street clearing away the smell of the cattle and rustling the leaves of the cottonwoods. Blevins had risen from the bench and was leaned with his shoulder against a post. He was saying, ". . .We've all been thinking murder because of the violence of being snagged and brought up by the dredge line. And well, she'd taken a hard blow across her face. It looks like murder, all right. But did we, any of us, consider suicide?"

"Well yeah, but Rose wasn't like that."

"If the girl was abused as much as we know she was, and let's face it, nothing else was going right in her life, either—an unwanted pregnancy not the least—well I think suicide should at least be looked at." His voice was deep and smooth, like Montgomery's when he explained things.

Munson turned his hat in his hands and pursed his lips. Ada closed her eyes. "No, it's not right," she said. "Rose was too strong."

"You never met the girl!" It was Munson, and he wagged his head in apology for the sharp tone.

Her jaw tightened, but he was right. She had never met the girl. She slid from the railing and hopped down from the boardwalk.

Munson said, "But Ada, Rose Braden wore a chain of weights around her waist."

She stopped and rested against her truck with her head down. "An albatross. An encumbrance of her own making."

"Well, damn," Blevins said. "And if Sergeant Braden saw it from his window, then he may have understood that his actions and behavior were responsible for his own wife's despair. Hence, the confession." No question marks ended Blevins' sentences; there were none of the second guesses and uncertainties that tangled her own thoughts. "Maybe he wheeled himself down there filled with remorse," Blevins went on. "Or maybe, damn, maybe he left those tracks thinking he might save her—that a whole man might have been able to save his wife." He sat on the boardwalk with his feet on the ground, sighed heavily, and lit a cigarette. "I think the boy still loves her."

"There's no doubt of that."

"He's a good kid. But he's half out of his mind due to his war wounds and to that damned loose talk around town." He spoke softly and leaned his elbows on his knees. "I'm sorry, do you mind if I smoke?"

The air had calmed, and the nicotine fumes drifted over as in old days when Montgomery and his deputies would sit in the driveway or at the kitchen table discussing evidence. Mont never seemed confused or hesitant, either. He was always so sure. Sergeant Blevins sat straight, looking sharp and crisp in his uniform. "Hell, you've had a lot dumped on you, Ada," he said. "You've been up and down that damned highway, maligned in the papers, shot at, and run through the woods. It's your nature to take the girl's death personally. That's what makes you special. But it's not unusual in a case where someone is personally involved, for that person to step back and let someone else take the lead. Let us carry the ball a ways, Sheriff. I'll keep you informed every step."

Munson agreed it would be best if Ada got back to all the calls she hadn't had time for in the last week.

Ada turned and watched for another breeze through the cottonwoods, but it didn't come. In the end, she nodded, and told them she would go back to Camas and get her notes together. "I'll let you see everything I have," she said.

THE MIDDLE YANKEE FORK VALLEY WAS CALM and sunny on Ada's return drive, with heat waves shimmering over the acres of dredge tailings. She made it as far as the cottonwoods where the bedrock was shallow and the streambed left natural, before she had to stop. There, she dropped the tailgate and pulled out a cigarette, but decided against lighting it and cried instead. She cried a good ten minutes sitting in the shade with the river splashing below her. The magpies brought her up eventually, and she wiped her eyes and lit the smoke.

She had not seriously considered suicide, not in all that time. There was so much dying—on the highways, in the mines, in Korea. And Rose had packed a suitcase! Ada had seen it full of summer dresses and sandals, hopeful things. It just made sense that Rose was still hopeful and still dreaming.

"An amateur mistake," she said aloud. She'd put her own feelings and motives into the case. The fact is, young girls left alone with child, especially in desperate households like Rose and Corey's surely was . . . She hated to think about it, but young girls can lose hope.

She'd been right about Corey. He wanted to be respected even if it killed him. It was pride and maybe remorse behind the confession, and nothing more.

She was obviously wrong to hold any suspicions with regard to Cuss Pearen; there was no felonious intent in any of his answers. And Lonnie Barr was as upset as she'd ever seen a young man. He had loved Rose, clearly, and was devastated knowing he'd done nothing to save her. He could have misinterpreted her concerns. And the gunshots? Well hell, there was a target range just up in the trees.

The cigarette butt sizzled where it landed by the stream. Ada stared at it for a moment, then jumped to her feet, kicked the tailgate closed, and banged the hooks into the locks. The wheels of her truck scattered dirt and rocks as she circled around, and she left a rooster tail of dust all the way back to Custer.

Munson met her at the office door. "Where the hell is Blevins?" she demanded.

"Well, he went to the Pinyon for lunch. Ada, what the heck? I thought you went back to Camas." He chased after her down the boardwalk with townspeople craning at the windows of the shops and offices to see who was stomping so loudly. "What's up, Ada?" he called.

She didn't answer. The Pinyon Bar was dark and cool, with knotty pine walls and elkhorn chandeliers hung the length of the room. The young trooper sat at a table in the middle of the room in front of a hamburger steak and fried potatoes. "I thought we were shut of you," he blurted.

"Where's your boss, Deputy?"

"Huh?"

"The one with the silver tongue: Blevins."

The trooper tilted his flat top toward the men's room door. Ada strode to it and pushed through.

"Ada, goddamn!" Sergeant Blevins was at the urinal and had to turn away from her, struggling with both hands to do up his trousers. She grabbed his elbows from behind and swung him away from the urinal and into the toilet stall, pushed him down, and dropped her knee into his back. "Who told you I was shot at?" she shouted.

"Are you out of your freakin' mind?"

"No one but me, God, and the shooter knew about it." Holding one of his wrists twisted back, she pulled his firearm from its holster with her free hand and slid it across the floor. With his hand still pinned, then, she pressed down on his head with her full weight. "I'm asking officially because you're now a witness in a murder investigation, who told you I was shot at?"

Blevins kicked, and bucked her against the side of the stall. She kept her weight on him, though, and his head poised over the bowl. He tried to twist away but she kneed him a couple times in the kidneys and pressed on his head till his forehead touched the water. His voice echoed from the ceramic bowl, "My supervisor called me from Boise! You want to slam him around?"

"What kind of a cop are you, Blevins? How the hell did your supervisor know about it?"

"I don't know. You need to ask him!"

"Right now I'm telling you, and make no mistake: this is my investigation. Stay out of my way or I'll lock your ass in jail!"

3:57 p.m. – ~~Back at the goddamned jailhouse~~.
Follow-up with Sergeant Braden

ADA REED STOMPED BACK TO THE jailhouse, rattling windows and raising dust. But she changed her mind again and sat back heavily on the boards just outside the office door. For half an hour she let the mid-afternoon sun bake her through her uniform shirt and slacks. She sat, elbows on knees with her head down, and kept her handkerchief wadded tightly in her fist so that if anyone had been watching they would not have noticed her wiping at her eyes— and laughing.

God, how could she have done that? She'd never done anything like that in her whole pitiful life! She'd never gotten physical, not even when Montgomery was rough with her. She laughed, but anger prickled just under the surface. Anger at herself as much as at Blevins. Damn her, if she wasn't going to respect herself, who else would? And she'd not only been willing to doubt herself, but to doubt Rose Braden. Rose was not that kind of victim. She had a free will, she had a suitcase and a ride out of town. Rose wasn't giving in, she was starting out.

COREY BRADEN HAD BEEN LYING ON HIS COT READING, his face to the wall, but he sat up when she entered and stuffed a handful of letters under the pillow. He swung himself into his chair and wheeled nearer.

"Hello, Corey."

"You're wound up," he said. "What is it?"

"It's nothing." She pulled a chair over and sat but then stood again with her head turned away. "They're sons of bitches—pardon my French."

"Don't let them treat you . . . you know, bully you."

"No one's bullying me! No one's treating me any damned way."

"You think I don't know how this shit works?"

She didn't answer, and for a minute there was just the squeaking of his rubber wheels on the stone. She sat back down and sighed. "I got a letter from Montgomery yesterday. His company was relieved, so he's in Incheon for a few days R&R. He wanted to know if I was getting out of the office at all or if I was growing moss there filling out paperwork and budgets. I'm not sure what I should write back. Should I tell him about the case, about Rose and you?"

Braden yanked one wheel and pushed the other, spinning himself in a full circle and a half. A smile faded as quickly as it appeared. "He doesn't want to hear how you're doing fine and how life is working out. Tell him the music at the dance hall is dull so you stopped going, and the church socials last forever because no one has a damned thing to say. Tell him you can't even read a book because you don't care how it turns out."

"What if some of that isn't true?"

"What the hell is truth?" He took a deep breath and looked away. "Sorry, ma'am. I don't mean to be that way."

"Don't worry about me." She closed the notebook on her finger and, glancing at the pillow where he'd just hidden the letters, asked, "What did Rose write to you?"

"To me? What did she write to me?" The smile came and went again. "You know, 'Be careful, keep your head down'—which is a waste of ink, by the way—and, 'Don't worry, I'm taking care of the roadhouse; business is good.' That shit." He sighed. "Nothing about the quiet and the darkness."

Ada nodded. "Or the brandy."

"Nothing about the moon racing against the night, or how bright the stars can be at two in the morning, or how lonely the world feels waiting all alone in the dawn."

She put the pen down and sat up, suddenly tangled up in her feelings. His words could not be his own, they were not the words of a young Marine.

He spun his chair in another circle. "She didn't write any of that stuff. Not in her letters to me." The chair shot backwards across the cell, banging him into the wall. "Fuck me! No poetry for Corey!"

He spun in his chair. She squeezed her eyes shut and let him spin. What else could she do? They had to be Rose's words, and it was as clear to Ada as the nails digging into her own palms that they were meant for someone else; that Rose had loved someone else, and she no longer loved Corey. How else could things have worked out as they had? But Ada had not, even after learning the girl was pregnant, even after seeing the suitcase, she had not conceded the obvious. She hadn't let herself understand Rose had left him, even if she hadn't yet gone, and it happened long before San Francisco. It happened before she saw him ghostly and legless in the hospital, before his angry return.

She wanted badly to get up and leave, to find some air, but she moved only as far as the coffee pot, where she stood with her back to the cell wiping clean two cups. Rose had given up on her marriage. She had outgrown it and become someone new, and had stopped needing her husband. A sudden panic twisted Ada's insides, because maybe it started for Rose when she found herself up on a roof or under a sink, and realized she could swing a hammer or turn a pipe wrench; when she discovered she could dream and make plans and make the plans happen all on her own. "Coffee?" she asked.

"No thank you, ma'am."

Or maybe all the love, left untended, had just gone to seed and the seed had blown somewhere else. She carried her lukewarm coffee back and sat, but could barely look at the boy. She crossed her leg over her knee. "You married right out of high school. Did you think things through all the way?" she asked. The coffee was bitter.

He was slumped forward but turned back and gaped at her. "I did. There was never any doubt with me."

"You loved her?"

"I wouldn't be here otherwise, would I?" Tears welled in his eyes, and they both had to look away. "What the hell does any of this have to do with a murder investigation?" he asked.

"Do you want me to leave you alone?" She was ready to go.

Braden backed his chair up to the wall and balanced with his shoulders against the stones. After a moment he said, "She was a dreamer. That's the thing about Rose, she could start dreaming, and you had to watch out or, man, you'd be dreaming right along with her." He grinned up at the rough timber ceiling, and she ached for him. She ached for herself, and for Rose, too.

He said, "Rose thought we could move to Los Angeles and go to college. 'Hell's bells,' I told her, 'we aren't college material and we're sure as heck not made of money.' Did you ever go to college, ma'am?"

A bird abandoned the wire outside the cell window and another one lit, and then another. Ada watched them for just a moment. "Yes. College is where I met Monty—met my husband."

HER MOTHER HAD INSISTED ON IT. And no one would ever say, "What else is a woman good for when she's been shot up?"—but they might as well have. Everyone in the valley knew of the accident and what it meant, so what possible future would she have. "Still, wouldn't it be fine for Ada to get out and see the world, to get some ideas about all the different careers out there?" It was modern times, after all, and ladies with brains had all sorts of opportunities—out there.

A small scholarship got her to a college back east, and for a few years philosophy, literature and history filled her days. And boys her evenings, unexpectedly. And it truly was modern times;

it was carefree, exciting, and . . . God, he was dazzling in his ROTC uniform; tall and handsome! They danced, and there was barely a floor under her feet. And he was gentle—he was, and she loved him . . . back then.

"Ma'am?"

"Hmm? Yes, I attended college for a few years." The coffee was cold, and she set it down, again glancing toward the door.

Braden stayed against the wall, staring at the ceiling. "Anyway, I knew Rose since as long as I've known anyone. Her old man was a miner up Jordan Creek, and him and my old man had some partnership dealings. She was smart, boy. She had something going all the time; not at all like a girl at some things." He cleared his throat. "I mean, don't get me wrong, Rose was plenty like a girl. But she was . . . We'd hike and fish. She loved climbing above tree line." He dropped his wheels to the floor and rolled a few feet. "Gosh damn, and she was a rockhound, too. We'd go collecting, just the two of us; we'd sneak into some of the abandoned mines and find malachites and turquoise. She made jewelry out of some of it."

"Is that how she got to know some of the old miners?" Ada opened her notebook and fumbled for her pen.

"She thought she could make some money at jewelry, but I told her it was stupid. 'A damned waste of time,' is what I told her; 'We got a business right in front of us to concentrate on.'" For just a moment his face twisted, and he squeezed shut his eyes. But he breathed in hard and said, "Yeah, she was always conversing with the old coots."

"That include Custer Pearen?"

"She got to be as looney as some of them half the time. She came to me about investing in mines. Can you believe that shit? I told her, 'Not with my money!'"

"Had she taken money from you? Emptied your savings or anything?"

He stared at the floor shaking his head. "No, none of that. The savings are all there in the bank, little as they are. If she'd have wanted money to skip out, she could have signed the papers with Mansfield. I had a deal to sell him the roadhouse. But when the time came to sell, she wouldn't sign the papers. I guess they had words over it."

Ada said, "I'm told Dee Mansfield has big plans for the valley. How'd that get on with Rose's dreaming?"

"Dee isn't just a businessman. He's a Marine, and you're better not forgetting it." His tone changed in an instant from pensive to martial. He rolled to the back of the cell again and spun around. "Sometimes a campaign is going to come down to scorched earth."

She shrugged. "Sounds rough."

"This town is a bunch of damned sheep."

"Rose was not a sheep?"

"Rose was a dreamer, like I said. Then she became a screwer-arounder."

Ada closed her notebook and stood. "I should get going, probably."

"That's all?"

She leaned against the bars for a moment. "You said you never showed Rose the irrefutable evidence. Did you show anyone else?"

"What's that supposed to mean?"

What was it supposed to mean? "It's a pretty heavy burden to carry by yourself."

"If I passed a letter on to a friend, gave him a heads-up, why shouldn't I? He's always been square with me. Never sugar-coated anything."

"Who?"

He didn't answer but backed his chair up and rocked back on his wheels, leaning and rolling his head on the stones. "A screwer-arounder," he said. He closed his eyes. "Yeah, I showed Rose the letters. The whole damned stack of 'em."

"The letters you got from her room in the carriage house?"

"I figured she'd shit or go blind, but it was like she didn't even care. She just walked out. So, forget you, Corey! She didn't come home till morning, then left again for most of the day. That was the night she died."

"The night she was killed."

Braden dropped his wheels and pushed forward. "The night I killed her!" He gripped the bars and hung his head. "I'm done, Sheriff. No more, please."

"I'll stop by tomorrow if you want me to."

"It's up to you."

Chapter fifteen

11 July – 10:35 a.m. Full time on the Yankee Fork case.
State Police assistance declined for now.

T HE BOARDWALK THROUGH CUSTER once had been painted—
back when the mill was running two shifts and the town felt
a spring in every step. But the boards now were worn and cupped
by years of shuffling and dragging of feet. The mid-morning sun
already baked the pine and the tarpaper walls of the town, and
though a musty smell, it was better than the cyanide fumes and the
sickly smell of isobutyl carbinol when the mill had been running.
Vapors rose from the oiled gravel of Main Street, too, but that was
an improvement over the mule shit permeating everything forty
years ago.

Margaret Li struggled to get her grocery cart down off the
boardwalk, nearly tipping its few contents into the street. She
leaned heavily on a red and blue-painted post, caught her breath,
and pulled her cart across the street. From there, she dragged the
cart six more steps to a signpost, caught her breath again, and made
it to a light pole. And in that way, post to pole dragging her cart,
she made it to the west end of town. Her knees and ankles hurt by
then, so she sat down on a bench where the southside boardwalk
passed along the edge of the mill-tailings pond. A breeze drifting

down from the headwaters brought the sweet smell of Douglas fir, alder, and syringa.

The pond, all five acres of it, lay calm and chrysocolla blue—a lovely and mostly benign shade imparted, Mrs. Li knew, by solutions of hydrous copper carbonate. It was an expansive view from where she sat, and she supposed the bench had been positioned just so for townsfolk and visitors to take in and enjoy the scenery. The shores and islands of the mill pond were of putty-gray sludge banded orange with iron-sulfates and red with hydroxides, and picketed all around with white skeletons that once had been trees. Magically, and Li had seen it happen, the blue pond could turn over on windy days to a mustard yellow and a somewhat alarming garlicky stench. The color and stench, she was well aware, were due to hydrated arsenates released from anoxic bottom sediments, and that in turn explained the dead trees along the shores and the occasional dead waterfowl. But townsfolk seemed not to mind the odor or the toxicity, and Li didn't give a goddamn either.

A light breeze rippled the pond and the sulfur dioxide fumes scratched at her throat. She coughed deeply and had to spit. On her side of the road there were just a few places of business still standing, including the assay and post offices near her. At the east end of town, the old Lucky Boy mill lay rusted and blackened by fire, its corrugated skin slumped over a stone and iron skeleton. It had burned in the bleak midwinter. God, it had burned, and all night long! The smoke had hung in the valley for days under a frozen sky. When a north wind finally cleared out the filth, it brought with it four feet of snow and, unable to get out to the store, she had nearly starved. But Rose had come. She'd brought food and medicine, and even milk for their tea. They'd talked, and Rose had been angry—murderously angry. But mostly they had wept for the impermanence of dreams and the evanescence of hope. It had all befitted the darkness of the season.

Now Li dared not sit on the bench for too long or the good citizens of Custer would whisper, "Lazy Chink." Enough of them stared out now from the barber shop and the insurance office, their round eyes as glassy and hollow as the windows of their shops. She tried to rise, but her legs were not yet under her, so she sat and watched the townspeople watching her. The people went about their businesses deliberately, shifting from automatonic tasks, peering and ducking from the strange woman who peered back. *Wee timorous beasties,* Li thought. *Watching out on their town dying beneath them like lemmings who've somehow missed the migration.*

A red pickup truck with a cherry top and law insignia rolled into town from down-river, bringing a little dust and the smell of exhaust. It passed her and stopped across from the jailhouse where the Braden boy was being held for Rose's murder. "We'll see," Li said aloud. She forgot about her neighbors, then, and watched a tall, slender woman step out, set her Stetson, and pin on a badge. The lady sheriff sprang up onto the boardwalk, surprising and pleasing Li with her vigor. "We'll see," the old woman said again, struggling to her feet.

"WHAT'S THIS?" MUNSON ASKED. He swung his boots down from his desk, nearly upsetting the swivel chair. Acting Sheriff Reed and a lot of sunlight had come bursting through his front door, and she carried a plate covered with a linen towel. "What's this?" he asked again, righting himself.

Barely reigning in a smile, Ada kicked the door closed and carried the plate over to the coffee-break table. "Good morning and how are you boys doing?" she said. "Well, I thought I would just light a fire in my oven this morning before the squirrels build a nest in the flu." Braden was rocked back against the stone wall, staring at the ceiling. Ada glanced his way, still smiling. "And since I was up at four o'clock anyway, I thought I would do some baking." She pulled off the linen to reveal half a dozen large, heavily-frosted cinnamon rolls.

Munson scrambled over. "I'll make a fresh pot," he said. Braden glanced down and nodded to Ada, but said nothing.

"Are you resting okay, Corey?" she asked.

"Yes, ma'am. Thank you."

Munson said, "I didn't know you baked."

"Of course I bake. Why would you think I don't?" He didn't answer but busied himself with the coffee grounds and water. She said, "I've been cooking my whole life, you know. Just because I have a job . . ."

He set the pot on the hot plate and his hands on his hips. "Ada, what happened yesterday? We had a deal with Blevins. What the heck happened between you?"

"I'll explain it all to you, Kellen. Let's just have a coffee first."

But she didn't explain it—not the shooting, or Rose's room being searched, or the medallions maybe being worth a lot of money. There was nothing certain, after all, to any of it. Munson, too, let it drop, and the two of them discussed new State regulations and paperwork while the pot came to a perk. Ada glanced over from time to time, but Braden seemed lost in his own thoughts.

Munson poured coffee into three mugs, then carried his cinnamon roll on a paper napkin back to his desk. Ada brought one mug and a roll to Braden's cell, and slipped them through the bars to the small table by his bunk.

"Thank you," Braden said. He wheeled to the table and picked up the coffee cup but kept his eyes to the side.

She returned with a cup of coffee for herself, and a chair. "It might be a little burned on the bottom," she said. "I ran out of pine for the kitchen range and had to use aspen, and the aspen was dry, so it burned way too hot. So anyway, the rolls might be a little burned."

"They're real fine, ma'am." He took a small bite. "We used to have them at the roadhouse, Rose and me."

HALF AN HOUR LATER, Ada stepped from the jailhouse, jumped off the boardwalk into the street, and started kitty-corner across Main to her pickup truck. But in the middle of the road, she stopped short and gaped: a fresh set of narrow tracks curved down the road. The tracks were crossed by a few automobile tires, including her own, but clearly had been made since the last night's rain. She dropped to a knee. They were left by two-inch wide wheels, about thirty inches apart—the width of a wheelchair—and were cut an inch deep into the soft dirt. The tracks clung to the south edge of Main Street and continued westward. Following on foot, she passed the assay and the insurance offices and hurried on toward Corey Braden's roadhouse. The tracks led south from there, toward the dredge pond.

At a trot now, she caught sight of Mrs. Li coming from behind a pile of building debris and tree limbs. The old woman was pulling a heavy cart behind her, following a path near the edge of the pond but struggling in the mud and deep grass. Ada picked up her pace. "May I help you," she called when she was close. "It was you; it was your cart!"

Li turned as Ada trotted up. Her face was as yellow as the day they'd talked, and her motions as slow and labored. The dredge towered above her but floated eerily silent. "Thank you," the woman said. "I would not refuse the help, if you don't mind." The cart carried a few groceries: cans of vegetables, bags of rice and flour, tea, and canned milk.

"I don't mind at all." Ada took the handle of the cart in one hand and offered her other arm to Li for balance. "Let's get you home."

They entered through a gate into the backyard. The white picket fence along the back of the property, which earlier had been slumping toward the water, was now floating. The lawn was grown tall and going to seed, but rows of flowers were still cared for.

Ada packed the groceries into the house, then made tea while the old woman retired to the parlor to catch her breath. She found a porcelain teapot, two small handle-less cups, and a crystal creamer, all of which she carried into the parlor on a lacquered tray. The room was brighter than before; the window had been left open, with the dredge sitting quiet, and mid-day light livened the place. A bright pattern of bamboo and exotic birds covered the walls. Almost in reflection, Ada said, "We forget to look for nice things, stop expecting them, and then we're pleasantly surprised, aren't we?"

Li considered her for a moment. "It is better to expect them, though," she said. "It helps to bring them about, I think."

They drank their tea quietly, hearing birds rather than boulders, and wind instead of splashing water. Ada waited, and when at last it was time to speak, she didn't ask about the dredge workings or the Braden case, but about the peonies and roses in her garden, and the difficulty bringing them through the mountain winters. Li nodded. "Peonies are easy enough," she said. "You can cut them low and bury them, and they will find their own way back in the spring. Roses are most difficult. It takes much time and burlap to wrap them in the fall."

"In my garden as well."

"Many times in the winter I have been out in the storm shoveling snow over them for insulation. But they are so beautiful if they live."

"A favorite," Ada agreed. There were a hundred questions, but she touched the napkin to her lips and said, "I don't remember the Bottoms in the time before the dredge. Was it like your yard here? Did you have gardens in the old days, and were there parties and celebrations?"

The old woman turned toward the open window, and when she spoke it was with a wistfulness that made Ada smile. "It was a beautiful neighborhood once," she said, "and a happy place. My father was a leader, and well respected, so yes there were many elegant occasions in this house." Her eyes focused beyond the curtains to a few lilac hedges still standing, and to scattered forsythia just beginning to drop their flowers. "It was in the springtime when everyone's yard flowered and the apples and plums blossomed that we would hardly breathe lest the days and nights pass too quickly. There were noisy festivals, even fireworks when we could afford them. Soft petals would cover the ground, and under the moon the air was sweet, and laughter could be heard behind every tree."

"What happened, Mrs. Li?"

"It was not only the dredge. That monster came mostly to desecrate our graves. We grew old, and the young grew restless."

Ada nodded, and they sat quietly for a short while longer. Ada said, "Rose Braden did not grow old."

"No, but restless."

"The night she died, her husband, Sergeant Braden, did not come down by the water."

"No. I never saw him down here. The ground is too soft for his chair, I'm sure." The old woman found her pipe and filled it with dry leaves from a folded handkerchief.

Ada said, "Rose had packed a suitcase. She was leaving town, but I think it was more than just running. It was important. The trip meant something to her."

"That is very Eastern of you. *We are all wandering, and every journey brings us closer to the truth.*"

"That's not Chinese, it's Hindu," Ada said.

"Sue me." She looked up and winked, and Ada laughed. The old woman lit the pipe, puffed it up, and blew out a long smoky breath. She said, "I saw Rose the day she died. She was quite unreasonable, I'm afraid. Excited and angry at once. *'He stole them all!'* she said. Quite unreasonable."

"Upset her boyfriend might be lost to her?" Ada asked.

Li shrugged.

"A woman in love, who'd been found out . . ." Ada turned to a warm breeze through the open window.

"Yes, but a woman, Ada Reed. Rose was not so one-faceted as you make her to be."

Ada hesitated for just a moment, then without turning from the window said, "Rose was pregnant."

"I thought she might be. Still, that's not all there is to a woman.

Let's agree there was a young man. But Rose was finding her own life beyond just wife or lover, or even mother."

If Li's words stirred anything at all in her, Ada didn't show it. She waved at the sweet, acrid smoke and after a moment asked, "But why did she stop that night? She was going. For whatever reason she was on her way. What else was so important she had to turn back?"

Li puffed on the pipe and struggled not to cough. "Rose had been excitable for some time. But that day she was quite upset, and it worried me. She'd been up to the Sunnyside Mine that morning."

"The Sunnyside? Pearen's mine?"

"Yes, poor Cuss. He and I grew up here, did you know that? He asked me to dance once at the Lilac Festival." Her head lolled gently. "When I saw Rose that night, she looked like she'd been in a fight. Cut and bruised. She was angry and swore he would not get away with it." Li closed her eyes and rested. "In the end it was she who could never get away. Never quite get away."

Ada wrote a few notes as Mrs. Li went on smoking and talking, sometimes indecipherably. She started to interject several times, but in the end put her pen down and asked, "It's cannabis, isn't it? Your dàmá, your medicine. Rose got it for you, didn't she?"

"Are you going to arrest me?"

"I've no time to arrest you. Nor any desire."

The old woman's eyes peeked open, and she managed a thin smile. "You have no place to incarcerate me if you did, although that would not stop the resolute Montgomery Reed. And arresting me would put you back in good graces with your constituency. I'm sure the judge could be convinced to levy a big fine, which I could not pay. My land would have to be auctioned on the courthouse steps."

Ada stood, and said gently but firmly, "I am not Montgomery."

Li showed another bit of a smile. "We'll see. In any case, this is the last of the dàmá. I'm burning the evidence."

2:15 p.m. – Site investigation, Jordan Creek canyon:
Cuss Pearen's Sunnyside Mine.

THE OILED GRAVEL OF MAIN STREET shined in the midday sun, but the air held onto the cool of the morning, so a number of townspeople had come out onto the boardwalk. Two old men sat in front of the hardware with a cribbage board between them, and Ada listened for a while to their rhythmic counting. She should talk with Corey Braden again, contradict him over the cart tracks. But not yet. She couldn't just tear off whatever bandage he'd found to bind his wounds. And between Blevins yesterday and Margaret Li today, she felt drained. It would be good to sit and rest in the bright sunshine. But now more than ever she had to move. Rose had lost her composure while visiting Cuss Pearen's mine. Something had happened to her at the Sunnyside.

Chief Munson was nowhere to be found, so Ada headed up alone. The road up Jordan Creek ran most of its length between high canyon walls that baked hot as an oven. In the tight curves the dust swirled around and choked and blinded her. The road rose and fell through deeply scarred hills; it crawled over rocky stretches dynamited into the canyon walls, and it splashed through the creek at a dozen places where there was not room for road and stream both. The going was slow, and she did not push it.

Five miles above Custer she found her turnoff. The main road continued up and over Loon Creek Pass to disappear into trackless wilderness, but just as the road started into the switchbacks she turned left onto the narrow, rocky, Sunnyside mine road. A chain across the entrance was unhooked and lying in the road. Ada left it as she found it and drove through. Beyond the gate, the truck bounced and swayed over a badly washed-out two-track road that twisted up an aspen choked gulley then up the steep side of a bare rocky ridge. The rocks everywhere were bleached white, and the glare nearly blinded her as she crossed over the ridge and dropped down the far side.

THE RED SHERIFF'S PICKUP CRAWLED DOWN the steep mine road, skidding here and there in loose rocks and taking it slow and careful around the tighter curves. The man watched from behind a boulder until the truck dropped out of view behind a bend. He lowered the hammer of his rifle and clicked on the safety, then ducked behind the boulder and boot-skied down a gravelly chute, grabbing at pine boughs with his free hand to stem his slide and keep the dust low.

Four rough-timber shacks made up the mine site. There were half a dozen broken-down trucks and wagons parked in a row, and an equipment boneyard. The sheriff's truck pulled to a creaking stop in front of the bunk cabin. He skirted behind a screen of trees and moved in closer, inching along the side of the machine shop.

The sheriff climbed out of the truck and stretched, and her hair flew up in a breeze, flashing yellow in the midday sun. There was no gun on her hip, but after looking around, she reached back into the cab for her holster and belted it on.

She called out for "Anyone here?" He kept quiet in the shadows, letting her search around the machinery and look into the buildings and sheds. He crept from cover to cover as she moved, keeping an eye on her activities. She stopped to take pictures all around the minesite: pictures of the doors, roadways, and footpaths. She knelt to photograph vehicle tracks and bootprints. For a half hour Reed poked her nose into the Sunnyside business; writing her notes in a small book and ignoring all the 'keep out' signs and the signs warning of danger. She crept between the buildings, the so-called sheriff, glancing quickly into windows and poking through the cluttered back porch of the cabin. The front door was unlocked, and she pushed it open, then called "hello," but did not go in.

At the entrance to the mine, she knelt in the soft earth and touched with her fingers the sediments there. She lifted a piece of trash from the slime of the mine effluent and examined it. He watched from behind the spring house as she took the flashlight from her belt and entered the mine without the least show of sense.

THE SUNNYSIDE WORKINGS WERE IN BETTER SHAPE than the Pirate's Gold had been. The walls and roof were well braced and there was very little sluff on the floors. The mine, at least the main entrance to it, had been well maintained. Ada's interest, though, was not in the walls and roof, but focused on the footprints pressed into the mud of the floor. A trail of miners' footprints kept to the middle of the adit, between narrow iron rails. To one side of the rails, though, she found what she was looking for. They were the footprints she'd seen in the Pirate's Gold mine—the Lady Lane Oxfords—and they must surely be Rose Braden's. Margaret Li said she had visited there.

The man's western boot prints were there as well. She followed the tracks in. One hundred yards into the mine not a drip of water could be heard, and all was pitch black but in the narrow circle of her flashlight beam. On her knees, she immediately recognized what had bothered her about the footprints in the Pirate's Gold. And it wasn't the woman's prints. With the darkness and silence closing in, she reached to touch one of the larger boot prints that seemed to follow Rose's. In the heel of the man's print, a clear crescent shape was pressed. She hadn't taken notice before because they were common enough marks, the kind made by metal taps— heel protectors. But sure as anything, they were the shape of the crescent moons on the backs of Rose Braden's hands.

She fumbled the notebook from her back pocket and, tucking the flashlight between cheek and shoulder, flipped through the pages. Barely able to keep the book from shaking, she compared the sketches she'd made on the first day of the investigation to the heel prints in the mud. The crescent marks were identical in size and shape!

THE WOMAN SHERIFF CAME OUT OF THE MINE at a run, turned a complete circle, then leaned forward with hands on her knees, breathing hard. She rose up and hurried back to her pickup, but dropped to a knee, listening, he thought. He raised the rifle to his shoulder. The sheriff jumped up, drew her gun, and sidestepped to the driver's side door. She stopped, with the truck door open, and scanned the treed hillside above her. He searched the trees as well. The air was warm, dry, and deathly still, and the shadows were beginning to lengthen. She called again, "Who's there?" He clicked off the safety and aimed.

But the goddamned truck horn blared! Crows and jays scattered on the wing and a lithe shadow darted through the undergrowth. The man looked up over the iron sights as the sheriff dove into the cab of her truck with a shriek.

He lowered the rifle, eased the hammer down, and watched the pickup truck bounce and sway back up the side of the hollow. He'd had a good shot. He should have taken it.

ALL THE WAY DOWN THE ROCKY, DUSTY ROAD toward Custer, Ada gulped her breaths and struggled with tears. The tears were not for the panic that had gripped her, but for what she'd seen underground, and the horror of what it meant. Her hands—Rose Braden's hands—had been stomped on by the owner of those boots!

There'd been no scabs or deep bruising with the crescent marks on the girl's hands, either, so it probably had happened in the seconds before death; before she'd slipped under the water. She hit the brakes and skidded to a stop in the middle of the road, breathed in deeply, and laughed through her tears at what else it meant: Sergeant Corey Braden was the one person in the county perfectly incapable of having done it!

Rose had been inside the Sunnyside Mine. *For what purpose?* And clearly her killer had been in there too. Rose had seen or heard something inside; something had happened to make her lose control, according to Mrs. Li. *What was it?* Damn her, Ada had panicked and run out before she'd seen what she needed to see.

She put the truck in gear and continued toward town slowly, trying to keep the dust down and her thoughts clear.

CHAPTER SIXTEEN

*4:55 p.m. – Yankee Fork Dredge: Mr. Mansfield has agreed
to see us again (follow-up interview)*

DEE MANSFIELD HAD CONSENTED to a second interview, but
it couldn't have come at a worse time for the acting sheriff. Ada parked in town, still jittery from the scare she'd had at
the Sunnyside, and she walked to the dredge hoping the fresh air
would settle her nerves. She poked among the willows and rushes
above the culverts, cooling in the shade and sharing the river-
bank with a family of ducks. But the jitters wouldn't go away, so
she took to the bare hillside on the south side of the river instead,
climbing until her legs hurt. The air was sweet with sage still wet
from the last night's rain and with yellow balsamroot glowing
in the sun. She found a smooth boulder where she could sit and
catch her breath.

A wind blew from the east, bending and slapping the loose
sheets of siding in the town below her. From her rock vantage it
sounded like doors opening and slamming shut. A hawk soared on
the east wind, and it circled and looped, watching for rabbits and
ground squirrels. Ada closed her eyes to the hawk and covered her
ears against the banging sheets of tin. She needed a clue; anything
that could help her put things back together.

Corey Braden could not have done the crime, which left her no longer with a prime suspect. Her secondary suspect was a nameless, faceless man in cowboy boots. But she did know a few things. Rose's killer had to have known her, and had either accompanied her into some odd places, or had stalked her. Rose had drowned, so it was reasonable that she had died where she was found, at the dredge pond, her hands stomped on as she tried to save herself.

Okay then. Had she come to the pond on her own, and if so, what did Rose need to get from there, or whom did she need to see? Ada took the field book from her back pocket, turned to the end of her notes, and wrote:

Why go onto a gold dredge at night?

Leaving aside, for the time, why anyone would wear a belt of heavy medallions onto a dredge, she listed:

1. *Steal gold.*
2. *Meet friend or confront enemy.*
3. *Look for something.*

She paused, then added:

4. *Revenge, sabotage.*

It probably was not possible to steal gold from a shut-down dredging operation. The crew were pretty adept, she reasoned, at cleaning the riffles at the end of a shift. She crossed it out.

But had Rose Braden even made it onto the dredge? Impossible from all appearances, unless she'd been invited on by someone with a key. That would be Mansfield or Dar Colemaker. A friend? A secret lover? Ada made a face. But Mansfield's assurance notwithstanding, the grease smears on her dress suggested she probably did visit, and maybe retreated hurriedly from the dredge. So, she might well have died trying to get off the dredge, and the marks on her hands—Ada swallowed hard—proved she didn't die accidentally. That part was certain.

Rose was not dumb and would not have gone onto unfamiliar ground to confront an enemy, nor to commit some sort of vengeful act. So, 'look for something' it must have been. Ada circled it in her notes.

But what kind of something? Evidence perhaps—but of what?

The hawk flew on and Ada shaded her eyes to follow its course. The bird caught a thermal, circled, and climbed until she lost it in the sun. The town lay below her, its businesses and shanties, and ruined foundations deposited like a logjam at the narrow mouth of the upper Yankee Fork canyon with barely room for the river still to flow. She could mark the empty lots of three or four properties, including the mill, that had burned down in just the last year or so. The map she'd seen on Mansfield's table had highlighted a number of properties, but she did not know if they were the blackened lots she could see. It didn't matter; it wasn't the case she was working on now.

Except, the old miner, Jubal Mason, had thought them connected. He'd told her the mill fire was no accident and was meant to starve out the town. She banged the notebook against her head, opened it again, and below her last notes wrote:

Arson? Who, Why?

Downstream from the jumbled logjam of a town, the canyon opened wide where Jordan Creek flowed in. But there was no town there, at least not anymore. Where once lay streets and the neat Chinese gardens and fruit trees of the Bottoms, there were backwater ponds between row after row of tailings. And now the dredge, straining on its cables below her, was nearly done, its appetite satisfied.

But was it satisfied? Ada jumped up and nearly choked. For heaven's sake, the river valley continued broad and flat above town, too! The General Custer Mine stood two miles upstream and was certainly a principal source of placer gold.

She opened the book and after the words, *Arson? Who, why?* wrote:

Open up more Dredging Ground ?!

She stuck the book in her back pocket, jammed her hat on her head, and hurried down the hill, sliding in the rocky soil and tripping over sagebrush, going nearly ass over tea kettle a couple of times. She stumbled onto the road breathless and found Kellen Munson waiting for her on the tailgate of his pickup truck.

Munson's yoke-back western shirt was pressed and starched: an eye-punching tartan of fuchsia and pineapple with black pearl snaps. Ada said, "Let's beg off, Kel. Can you thank Mr. Mansfield but tell him we'd like to reschedule?"

"We have an appointment now. Mansfield is a busy man." He straightened his cuffs and got to his feet.

"But Kel, I'm not ready."

"It's now or never, Ada." He closed and hooked the tailgate.

THERE WERE OTHERS IN MANSFIELD'S OFFICE, including two white-shirted engineers and Sergeant Ken Blevins of the State Patrol. The door to the sleeping quarters was closed this time, but otherwise the office looked the same. "Hello, Ada," Mansfield said. Blevins didn't acknowledge her but leaned against the wall with his arms crossed. Mansfield nodded to the engineers, who gathered their papers and left the room. "Still working on the Braden case?" he asked.

"I'm afraid so, Dee."

"It's been what, ten days? I'd have thought we would have that put to bed by now."

Ada found no words at all. She stuttered, "Eight days. It's still ongoing. I'm . . ." Then stood with her hands at her sides feeling a warmth and surely a redness growing around her head and neck.

"Sheriff?"

"Sorry, yes. I meant to ask last time, if the mining district is all played out, then why did you accept the Sunnyside Mine in payment from Mr. Pearen. I mean, versus fifteen hundred dollars cash?"

"Your business today has nothing to do . . ." Mansfield sighed and crossed the carpeted floor to the starboard windows. "It was the mine or nothing. I presumed I would never see a sawbuck from that old thief."

"So now with the mill burned down, you own a worthless mine?"

Mansfield turned with a shrug. "I don't own it. The old bastard came up with the cash after all." He wore an amiable smile back to his desk. "What else, Sheriff?"

There were so many loose ends! Blevins stood with a smirk on his face. He'd let slip the other day that the State Police Commander in Boise knew she'd been shot at. Who could have told him? Who in the whole county could pick up a phone and call the State Police Commander, besides Mansfield? But how would that make sense, even if . . . And what exactly had Corey Braden meant by 'scorched earth?' She raised her eyes and asked Mansfield, "You are friends with the attorney general in Boise?"

"Bob Smylie; had dinner with him last month. I have his phone number in my book."

"Do you have the number of the State Police commander in Boise, as well?" She glanced at Blevins, who froze for an instant, eyes closed. Ada breathed in through her nose and out through her mouth. The notebook was shaking in her hands, so she closed it and stuck it in her pocket.

"I suppose I could find it if you need it," Mansfield said. "Do you mind if I sit? There are a few papers Ken needs me to sign."

He stepped around her to settle into a swivel chair. As he sat, the cuffs of his slacks pulled up to expose the elaborately tooled tops of a pair of western boots. He opened the wide, flat drawer of the desk, where he sorted through papers, envelopes, and ledgers. "I am sorry to be so busy," he said.

Ada stared at the boots, open-mouthed. She said, "The, uhm, commander who knew I was shot at almost before I did?"

"You were shot at?" Munson asked. He hurried over and reached for her, but she pulled away. Blevins took the toothpick out of his mouth.

Mansfield set down his papers and leaned back in the chair. He sighed and pursed his lips. "I appreciate a spirited investigation, but . . ." He sighed again in Blevins' direction. "The girl killed herself. It is a tragedy, but it happens. And it's silly and just a little distasteful for you to try to make it into something more. You need to do your job, Mrs. Reed, instead of chasing some phantom of the lagoon."

Ada stood her ground. "It's not a phantom. I have proof positive Rose Braden did not die willingly."

"What proof?"

"I'm not ready to divulge that yet."

Mansfield looked over at the grinning Sergeant Blevins, who asked, "And did you find this evidence doing your undercover work?"

Mansfield shushed him. He asked, "Any witnesses whatever, Ada?"

"There's Lonnie Barr. He . . ."

"That little drunk? Mansfield stepped from behind the desk, his boots again catching her eye. "What exactly did he tell you? Did Mr. Barr give you a reason why Rose Braden would want to trespass here? Do you have a reason, *Acting* Sheriff, for any sort of enmity between me and the girl? Any reason she or I would want to do harm to the other?"

Ada stepped back, confused by the rapid questioning. "The

town map," she sputtered, "the one I saw the other day before you rolled it up. Some of the properties you highlighted have recently burned. Your mill, which incidentally was keeping the whole district going . . ."

"What the hell are you saying?" He grinned again Blevins' way, but not pleasantly.

"I'm just pointing out some troubling coincidences." She cleared her throat again and tried to keep her breathing even, but her head had begun to pound and her stomach to knot up. She wasn't ready to push forward, but she didn't know if she could go back anymore, and she knew they were all thinking her just a silly amateur. It made her angry, and that helped a little. She said, "Mont would do the same thing. He would look into coincidences like this."

"Why the devil would I or anybody . . .?" Mansfield asked, now testily.

"There are probably a number of reasons any number of people might want to clear out portions of the town." She stopped to gulp a breath. "Maybe the most obvious being so that a dredging operation could continue to mine through the town site, all the way to the General Custer Mine."

Nobody spoke. Even the muffled grinding of rocks ceased. Ada, still a little miffed, looked down and shuffled her feet. "It's a circumstantial coincidence, I understand, but there are people in town who think along those lines."

Munson reached for her arm again, pulling her back, clumsily, a couple of steps from Mansfield. Blevins leaned against the back wall with his arms folded, and now his head wagging back and forth. Mansfield, though, freshened his smile and nodded. "I see where you're going," he said.

All heard the sudden screeching of winches and felt the room turn under them as cables strained to re-position the floating factory. Mansfield walked to the window, listened for a moment, then closed it. He said, "I don't know why the girl would be saying things about me, if indeed she was. But she spent a lot of

time with the unstable Mr. Pearen, and that could explain a lot."
He went to the map rack and sorted through the tubes. "Now, as
to your . . . We'll call it a flight of fancy . . ." He found the map
he was looking for, brought it to the drafting table, and unrolled
it. "Do you know what an isopach map is, Ada? It's a contour
map of overburden; it shows the thickness of gravels sitting atop
bedrock."

Blevins and Munson stepped in close. Ada took a step toward
the table, her arms crossed, and craned to see.

Mansfield said, "This map shows the thickness of the placer
gravel in the valley from just around the bend behind us, eastward
through the townsite. It was put together—at considerable expense
I might add—from drillhole data, from well diggers reports, and
from Paul and Dwayne's notes over at the town works. You know
Paul and Dwayne don't you, Kellen?" Munson scrunched his lips
and nodded. Mansfield said, "Of course you do. Between the two
of them they hand dug most of the sewer and water lines under the
streets. Take a look here."

They all leaned in. He said, "The river gravels are twenty feet
deep right here where we're digging. But there's a fault line running
down Jordan Creek. You all know what a fault is? That fault raises
up the bedrock on the east side so that the gravels under the town
are no more than three to five feet thick before you're down into
solid rhyolite. This barge by itself draws six feet."

Mansfield left the map on the table for the three of them to
study, and poured himself a Scotch at the credenza. Blevins said,
"Well hell, Dee, if you want to mine through the townsite, you'll
have to put the dredge up on wheels and roll it over that bedrock."

Mansfield laughed. "Now you're talking, Ken. We'll go into dry-
land dredging. Hell, we'll start a whole new industry."

Blevins stepped away from the map table and helped himself to
a whiskey. Munson stood with his hands in his pockets, not looking at anyone. Ada glanced at Blevins across the room and felt her
knees go wobbly. Blevins wore sharp-toed western boots under his

blue uniform slacks. She turned back to Munson, and of course he wore the same kind of footwear. Good lord, half the men in the county wore western boots! The knot in her stomach wouldn't go away. She crossed her arms more tightly and felt herself flush from her neck to her wrists.

Mansfield said, "I don't hold it against you, Ada. Hell's bells, we all make mistakes." He sat back at his desk and waved them away with a good-natured smile. "Good day, please. I do have a lot of work."

MUNSON TOLD HER TO GET INTO HIS TRUCK and he'd drive her back to the office. She told him she'd rather walk.

"Please get in." He slammed his door. "We need to talk."

She climbed in the passenger side and held her hat on her lap. Munson said, "I know this is your jurisdiction, but it's my damned town, and I have to live and work with these people."

"Please don't lecture me right now, Kellen."

"Pardon my language. But this is my gosh-darned job, Ada. It isn't a hobby for me." He started the engine, but when he saw her wince at 'hobby,' he exhaled and slapped the steering wheel. "Fine," he said. "Okay, then." He put the truck in gear and let the clutch out slowly. "I think you need to focus your investigation on one, the admitted killer, or two, the mystery boyfriend. And we need to forget these theoretical dissertations."

Ada rolled down the window and rested her head on her arm, letting her hair swirl in the breeze.

"Ada," Munson said, "Rose Braden was out seeing somebody she obviously knew a little too well. The most reasonable thing is the baby's father wanted to end the relationship—to keep her quiet, or just make the problem go away."

"But she was already packed and running, Kel. An un-willing father would have given her money and bought her a bus ticket."

"Then it's Corey. Wheelchair tracks at the crime scene, a motive, a weapon."

"I have other evidence: the marks on her hands. I'm certain it shows it could not have been him. It has to be someone else."

He looked over, and her head was cradled in her arm, leaning on the frame of the open window. More gently he said, "Ada, are you identifying too closely with the suspect?"

"Cuss Pearen knows more than he should, and he's broke. And I don't know, listen to what Mansfield says, Cuss is a dangerous con man."

"Cuss? Pearen didn't leave wheelchair tracks at the crime scene!"

He had to be told, *it was Li's grocery cart, it was never a wheelchair,* but she didn't have the strength anymore to explain things. Munson stopped a block from the jailhouse between the rusted carcass of the mill and the assay office, where Ada's pickup was parked. She stepped out and shaded her eyes at the low afternoon sun burning over the trees. A pair of mallards settled on the blue mill pond.

"Good evening, Millie," she heard Munson say. From the corner of her eye, Kellen's shadow swiped the hat off its head. A long, thin shadow joined his. "I haven't time to talk Kellen," a woman's voice said. She appeared to eye Ada up and down.

"Mrs. Niedermeyer, this is Sheriff Ada Reed." Munson turned to Ada and cleared his throat. "Sheriff, you remember we met the Reverend Niedermeyer, the other day?"

Ada nodded.

Mrs. Niedermeyer held a coarse cane basket half filled with zucchini, carrots, and new potatoes. She said, "I heard you wear pants."

Ada didn't answer but leaned again on the boardwalk railing and watched the colors deepen in the west. Sunlight stabbed straight through the windows of the assay office. A shadow crossed the light; it would have been the assayist working inside. Her stomach tightened. Fifteen dollars for a medallion, according to Lonnie. It had to contain gold, and she needed to call the Idaho City assayist for the test results.

Munson said, "Millie I don't mean to keep you, but I'm still a little curious about Aaron's last visit."

Ada's head pounded. She didn't turn, but said, "Mrs. Niedermeyer your husband was not truthful when he told us Aaron hadn't been home since Christmas. Aaron was seen at Easter service and at the town picnic afterward."

Millie Niedermeyer set her jaw and looked as if she could swat at the sheriff. "Ada!" Munson snapped. More calmly, with hands on his hips, he said, "Sheriff Reed, would you mind over much letting me ask questions of my own townsfolk."

Ada rubbed her temples and focused on the honey rays reflecting off the mill pond. Her hands and knees began to shake as she re-traced every word spoken in Mansfield's office. Birds chattered in the dead trees across the pond, and a slight breeze whispered through live branches behind her. Rose had been warning others of Mansfield, according to the old miners. Could Rose Braden have made the same stupid mistake she'd just made?

Behind her, Munson was asking, "Millie, pardon me, but why were you not at prayer supper last Tuesday night? The Reverend said you were feeling poorly, but I've seen you there with a raging fever."

Niedermeyer brushed the plaquette of her blouse and scoffed, but Munson waited with raised brows. The woman said, "Because my heart was filthy with gladness that whore was dead. I could not bring such filth into the house of the Lord." She cleared her throat and turned to Ada, who continued to study the lake. "Yes, our son was home for holy Easter. Just for a few days. It's such a long bus ride back to Berkeley, you see, so he could not stay longer, although he would have liked to, and of course we did wish it as well. My husband simply confused the dates under the many burdens he carries for this unhappy town."

The woman's voice sounded distant. She stood stiff and red in the sun's rays, her knuckles turning white on the handle of the basket. Ada asked, "Berkeley? Aaron attends university in Berkeley, California? In the Bay Area?"

"He does."

"The Bay Area." The breeze stopped and no birds called, and it seemed she could hear her own heartbeat. "Does the Reverend sleep deeply, Mrs. Niedermeyer?" she asked, looking up now and noticing the clouds catching a red glow. "Or does he find himself up late some nights listening to the crickets and frogs and worrying over little things that might never bother a person in the light of day?"

"He sleeps fine. I'm sure he'll thank you."

Ada turned to face the woman. "And you? Late at night when little things won't let a person be, and every worry becomes a certainty; when all one's work has gone for nothing . . ."

"Some nights are more restless than others. That's true for anyone."

Munson pushed his hat back on his head and crossed his arms. "Ada?" he asked.

Ada glanced at him but turned back to Mrs. Niedermeyer. "Do you step out, then, if the weather is fine and the night is quiet but for the insects and all your worries?"

"I have, for the air. Without bothering no one; it's no one's business." Millie Niedermeyer glanced sideways at Munson and clutched her collar with her free hand.

"And might a person hear and see things then that would never be seen in the light of day?"

"You can go to hell, Ada Reed, if you haven't one foot there already!" She squared herself and looked for a way between the two lawmen.

"Aaron was with Rose Braden that Easter visit, wasn't he?" Ada asked. "They were friends—a lot more than friends. Did you see them together?"

Millie Niedermeyer cried out and swung the cane basket, catching Ada on the head and shoulder before she could fend the blow, knocking her to the boardwalk. "And he left town with that whore still wet in his pants!" she cried. "What kind of a man is he going to be now?"

MUNSON WAS ON HIS KNEES HELPING HER TO SIT UP. Her head spun, and her right eye felt sticky. "Lord, Lord," he was saying, "Mary and Joseph!" He held a handkerchief to her forehead with shaking hands. "Are you okay, Ada?" A bullfrog croaked, and a pair of ducks flew by not ten feet over their heads. "Are you okay?" he asked again.

"Well, there you go," she said, her own words sounding distant. She tried to rub her head, but he pushed her hand away.

"There you go, what? Are we supposed to take Millie Niedermeyer for a suspect now? Sure, she's mean as a snake, but . . ."

Ada took the handkerchief from him. "No, of course not. Her feet are too small."

"Huh?" When Ada only laughed, he asked, "Aaron Niedermeyer, then?"

She made it to one knee. "No, that's the point. He was in California." She gritted her teeth as he helped her to her feet. "I mean, there you go: the boyfriend didn't do it."

CHAPTER SEVENTEEN

12 July – 9:00 a.m.,
One step forward, two steps back.

D R. MINK HAD THE DRESSING OVER HER EYE CHANGED before he officially opened at 8 a.m., and Ada was able to slip out of his office, back to the courthouse, and into her own office without a lot of witnesses. The new *Canyon Courier* lay open on her desk— a gift, most likely, from her uncle Ephraim. She started a pot of coffee.

Page two of the Courier was headed, *WE NEED A SHERIFF,* in inch-tall letters. There was nothing new about that. But this time the story included almost word for word what she'd done and said in Mansfield's office, and it just made her cringe.

The blinds stayed closed, and the door locked, and she didn't answer the telephone until well past ten o'clock. She drained the coffee pot and made another, and managed to complete no paper-work at all but read over and over the newspaper story. At first she thought it was Blevins who had spilled the story. He was bound to have it out for her. But as she read on, the story included refer-ences to the first meeting with Mansfield as well as the second, and Blevins wasn't at the first meeting. Only she, Munson, and Mansfield attended both meetings.

For half the morning Ada swore at the paper. She cried some, too, because Dee and Kellen were supposed to be her friends. They should both know better. It was one thing to be left out of Betty's golf outings and Cheryl's damned picnic socials; she'd come to expect that. But Kel and Dee knew what it meant to work hard and do your job. Even if you do make a stupid mistake.

She cried and swore, but by eleven o'clock she also had to admit the story was mostly accurate. And it was awful, what she'd done—such a dumb mistake! How, in heaven's name, was she going to live it down or face Dee Mansfield again? She sat at her desk with the blinds pulled, used her private john, and didn't answer the door even when Ethel knocked.

Clearly the time had come to give up the sheriff's job; to turn in the badge as Uncle Ephraim and the Courier and apparently her friends thought she should. It had been a conceit from the beginning to think she could do it. Now, looking back on her three and a half months in office there was not a single accomplishment to point to but to get behind in her paperwork and to screw up the only real case she'd had. She'd managed to take a clear and probably simple tragedy and in ten days totally confuse herself and alienate half the county.

But at least she'd found enough evidence to ensure Corey Braden wouldn't be railroaded, no matter how much he wanted to be. Now there was just one more part of it that needed looking into before she could package it up for the next sheriff. She checked the hallway for foot traffic, and when clear, scurried down to the clerk and recorder's office.

"ETHEL, I HAVE A BIG QUESTION and you're just the person to know the answer."

Ethel Grimes laid her glasses on the desk and leaned back, folding her arms as she tilted toward Ada. "And just what does that mean, sheriff-lady, that I'm in everyone's . . . What, for heaven's sake, did you get on your head?"

Ada's hand went to the bandage, and she half turned. "It isn't as bad as it looks." She leaned on the clerk's counter and stared at her hands. "Ethel, do you remember Custer Pearen from last year's lawsuit?"

"I heard Mansfield roughed you up yesterday, but I didn't think he used brass knuckles."

"How in the world did you hear that? Never mind. Where would Cuss Pearen get hold of fifteen hundred dollars?"

Ethel shrugged. "Easy. He had to sell shares in his mine."

"To whom?"

"Whom?" Ethel rose and, with a heavy sigh, descended the stone steps to the records room. When she'd gone, Ada smiled for the first time that morning. Gruff as she seemed at times, Ethel was a rock. The clerk was different from her other girlfriends. There was nothing silly, or vain, or jealous about her. She was capable and steady, and a person ought to care what she thought about things. She was going to miss Ethel, day to day.

The clerk returned in just a minute with a ledger two feet tall and fully four inches thick and dropped it with a thud onto the counter. "The Sunnyside Mine was running at a loss for years," she said. "That's why it was so surprising the old crank found investors." She carefully turned the heavy pages to the one recording the change of ownership. "I heard you did a little roughing up yourself on Tuesday. State troopers, no less."

Ada scoffed. "Is there anything at all you don't hear?"

"Not a lot."

In fact, there was probably not much at all, and Ada's chest ached a little. She gave a half-hearted smile and explained, "They wanted me to hand over the Braden case."

"Why?"

Suddenly unable to meet Ethel's eyes, she turned and said, "So they can close it."

"Damn it, don't you let them do that, Fancy Badge."

Ethel had raised her glasses and was giving her a serious look.

Ada said, "You've read the paper; folks don't want me."

"The Courier? Ignore that rag. Folks like you. And let me tell you, Sheriff, we need someone like you for a change."

Ada almost laughed, but then had to look away again. She took a deep breath, wiped at her eyes, and put her hands on her hips. "I'll see what I can do, then," she said.

And that's all there was to it. Smiling a little, Ada ran her finger down the page of the claims book. "I don't understand. To whom did the mine ownership transfer?"

"To whom?" Ethel gazed heavenward as she rotated the book back toward her. "Well, I guess Pearen retained a portion, and he took on half a dozen new partners, as I recall." She leaned in with her glasses. "Sure. Jubal Mason bought in, that no-luck old scrimp; Adolf Slater, and several others."

Ada leaned in and studied the entries. "Do you have the original signed deed-transfers, sales agreements, and such?" she asked.

In just a few minutes Ethel returned from the records room with a document folder fastened with string. The top few pages constituted the recent transfers of ownership and were signed by Custer Pearen, Jubal Mason, and half a dozen others. Mrs. Rosalie Braden was on the list. She'd invested two hundred dollars. "All of these people invested in the Sunnyside? Rose Braden as well?"

"Looks like it. A lot of good it will do them, though, with the mill burned to the ground."

"Is Cuss Pearen running some kind of a scam?"

Ethel shrugged. "He's a known troublemaker."

BACK AT HER DESK, THINGS MADE LESS SENSE than ever. What was Rose doing poking around in crumbling old mines, and what in the world was she thinking putting money into a mine everyone agreed was worthless? The leak to the Courier made Ada sick to her stomach, but she still needed to confer with Kellen Munson.

The operator connected them. "Kel, where could Rose Braden have gotten two hundred dollars to invest in an old mine?" she asked.

The call was staticky, as were all switchboard calls between Camas and Custer, so Munson's answer was garbled: *Did she take it from Corey's savings?*

"Corey said his savings are all there."

It sounded like Munson pushed back in his squeaky chair and put his feet up on the desk. *Well, I mean—and don't get mad at me Ada—but maybe 'whoring around' was more than just an expression.*

Ada sighed. "She wore no makeup, a plain house dress, and low-heel work shoes. Is that how a prostitute dresses, Kel?"

He stopped squeaking. *I don't know how a prostitute dresses. Why ask me?*

"I'm just saying, she was not engaged in prostitution."

I mean, why would you even ask me that?

"Never mind, Chief. We'll talk tomorrow."

BY EARLY AFTERNOON HER HEAD WOUND had begun to ache, so she left work early. It might have been guilt, or the idea of returning to civilian life, or maybe it had just been months and the place badly needed a scrubbing, but she spent the rest of the day doing laundry and cleaning the house. She filled the wood box as the sun paused over the foothills, then re-bandaged her head and took a glass of brandy out to the bluff as the few wispy clouds turned to gold.

The sunset was lovely, as usual, and a few robins showed up for an evening chorus. But where once that place and quiet time had been her secret refuge, now it just felt lonely. And she had no one to blame but herself. She had not been forced to take the sheriff's job; she'd been lying to herself about that the whole time. Montgomery had told her straight out it was probably a cockamamie idea, and she didn't have to do it. Uncle Ephraim and especially Aunt Corrine told her it was ridiculous, and she shouldn't do it.

But she'd wanted the job, and that was the truth of it. She stretched her neck one way and the other, then shuddered as a cool breeze swirled down from the high country. It had scared the hell out of her, at first, just to think about it—about standing up and being in charge. But that had just made her want it all the more. In all these months she hadn't told anyone, not even herself, but the truth was, she'd wanted the job more than anything she could remember. Well, she had the damned thing now, and it was too late to pretend or to wish it away.

The air cooled and the shadows grew, and in less time than a smoke the sun filtered red through the scrub oak, and she was able to put the day behind her.

CHAPTER EIGHTEEN

THE RANGER STATION WAS OPENED UP as if for an air-raid drill. Windows and doors were thrown wide so that the Friday morning sun shined through the back door, reflected off wet linoleum, and nearly blinded Ada as she approached the open front door. She stepped over hoses and through flowing puddles and met District Ranger Ben McGann in the lobby. "Hello again, Ben," she said. There was a moment of fluster, so she added, "You just open the doors and hose out your office? Maybe I should try that at home."

He said, "Ada Reed, I do believe you have a new look every time I see you."

"Yes, the uniform, it uhm . . . But you saw me in it at the fairgrounds."

"You look swell. I was teasing."

"Thanks again for dinner." She glanced around. "The hoses?"

"The bandage?" he tapped his forehead.

"It's nothing. A gardening accident."

He indicated a hallway to the left and pushed aside a bucket to make way for her. He said, "We've had some unusual traffic come through lately. But how can I help you Ada Reed?"

"You called the sheriff's office for help; one of your rangers is missing?" She had to raise her arm to her nose as they turned up the hallway. "It was a skunk, the unusual traffic?"

"It was. Can I get you a coffee, by the way?" He considered his words for a couple of steps. "I can't get over you're the darned sheriff."

There was a lot about him she couldn't get over, too, and she turned to hide a grin. "Acting sheriff in a temporary capacity—just until Mont . . . you know, until the sheriff gets back from Korea."

"Sworn-in, though, right?"

She laughed. "Sworn-in, Ranger McGann. For the time being, anyway."

"Damn, wouldn't your father love that!" He grinned a big Jimmy Stewart grin and nodded to his office door, almost putting his arm on her back but dropping his hand to his side at the last moment. "I probably shouldn't have bothered you all just yet," he said. "One of our lookouts hasn't called in on schedule. Hogan and I are going to saddle up this morning and go check on him."

She took out her notebook and, fighting back tears as a whiff of the skunk caught up to them, said, "It's good you called. I'll make an official note of it and wait to hear what you find. How long since he called in?"

"He's more than a day late."

"Is it unusual not to call for a whole day?"

"Not awfully unusual. It's a quiet fire season; nothing really to call in about. Except Barr generally chatters more than most. He's a nervous sort; gets lonely. I don't know what the hell he was thinking when he signed up to man a fire lookout."

"Not Lonnie Barr?" She put down her notebook.

"That's him."

"Dammit!" She walked to the open window, pushing her fingers through her hair and feeling a sudden knot of panic. Had the young man run again? Or had whatever Rose tried to warn him about caught up to him? She said, "Well, saddle an extra horse. I'm afraid I have to go with you." Her hands began to tremble to where she had to stuff them in her pockets. "Can I make a telephone call from here?" she asked.

The call was to Chief Munson, but he had not seen Barr all week. "Keep an eye out," she told him. "We're going to check up at the Greylock lookout."

McGANN AND HIS WRANGLER, A MR. HOGAN, trailered four horses while Ada checked what gear she had with her in her pickup. The fourth horse was "in case our guy needs a lift out." The three of them kept quiet about what that might mean. They were outfitted by nine o'clock.

Hogan, a barrel of a man on and off the Forest Service payroll for thirty years, rode with the district ranger in a big Power Wagon with the horse trailer in tow. Ada led the way in her pickup truck, topping Mill Creek Pass and dropping into a cool fog all the way down to the Yankee Fork headwaters. The road followed the river west from there, downstream through dark stands of Lodgepole and towering volcanic outcrops. They rumbled over timber bridges where the road crossed the stream in a dozen places.

On the broad gravel bar of Eightmile Creek, Ada leaned her head on the steering wheel for a minute waiting for McGann and Hogan to catch up. Her stomach felt jittery as it had since she'd heard Lonnie Barr might be missing. The boy had been concerned about something. It was a cinch he was caught up in something—he and Rose.

The squeak and groans of the horse trailer brought her around. The Power Wagon crunched into the gravel behind her, and the guys got out to check on the horses and to relieve themselves behind the trailer. Ada started her engine and eased on up the broad gravel bar.

Much of the two-track road up Eightmile Creek made use of the rocky stream bed. Where the road cut up into the hillsides or turned tightly through treed gullies, she expected a dozen times for the long four-horse trailer to be stopped, but the Power Wagon kept it coming. After a quarter hour, she let them disappear in her mirror and drove ahead. At the very top of the pass she pulled off onto the broad, flat saddle looking down into upper Jordan Creek, set the brake, and got out to stretch.

A dark-colored pickup was raising a plume of dust across the canyon, heading down the other side of the pass. She watched it for a minute. It stopped on a straight stretch, and it appeared the driver leaned out the window to watch her for a while in return. But it was half a mile away as the crow flies, so she couldn't really tell.

The Forest Service truck and trailer were still a mile behind her, so she found her cigarettes in the jockey box, grabbed her thermos and, leaving the driver's side door open, walked back and dropped the tailgate. It had rained in the night, and the high country smelled of rock flour and pine pitch, and of something flowering down-valley. She sat on the tailgate with her feet hanging down, poured herself a coffee, and lit a cigarette. The dust from the horse trailer billowed slowly up the shadowed canyon toward her. Radio reception was decent up on the ridge, and she heard that peace talks had begun in a place called *Kaesong*. She didn't know where that was. Anyway, it was peace talks, even if that was no help to her today.

At nine thousand feet the coffee and cigarette spun her head a bit, and the thin air had a bite to it even with the sun baking her shoulders through her uniform. She hung her head and knocked her bootheels together, trying to make some sense of things. What in the world, she wondered, had Rose been warning Lonnie of? Who was he supposed to be wary of? Could it all have been just a dumb mistake—the same mistake she had made about Mansfield's business dealings? In any case, there was probably no need to get herself worked up. Most likely Lonnie's two-way radio had conked out. That's why he hadn't called in, and they would all look silly barging in on him. And maybe that black pickup truck belonged to a geologist who'd driven up to look over the Estes Mountain prospects. Maybe. She finished her coffee and flipped the cigarette butt into the rocks.

She managed a wave to the rangers when they arrived, but stayed on the tailgate with her arms around her knees while they unloaded and saddled the horses. The wrangler, Mr. Hogan, uncased two Winchester rifles, loaded each, and checked the sights and lever actions. He stuck them into leather scabbards on two of the saddles. "You packing your revolver?" McGann called over to her. There was nothing teasing in his voice.

The thought of riding through trees and brush with a gun on her hip made her wince. She said, "Your two rifles should win the war, don't you think?"

"We'll be fine. It's just procedure."

ADA MOUNTED A BUCKSKIN MARE AND FOLLOWED behind McGann. Hogan brought up the rear, leading the fourth horse. They stuck to a good trail southeastward through scrub pine and volcanic hoodoos, and within a mile came upon the tracks of two shod horses. Snow clung to the higher ridges and talus chutes, and the horse tracks showed clearer in the soft soil fringing the snowfields.

Hogan dismounted, and after a brief look, told them the horse tracks were not today's, but they overlaid the last boot prints. Ben looked over and shrugged. "Could be prospectors; could be surveyors." he said. "Hell, it's huckleberry season. It could be anyone." The tracks of the earlier horses disappeared again after another mile, although Hogan spent a few minutes back-tracking, trying to find the direction they'd taken.

Winter-felled trees had been cut and cleared from the well-used lookout trail, and the sap from the dying branches kept the air spicey sweet. At two miles, the trail climbed out of the thick lodgepole pine and topped a high ridge. The three dismounted to rest the horses. Ada climbed a rocky promontory from where mountains and ridges stacked up one behind another in every direction. As she turned back, a movement caught her eye in the distance to her right; a dark brown haunch disappeared into the brush. An elk, most likely.

Four miles in from the pass, they reached the Greylock summit, where the door to the lookout shack hung banging in the wind. They hitched the horses to the railing and climbed onto the lookout porch—except for Hogan, who took a Winchester from its scabbard and stayed among the horses. The floor of the shack stood six feet above the top of the mountain, and Ada had to catch her breath just climbing the stairs. "Ten thousand feet," McGann reminded her. A copper mast towered over the lookout, and four heavy steel cables led down from the mast into the rocks. She let McGann enter his lookout first, then followed him in.

The room was square, maybe twelve feet on a side, with windows filling the walls almost continuously. A waist-high table took up the middle of the room, covered with a topographic map under glass. A bunk filled the remainder of the room on the right, and a narrow table, water tank, and grub box took up the left side. There was room for a shelf of canned goods: peaches, tuna fish, evaporated milk. But that was about it.

McGann went straight to the two-way radio, flipped a couple of switches, and called into the ranger station. A short, staticky conversation crackled through the shack, and Ada's heart sank.

"Shouldn't he have a horse tethered here?" she asked.

"No. The lookouts hike in with their personal effects. Provisions are delivered by pack string every few weeks."

"His truck wasn't at the pass." She moved farther into the small space. There was barely room to squeeze between the bunk and the table.

"He drove a Forest Service rig to the pass," McGann explained. "His cross-shift drove it back to the station." He pulled a quart bottle from behind the canned peaches, opened it and smelled, and shook his head. "This sure doesn't belong here."

"Whiskey?" She shrugged. "I've seen Lonnie Barr wet as a fish."

"A lot of the guys drink hard when they get down off the mountain. But alcohol is never permitted at a lookout. Barr had to have brought it up with him, because his cross-shift is a pretty straight arrow."

The locker under the bunk held socks and underwear, dungarees, three shirts, a toothbrush, and a bar of soap. There were a few paperback books: A.B. Guthrie, Louis L'Amour—no surprises. But there was Carl Sandberg's *Complete Poems* as well. Ada fanned the pages of the Sandberg, and a photo fell from it. It was of Rose Braden.

In the photo Rose wore white shorts and a red checked shirt, its tails tied high in front. A ringlet of asters crowned her head, and she laughed, bright-eyed, at the camera. The picture had been taken at an old mine; the red-weathered timbers of a headframe towered in back, and a reed-choked mill pond lay to Rose's right. Ada didn't recognize the place. McGann thought it might be the Bayhorse District.

Lonnie had signed the log, in pencil, with an 'all clear' at 9:15 am two days before. McGann explained pens bleed out at high altitude, so the official logbook is always kept in pencil. Nevertheless, blue ink stains on the table suggested correspondence. "Do you see anything else written?" Ada asked. "Letters? A journal?"

"No, there's nothing else." The 9:15 'all clear' was the last entry.

A brass theodolite sat in the middle of the map table. She looked through the eyepiece, adjusting the focus and the stadia hairs, looked up and over the instrument, then through the eyepiece again. She could see into a mine site: at a forge, a rough-timbered machine shop, and a lot of rusted, abandoned equipment. Swinging the instrument around, the lens took in miles of forested and sage-dotted hills, hunters' cabins, and dredge tailings.

She and McGann were looking back through recent log entries when John Hogan's shout carried over the wind. "Sir, ma'am, y'all better come look!" He was still holding the rifle, and looking over a cliff twenty yards along the path to the outhouse. They joined him at the edge of a narrow, jagged avalanche chute. Fifty feet below, blue denim and green plaid showed from beneath a slide of snow and rock. An arm and a hand stuck out; a boot.

Ada sat down hard at the edge of the cliff and dropped her head to her knees. Her whole body shuddered, and she felt she would choke. Lonnie was a sweet, confused kid, and he'd needed help. He'd been scared, and obviously in trouble. He'd practically asked her to keep him locked up, and goddamn her, she hadn't listened. She hadn't been strong enough or wise enough to help him.

McGann said nothing for a long while. When he spoke, he said, "He must have got drunk and fell on his way to the toilet."

"Maybe." She fought to keep her voice from breaking, and to keep from tearing the badge off her chest and throwing it over the cliff.

THEY'D BROUGHT PLENTY OF ROPE ON THE PACK HORSE, so they fixed two lines to an outcrop, threw the coils over the side, and Ada and McGann worked their way down to the body. Hogan stayed on top to mind the ropes and the horses, and to keep watch, although no one said so. It was sure enough Lonnie Barr when they got to him, and he was torn and broken. He still smelled a little of whiskey, McGann noted. It was too damned bad.

Ada held herself together through the whole descent. The time of death was impossible to estimate, given the icy bed he'd come to rest in. The cause of death was most likely one or more of the rocks that struck and gashed his head on his way down. The boy's face was clean-shaven, though, so it hadn't happened too long into his shift. His flesh was white, almost a blue, as they dug him out of the snow. They found what otherwise might have been defensive wounds on the arms but agreed they could easily have happened as he tumbled through the rocks. The fingers of his right hand, though, looked odd. She brushed them clean of snow and looked again. There was blue ink on the fingertips. "You're sure you saw no other papers in the shack? A journal?" she asked.

The recovery took a couple of hours, with Hogan working a horse up top and Ada and McGann using guide ropes from either side of the chute to ease the body through the sharp crags. It wasn't until they had him on top that Ada noticed Lonnie Barr wore cowboy boots, and there were crescent-shaped metal taps on the heels. She stared at the boots a long while, then walked away and gazed over the deep Yankee Fork basin while the men fought the wind to wrap a tarp around the still mostly-frozen body.

They secured the boy to the saddle of the pack horse, then McGann led them down into a calm, golden afternoon. Again, Hogan hung back, watching to the sides and behind for company. This time, though, Ada did not watch out but kept her eyes on the trail ahead.

It was near sunset when they pulled the still-stiff young man from the back of the horse. Ada said she should take custody, but McGann argued Lonnie Barr was a Forest Service employee and he would by-God ride home in a U.S. Government truck. He laid saddle blankets in the bed of the Power Wagon, and he and Hogan tied down the tarp-covered body.

Ada would lead again, and she would meet them at the clinic in Camas. Jordan Creek was the slower route to town, but it was easier than the Eightmile side in the approaching darkness, and there was no longer reason to hurry. Nevertheless, at the third turn coming down the flank of Estes Mountain, her Ford did not slow down as quickly as she expected it to, and she nearly drove over the side. The tires slid on the hard-packed surface right up against the low dirt and rock berm and, bouncing and skidding, she looked down into a deep avalanche chute filled with boulders and tumbled trees. She managed to steer the truck through the rocks and back onto the road, fishtailed a couple of times, then found she had no brakes at all when she pumped the pedal again. The next bend was tight, but it was an inside turn. The Ford slid and bounced over the berm, jolting and careening between brush and boulders. It came to a hard stop nearly on its side in a scrub-pine draw.

She lay, or more accurately hung, in the cab of the truck gripping the steering wheel. Brilliant yellows and ochres of sunset shined through the road dust billowing around her, and but for the dust, she breathed air sweet with sage and pine boughs crushed under the truck. A knot was rising on her head from the rim of the door, but nothing else was broken, scraped, or too badly bruised. Hogan and McGann had her out of the truck before she fully understood what had happened.

She'd been damned lucky, both men agreed. Their voices sounded as from a deep tunnel. She staggered back and sat on the sideboard of the Power Wagon, where she tried not to show tears in front of the men. Hogan noticed, and excused himself to check on the horses, while McGann examined the underside of the Ford. She did cry then, when they'd gone, but just for a minute or two.

They rode down to Custer in the Dodge Power Wagon with Ada sitting between McGann, who drove, and big Mr. Hogan. The men talked, but Ada kept quiet, hugging one knee to her chest. They passed old headframes and loading chutes, and the chained and locked gates to a dozen closed mines. The chain was down when they passed the road to Jubal Mason's War Eagle mine, and dust hung in the air. The road to Cuss Pearen's Sunnyside was untracked since Ada's hurried retreat a few days earlier.

Hogan got out at Custer. He and Munson would bring Ada's truck down that night while Ada and Ben McGann continued on, inasmuch as they were still escorting Lonnie Barr's body to the medical examiner in Camas.

All down the washboarded Yankee Fork Road, through the tailings piles and logjams, the clattering of the horse trailer made talking difficult. Once they got to Sunbeam, the smoother surface of the highway relieved the tension that had tied her in knots, and the quieter ride allowed her to think. She glanced over, and tall Ben McGann was leaned forward, arms draped around the steering wheel. "You like your job?" she asked him.

"I do." He glanced over and shrugged. "It gets lonely some-times. A lot of back roads; a lot of open range." He turned back to the road, and Ada focused on the river out the side window.

"A lot of campfires," he said. "How about you, Ada Reed, why'd you put on the uniform?"

"Oh, heck," she said. "I thought . . . Well, a lot of folks thought it would be simplest if I kept the job filled for when Montgomery gets home. Instead of bringing in someone else."

"So, you're just holding it until he can take it over again?"

"He's been gone longer than anyone expected. The war was sup-posed to be over by now." She slouched, putting her foot up on the dash. "I've sat home before, and I didn't like it. Through the last war, you know. It gets slow. It can be . . . difficult." She turned and marshalled a smile. "I liked the sheriff job at first—it wasn't cook-ing and cleaning, and it wasn't choosing theme colors for another church social. But I'm not as sure about it now. Sometimes I miss, I don't know, being softer."

He started to answer a couple of times, but let a mile roll by. He blew softly and said, "Your brake line was cut, you know. It was a saw blade."

Her chest started to tighten again, and she had to fight to keep her breathing steady. There was just the whining of the highway and the wind. She said, "Ben, it was too dark for you really to have seen that."

He turned back to the road, and she watched out the side win-dow, and the two of them rode without speaking the last few miles into Camas. They left poor Lonnie Barr in the big cooler at the sky-blue cinderblock clinic, then drove to the darkened ranger station.

McGann bedded down the horses while Ada searched through Barr's truck, which he'd left parked behind the stables. There was no journal to be found, and Ada gave up the search after just a few minutes.

She leaned heavily against the front fender, not surprised to be fighting tears. Lonnie wore heel taps, but what of it? Lots of people wear taps on their boots. Besides, Lonnie had secretly loved Rose. Ada had been so certain of it by the way he acted and spoke of her. She didn't want to stop believing it was true; she didn't want to stop believing she knew what love was supposed to look like. An all but full moon hung in the western sky, slipping between clouds, and she fought back the aching inside until it darkened into a fear even worse. She wanted to keep believing Lonny loved Rose, but she was afraid to believe it too, because maybe . . . maybe he did love her—too much—and Rose refused him.

She didn't know where to turn, and the loneliness seemed to ball up inside her. Ben McGann returned after what seemed forever, and Ada, without thinking, didn't step away as he approached but leaned forward and touched her head to his shoulder. He pulled back in surprise.

"Oh God, I'm sorry," she said.

"No, don't be. I just wasn't . . . It's been a pretty tough day on all of us."

The moon flooded the back lot, and it was suddenly too bright, so they moved to the shadows under an elm where Ben's pickup truck was parked. He leaned through the window for a pack of cigarettes he kept in the jockey box and seemed surprised when she accepted one. "Is your head okay?" he asked.

"It doesn't hurt. Is it a big ugly knot?"

"Not at all."

She held her hat in her hand and her hair back so he could light her cigarette. The air was still, and they stood for a minute watching the smoke curl through shafts of broken moonlight. "Did you ever come back to the valley?" she asked.

"I came back," he said. "You'd gone off to college."

"Yeah. I came back. You weren't here."

"She was waiting for me in Poulson right after the war. And there was the job and all . . . and I just settled in, I guess." He cleared his throat. "She left."

"I know."

Bugs flashed in and out of the glow of the stable light. McGann blew a stream of smoke and said, "Are you okay alone after everything? I mean, after all that's happened. Are you okay to just . . .?" He looked at his feet and scrunched his lips. "Look, I just mean, there are tears in your eyes. Will you be okay tonight?"

She wiped at the tears and laughed. "I'll be fine, Ben. Fine enough. I'm getting used to being alone. I guess we're both getting used to it, aren't we?"

"I don't like being used to it," he said.

Crickets chirped, and she took his hand. In the still air they could hear the crickets all the way down by Garden Creek. He was taller by a good three inches, and in the shadows she had to stand on her toes to look into his Hollywood eyes.

CHAPTER NINETEEN

14 July – 7:45 a.m., There has been another death in the Yankee Fork. ~~Possibly~~ Likely related to the Braden case.

SHERIFF MRS. MONTGOMERY REED STOPPED a couple of times, as she hurried up Main Street, to collect herself and to touch up her hair in the windows and check her tie and buttons. Her boots scuffed the sidewalk, and the morning sun in the shop windows nearly blinded her. The smell of fresh bread from the bakery on 7th Street gnawed at her but she was already so late. What could she have been thinking?

She took the steps of the courthouse two at a time. They were of old marble, and cupped from wear. The steps had already been worn when she'd climbed them with Montgomery twelve years earlier to get married, and worn a bit more six years after that, when Mont was sworn in as sheriff. He hadn't bothered to make the climb when she was sworn in, it being just a formality after all. From the top of the stairs she could see over the trees and across the whole valley. The snows were almost gone from the far Lemhi Range; the pastures beyond the highway were drying and brown, but the elms around the stables at the White Cloud Ranger Station were still green, and the shade beneath them cool and dark. She breathed deeply and for a moment longer didn't pull her eyes away.

She wondered how worn the marble steps would be the next time she and Montgomery would have to climb them.

It was close to eight-thirty and the sun was beating through the windows when she finally stepped into her office. Mayor Applegate was there and sitting at her desk. "You're late," he said.

"Ephraim!"

"Good morning, Ada."

"Yes, good morning to you, too. I'm late because it was a tough day yesterday; I got back late. I'm afraid there are more problems in the Yankee Fork."

His hands were folded, and he kept his eyes on the desk. "I know there are, Ada. In fact, half the world knows there are more problems up the Yankee Fork. Kellen Munson called from Custer. Good man—I've always liked Munson. He told me about the young fellow at the lookout. He also told me your truck was monkeyed with and you damn near got yourself killed."

Her uncle didn't make a move to get out of her seat, so she walked over and filled a cup with lukewarm coffee. She sat on the edge of the empty desk across the room. "It wasn't that serious," she said. "Kellen gets excited sometimes. What do you mean half the world?"

"He'll have your truck back to you tomorrow or the next day." The mayor leaned back and put one foot up on the edge of the desk, which was as much as his middle could accommodate. "Ada, I spoke with Montgomery this morning."

She jumped up, nearly dropping her coffee. "What? With Monty? How in hell did you do that?" She sat again. "Is he stateside?"

"Hold on. No, he's still at Inchy-on, and he had to pull all kinds of gosh-darned strings to radiophone the States, I guess. Twice!"

"Twice?"

"He called your place, Ada, about six this morning, he told me. There was no answer."

Ada's face went slack and then red. "I . . . Sometimes I go out and watch the sunrise; take a coffee out to the bluff and sit and think." She rose a second time and faced the coffee table and the back window. "About six? Are you sure?"

"Ada, what he called about is more important than when, or whether you were sitting on schist or the . . . in the bathroom. He said he's heard from a number of concerned citizens about the Yankee Fork mess, and he thinks you're getting in over your head. Way over your head. He wants you to give up the badge."

Over my head; good God! She stopped trembling and asked, "Who'd he hear from?"

"Why would that matter? He sounded very decided, and he's going to shoot you a telegram if he can, or an airmail letter."

"Who was it, Mayor?"

"Hell's bells, who wasn't it? Step back and look at what you've been up to, young lady. Spending tax money on coroner reports—I assume there'll be another one—when there's a clear-cut confession. Interrogating good citizens and implying all sorts of fool accusations, when there's a clear-cut goddamned confession! And then going out and nearly putting your truck over a cliff."

"Lonnie Barr's death may be related. And the brake line wasn't just cut randomly."

"All the more reason! What in heck am I going to tell Corrine? That her sister's little girl was found dead in a ravine somewhere?"

"Makes you wonder who wants me off the case, doesn't it?"

"It makes me wonder no such thing! It's all the more reason for you to give me the badge, and right now, Ada! I've already talked to Wickers. He's going to take over."

She raised her arm against the glare from the street-side window. The heat was already building, and she walked over and stared a moment before closing the blinds. Still with her back to him she said, "I've given a lot of thought to turning in the badge, Mr. Mayor. But the investigation is on-going. I'll stay the course until it's finished, and then further consider what you've said."

"There is nothing to consider, sweetheart. The decision has been made."

She turned. "Decision? Made by whom?"

Applegate dropped his foot and sat up. Ada took the opportunity to jam her hands in her pockets and blow a couple short breaths. He was staring open-mouthed at her, his hands flat on her desk. "Are you not going to do what Montgomery told you to do?" he asked.

She gave it a couple more breaths. "I love you Uncle Eph, but I'm sorry. I'm the sworn Yellowpine County sheriff and only the County Board can dismiss me."

The mayor sat still but for his mouth, which moved without sound. "You don't even know the girl," he sputtered.

"I know her well enough," she said, grabbing her gun and holster from the file cabinet. "I know her better than I know myself half the damned time."

11:15 a.m. - Custer Jailhouse – Fourth interview with Corey Braden

A PATCH OF EARLY AFTERNOON SUNLIGHT WAS creeping across the floor of the jail cell. The acting sheriff's hands had long-ago stopped shaking, and her breathing by then was deep and even, but the word 'contemptable' still stuck in her mind. To be treated like a child in that way; to be ordered to do this and not do that. *'Am I not going to do what Montgomery told me to do?'* Lord, could she ever have been like that? She had let it anger her, and had driven too fast. She'd raised a plume of dust all the way up the Yankee Fork Road. She could have blown a tire on the damned Buick!

She was in Custer to see about her pickup truck. She'd come early intending also to confront Corey Braden with the crescent marks and the cart tracks. But when she found him in his cell detached and oddly at peace, she said nothing. Confronted, Braden might admit he had not killed his wife, and then what could she do? She would have to release him, and he was in no condition to be left alone.

He sat hunched in his wheelchair saying something, answering her, but she couldn't remember what she'd asked. He said, "Anyway, yeah, I got drafted to the Army, so I went right out and joined the Marines. I'd have gone anyway. She didn't want me to."

"I didn't want Mont to come back . . . to go back." She was facing the door and didn't see him turn and eye her. They were quiet again for a minute.

"Are you okay?" he asked. "You seem upset."

"Corey, Lonnie Barr is dead. I'm sorry. I know you two used to be friends."

He didn't say a word but stayed sitting with his head slumped down, keeping his breathing even. His hands lay limp on the wheels. He didn't look up, but after a moment asked, "How?"

Ada was just able to answer without tearing up. "We recovered his body yesterday."

"At the lookout? Up at Greylock?"

"Yes. He apparently . . . He'd fallen down a ravine."

Braden squeezed his eyes shut for a long time. "He was . . . Ah, shit, he was alright. We had some yucks back in the day." He cleared his throat. "You wouldn't have a smoke, would you, Ma'am? Munson said he'd get me a pack, but he must have forgot."

Ada went to fetch the cigarettes from her jockey box, but they were in the sheriff's pickup, not in her Buick. So she walked down to the Pinyon. The bartender and a couple old patrons looked at her funny when she asked for a box of Marlboros, but she really didn't give a damn. She dropped a quarter on the bar and grabbed a book of matches on her way out.

On her return, she considered a moment whether to trust Corey with the matches, but then sat and lit one of the cigarettes and handed it to him through the bars.

"A beer'd be fine too," he said, then laughed when she shook her head. His laugh sounded distant, a little unsettling. "You smoke?" he asked.

"No. Once in a while." She let him smoke for a minute before asking, "Rose had told Lonnie to watch out. Do you know what that was about?"

"I was not in that line of communication." The words came at a military clip. He'd straightened himself in his chair.

"She was at the dredge pond late the night she died, maybe even on the dredge. Why would she be there, what could she have wanted?" When Braden didn't answer, Ada asked, "You don't think she was working on something with Dee Mansfield, do you? Something maybe you didn't know about?"

"You don't know shit." He clutched the armrests and stared at the floor, his neck and ears flushing. "Do you know anything about loyalty, Mrs. Reed? Dee and I are Marines. He's hung tough by me."

He turned his chair back toward the wall; a maneuver Ada knew meant he was shutting down. But she needed him to keep talking. She said, "When Montgomery came home after the war—the last war—he kept to himself quite a bit. He stayed clear of friends more than I thought made any sense, and especially from Army pals. He never went to any of his unit's get-togethers."

"Well, maybe jarheads stick tighter than ground pounders. Dee has stuck by me; it's called *Semper Fi*."

She nodded. "*Ever faithful*. And you'll stick by him, no matter what."

"No matter. You see, the thing about loyalty is this: it's just a word when times are easy. It's when times get tough that loyalty earns its meaning."

"Are those your words or his?"

"They're mine now." He smoked his cigarette with his back to her, sitting upright and stiff. She waited, hoping he would ease up, but he stayed almost at attention. She said, "Mont ran around in circles for the longest time. Like he didn't know how to get started on anything. I guess he missed not having a regiment to order around."

Braden glanced at her over his shoulder. "So, he ordered you around." He turned the chair a quarter turn.

Her laugh sounded as hollow as his a few minutes earlier. "No, I wouldn't say that exactly. But until he got settled, things could be . . . difficult, I guess."

"He hit you, didn't he?" The cigarette bobbed between his lips.

"You think I don't know how that shit works?" Ada looked away just as he turned fully to face her. She said nothing. Braden insisted, "He hit you, didn't he?"

"Mostly not with his hand or anything. Mostly . . ." She flinched, feeling almost physically the rush of memories. Mostly he hadn't hit her at all—at first.

AT FIRST THEY'D DANCED EVERY SONG, and there was moonlight and roses; and he was gentle—he really was, back then. And she'd loved him. He followed her all the way from Virginia with a diamond, and there was never a question she would go away with him.

But the war came, and he shipped out, and she rode the train back to Idaho, alone. They seeded and mowed, she and her mother, and calved through the seasons. And she'd missed him so badly she hadn't noticed her own mother growing weaker every day until it was just Ada, all alone again, when Mont found her in '45.

But he didn't last long behind the plow: just for a year or so. And those were painful times. It had never been his idea, after all, to be a dirt farmer. It was her useless farm and her selfish dreams, and he didn't know how to keep the goddamned weeds down or keep cattle from freezing in the winter. The frustration and anger found its way into the house and into their bedroom, and sometimes a heavy dinner and a glass of brandy for him, and a hiding place in the barn was the best she could do.

BRADEN WAS WATCHING HER. SHE SAID, "Mostly he could be short with me—with his words."

"You mean he knew what things to say to make you feel like shit." He tried to wheel into her view, but she turned one way and the other. "What did he call you?"

"Not names." She jumped up and took a step toward the door.

"Just you were slow, and lazy. And dumb. 'A dumb country hay-seed,' right? And, 'why in hell did you do that, you stupid bitch!'"

She spun and grabbed the bars of the cell, but when Braden shot his chair forward, she flinched back a step. "And, 'This dinner is shit!'" He yelled. "And, 'This place is a pigsty!' And, 'There's no oil in the car, what the fuck was in your head?'"

She ducked and closed her eyes for just a second, then stepped forward again. "He was a son of a bitch! Is that what you want to hear, Sergeant?" She winced and held onto the bars to steady herself. "The war was tough on him."

"Yeah, war is hell."

"He had a hard time with it." She backed off and started again for the door. "He just needed some time to adjust to home life again."

"How much time did he need? He had all his damned parts!" Braden rolled after her as far as the bars would let him. "He didn't just need some time. It never got better, did it?"

She turned and stepped back from the door but said nothing. He asked, "Did he think you were screwing someone?"

"He . . . No, that wasn't why . . ."

"Were you? Were you screwing someone?"

She crossed her arms over her breast and looked away again. "Once I understood what was going on, I could take it from him. I knew how."

"So, you did, didn't you? You just took it." He shook his head, open mouthed. "You're still taking it!"

She threw the notebook, banging it against the bars, this time making him flinch. "You don't know a fucking thing!" She stomped back, fists clenched. "What the hell was I supposed to do?"

Braden glared at her, shaking his head again. "He had no right, don't you see that? God, you are dumb!" He tossed his cigarette butt and grabbed the bars. "The son of a bitch. He wasn't good enough to kiss the mud on your boots!"

He dropped back into his seat and wheeled back from the bars. "Why did you just take it from him, damn it?" His voice broke and tears poured down his cheeks. "Why did you let him treat you like that? Why did you have to be so damned easy?"

Ada backed to the far side of the office. Braden sat hunched forward. She turned her face to the wall and stood a long while, arms crossed. When her breathing caught up to her, she wiped her palms across her cheeks then poured two cups of coffee from the pot. She cleared her throat, waited, and asked, "Do you take cream or sugar?"

He wiped his eyes on his arms and after a moment said, "Sugar, just one."

She carried the two cups over, but again had no place to set them but the small table inside his cell. Kneeling, she reached both cups through the bars and set them on the table. She slid her chair to the wall and turned it to face the front door. He wheeled over, turned, and sat facing the door as well, with the table and the bars between them.

She lit two cigarettes and passed one to him. They sipped their coffee quietly, listening to the birds on the wires outside the cell window. He said very softly, to himself mostly, "I haven't done right by anyone, don't you see?"

A long minute passed. She said, "They're all pressuring me to end the investigation."

"What are you going to do?"

"I'm not ready to end it, Corey. It's not done."

He looked over and nodded. "Good."

"Good? Really?"

"I mean, it's good you're doing your job. It's good you're stand-ing up, you know?"

She blew a long stream of smoke. "Mont couldn't wait to get back to war. He tried to act disappointed, but there was no ques-tion he would go." She choked in a breath and almost whispered, "I was . . . glad he went."

Braden nodded. "I know." He took a couple deep breaths and said, "I wish I hadn't come home at all. I'd go back there now. God, if I could!"

He sat still, staring—at what? At a bloody, frozen forest? At his friends dying in the mud? "Why would you go back Corey? Why would he?" she asked. "To be whole again?"

He closed his eyes and barely shook his head. "Because that's the only place where not being whole is okay."

She let the cigarette burn almost to her fingers then crushed it out on the floor. She stood, explaining that she had arranged to call on someone. It wasn't true, but she had to go, to get out. He nodded but stayed hunched in his chair staring at the floor.

As she was leaving, he called out, "Ma'am?" She turned at the door, and he straightened himself. "*Semper Fi*," he said.

3:15 p.m. – A damned, bloody mess!

SHE JUMPED FROM THE BOARDWALK AND RAN to her car under a cloudless sky, and raced the Buick back across the Yankee Fork wasteland. A wind from the west caught up to her at Sunbeam, though, bringing with it the smoke of a distant fire. The canyon baked all the hotter for the brown haze.

Ada never made it back to the courthouse that hot, smoky afternoon but spent the rest of the day taking statements and keeping a rancher from killing a truck driver who'd plowed into his cattle. There were blood and manure and bawling calves all over the highway at Torrey's Hole, and traffic backed up a quarter mile in each direction. State Patrol Sergeant Blevins and his deputy were shooting the animals too broken to stand, then dragging the carcasses off the road. Blevins, too busy to quarrel beyond a few caustic looks, asked Ada to direct traffic.

By late afternoon the traffic had thinned to where Ada could sit in the grass by her open car door for a few minutes at a time and watch the grisly proceedings. It was quiet across the broad,

wooded oxbow but for the breeze in the cottonwoods, the bawling calves, and the rancher and the rancher's family arguing with
Blevins. She pulled out her thermos and her sandwich.

The sheriff's two-way squawk box was back in the pickup in
the shop in Custer, so she didn't have to listen for Officer Stengel,
or Ethel, or Munson calling for this, or that, or the next thing. The
car radio picked up a staticky Pocatello station, but after a couple of songs it was just news, and that was all about Korea, so she
turned that off too. The last thing she needed was to think about
Montgomery right then.

But people were dying on her watch, and she couldn't shut her
mind to that fact. She'd told Corey Braden she wouldn't quit the
investigation. That was easy enough to say, and it was easy enough
to act defiant in front of Uncle Ephraim, but what in hell . . . "What
are you going to do now, Fancy Badge?" she whispered.

She poured a coffee from the thermos, which was barely warm,
and jumped up when a produce truck and a station wagon full of
kids rounded the bend. "It was just an accident," she explained to
the family as she directed them through the carnage.

Just an accident, she thought. As though it might have been
worse for the cattle otherwise. Rose Braden's death surely had not
been an accident. Nor was it suicide, nor did Rose's husband kill
her. Those were certainties. And there were a few other facts she
could count on, as well. At the very least, Lonnie Barr could not
have been the perpetrator. He was behind bars the day Ada was
shot at, and it sure as hell wasn't Lonnie's ghost that had cut her
brake line. He was a victim, the same as Rose—another certainty,
and Ada breathed a sigh and thanked heaven for that bit of clarity.

Rose had been poking around in old mines, probably since
last fall according to Lonnie. To what purpose, and what had she
learned? Rose had told Jubal Mason and others not to sell out. She'd
even invested her own money. *Where did she get her own money?*

And how in heaven's name was Ada going to solve any of it?
Boot marks—someone else's boot marks—on the girl's hands and a

soldier's false confession got her nowhere. A miner with a possibly shady partnership arrangement; an oriental belt with maybe some gold—it just added up to a lot of dead ends.

SHE STAYED TILL EARLY EVENING, WHEN THE GORE was finally cleared and the rest of the herd moved off the road. She drove slowly back to town and thought about stopping at the ranger station when she noticed lights on there. But she dared not, and God, that was another thing she'd have to figure out.

CHAPTER TWENTY

15 July – 8:15 a.m., Sunday late start. Back to Yankee Fork.
I think Sergeant Braden is ready to talk.

SHE'D MISSED HER SUNDAY MORNINGS AT DOLLY'S CAFÉ and the unhurried breakfasts she used to enjoy there. It hadn't seemed right—until now, oddly—to go without her husband.

The café was louder this Sunday, and brighter sitting at the counter alone. She'd wolfed down her poached eggs on toast so quickly it made her laugh. She'd had almost nothing to eat the day before, so she ordered biscuits and gravy, too, which she ate more slowly, staring at her blurred reflection in the stainless-steel back counter.

She'd brought with her a paperback book, *It's a Cinch Private Finch,* and read from it as she drank her coffee. It was a joke book Mont seemed to like when he came home last time, and she'd brought it today thinking, well, maybe Corey would get a kick out of the Army humor; maybe it would help to ease his mind a little.

A woman passed behind her and Ada noticed in the metal reflection a long stare at her appearance. She tucked her tie into her shirt and pushed her hair back behind her ears. The waitress offered her a refill, which she waved away.

Just as she rose to go, Betty came in with Ken and sat with Cheryl and Tony at the booth by the window. She and Mont had sat in that booth with one or the other couple a dozen times. Today the ladies were dressed in bright summer outfits—cornflower and seafoam seemed to be the new colors. They wore shiny heels and ribboned hats, and their makeup was just enough, but no more than proper, for Presbyterian services.

There was no retrieving her Stetson and getting past the four of them without being seen, so Ada tucked Corey's book into her pocket and walked up to their table. "Good morning," she said. "Gosh I haven't seen you all in ages."

"Ada, join us!" Ken blurted, catching Betty and Cheryl off guard. There was half a moment of silence.

"Yes, do."

"Oh, no. I just finished. Have to get to work," Ada said. It might have been seafoam, perhaps a mint green. It sure as hell wasn't olive-drab they were wearing.

"You're not still doing that Sheriff business are you?" Betty asked.

Cheryl smiled but wanted to know why the County couldn't just find someone else. "There's lots of men in the valley who could do it."

"It's politics," Ken answered for her. "The next man in line was a Republican, isn't that right, Ada." He winked.

Ada started to explain that Montgomery would be home in no time, but Betty interrupted. "But heavens, do they make you wear pants every day?" The four of them, then, studied her top to bottom while she pushed her hair back and flushed red. Her boots felt like size twelves on her feet. "What would Monty think if he saw you in those pants?" Betty asked.

Tony said, "I don't think Mont would mind so awful much." Cheryl scoffed and looked away. No one could think of a word to say, least of all Ada.

She stuck her hands in her pockets and managed, "There's not but the one uniform style, you see. It just takes a little alteration here and there, and . . ." *Oh, to hell with it!* She caught a deep breath, pursed her lips, and asked as politely as she could if they were all going to the ballgame after church.

The two ladies both shrugged and Cheryl suggested, "We're keeping an eye on the weather, Ada."

Ada looked from one to the other and struggled not to roll her eyes. "Well, do wear your bonnets; the July sun can be ferocious."

Betty exclaimed she was just starving and turned to the menu. Silence followed for another moment until Ken broke into a big grin. "You're not wearin' yer sidearm, Sheriff." He spoke in an exaggerated Hollywood accent that made Tony laugh, although Betty and Cheryl did not. "What if you find yourself in a shootout?" He demanded, still grinning.

"What is that supposed to mean?" Ada asked.

Tony wagged a toothpick between his teeth, glancing still at Ada's pleated slacks. He said, "I think slim meant, what're you gonna do if you gotta wrestle down a bad guy?"

"Break his head with my flashlight." She didn't smile, and the silence stretched uncomfortably. "Well, as I said, I'm on duty."

The ladies nodded their adieus, and Ada got her hat from the rack. She turned at the door. "Get your taillight fixed, Tony," she said.

HER TRUCK WAS STILL WITH THE MECHANIC in Custer, so Ada drove the Buick again on the oiled and graded highway by way of Sunbeam, then the slow drive up the Yankee Fork Road. If she'd taken Mill Creek Pass instead, she would have seen the heavy gray smoke filling the valley an hour earlier than she did, and she would have been sick in her suspicions sooner than she was, and might have stopped and had her cry before she got to town. As it was, she had no inkling until she swayed around the last bend above the Bottoms that Rose and Corey Braden's roadhouse had burned—was still burning—to the ground.

The ashes were smoldering and a few flames still licking when she drove up. Volunteer fire fighters were chopping with their axes and hosing down the hot spots. Three stone fireplaces stood tall against the sky, but not a stick of the walls remained above floor level. The flames, apparently, had leapt and caught afire the carriage house—Rose's sanctum. It, too, was gutted and blackened, and the roof fallen in.

Munson found Ada standing at the edge of the county road with her arm raised against the heat of the coals. He asked her please to step back, inasmuch as the flames could lick up again. "Does Corey know?" she asked him softly.

"Well damn, Ada." Munson turned white as a ghost. "Well shoot, we suppose he was inside when the place burned."

She stared at him, shaking her head. He said, "There's the frame of a wheelchair right there, and we're fixing to dig for his remains just as soon as we can get into them coals."

She caught her breath a couple times and said, "He had two wheelchairs."

Munson said, "Yeah, but . . ." then just shook his head.

Her knees felt like they would buckle. They stood in a whirl of ashes and sparks and in the reeking smoke of burning paint and plastic, and she could only gulp for breath and stare into the shimmering heat. "What the hell do you mean he was inside?" she nearly shouted. "He was locked in your jail!"

Munson's face was streaked black with soot and sweat except for a white band halfway up his forehead that showed when he yanked off his hat. He made a half turn, raised his arms, and let them drop. "I called you yesterday afternoon, Ada. I called on the telephone half a dozen times, home and office both. I called on the police-band, but of course your truck was in the shop. Corey's lawyer came by and bailed him out. He put down two thousand dollars cash, and I had to let the kid go. The money and all the signed papers are in the safe."

"Two thousand dollars? Where in hell did Corey get that kind of money?"

"The lawyer—and he was from Boise, the pushy son of a

bitch—said Corey sold the roadhouse and all the contents."

"To whom?"

"Who do you think?" It was the old miner, Jubal Mason. He and Cuss Pearen sat watching them from the tailgate of an old GMC half-ton. Half a dozen others hung around the scene, including Reverend Niedermeyer who stood apart, brushing ash from his vest and polishing his boot on his pant leg.

Munson ignored them all and said to Ada, "The lawyer didn't say. Corey left you some personal things at the jail. You'd better come have a look."

She felt dizzy, and like she wasn't really hearing or seeing properly. "Not yet," she managed. "I can't look at personal items just yet." Her voice broke in a sob. "Corey had two wheelchairs!"

"I know, Ada, but after I released him, he wouldn't accept a ride from me. He said no offence, he bore no ill feelings to anyone, but then he pushed himself right down the middle of Main Street with folks watching him through the doorways and windows. I seen him go inside at his place, and then again sitting in the window upstairs when I made my late rounds. He had his uniform on. I mean, the part I could see in the window."

She stood silent for a minute with the ashes of Corey's and Rose's home blowing around her feet and the glow of the embers burning her face. "Kel, I'm sorry if I sounded . . . I'll watch out here for a bit. You go clean up. And I guess you'd better start the . . . I don't know, whatever the hell we're supposed to do." She turned, crossed her arms, and couldn't say anything more.

Munson squared his hat and walked back toward town, and most other folks cleared out as well. Jubal Mason hung behind. He yelled, "Who do you suppose bought the roadhouse?" Ada waved him away and started for her car. The old man followed until she had to yell at him to leave her alone.

In the driver's seat of the Buick with her boot braced on the open door, she lit a cigarette and didn't give a damn who saw or whether anyone noticed she was crying. She finished the smoke and tossed the butt to the ground, then nearly choked when she saw where it landed. There in the ash and dust was a clean imprint of a large, smooth-soled and pointed-toe western boot. She jumped from the car and on her hands and knees examined the print. There was a two-inch crescent moon impression at the back of the heel.

"Who all's been here to watch the fire today?" she called, chasing after Jubal Mason.

He shrugged. "Everyone. The whole town."

"Damn it!" She hurried across to where Pearen had been sitting. She hadn't noticed what kind of boot he wore. Where he'd parked, though, the roadbed was heavily graveled; there were no prints to speak of. Neither could she find anything in the area where Niedermeyer had been fussing.

As soon as the fire chief allowed her, she stood with them in the black sludge and helped sift through smoldering timbers and twisted plumbing and wires. Late in the afternoon one of the volunteers gave a shout, and when they lifted part of a collapsed wall, they found the second wheelchair, half melted, along with the blackened bones of a double amputee. Braden was wearing his military dog tags, which the fire chief removed and handed to her.

IT CAME TO VERY LITTLE, REALLY, and was wrapped in a blue and yellow silk scarf. There were half a dozen letters, a bronze star and a purple heart, an engraved zippo lighter, and a couple color photographs. It had been Rose's scarf, Ada recognized it from a photograph she'd seen at the bar.

The letters, she supposed, were those Corey had with him in his bedroom and later in the jail cell. They were all addressed to R. Wilde at a post box in Sunbeam, and all showed a return address to one Fitzwilliam Darcy in Berkeley California. It didn't take her long, nor would it have taken Corey long, to determine Mr. Darcy was Aaron Niedermeyer, Rose was the addressee, and the two young people were in love.

One photograph was of Corey shipboard with his platoon, with a storm angling down in the distance. Bare to the waist and solid bronze, Corey wore a tee-shirt tied over his head and held a smoke between his teeth. He was not the oldest of the group, nor the biggest. But the other boys gave him room, and they watched him and smiled with him as he mugged for the camera. His eyes were those of a young warrior, not yet tested, with a home and a family still to protect.

"We need the coroner to examine Corey's skeletal remains," Ada said. "I want to know how he died."

"Jeez, Ada, he died in the fire."

"He was consumed by the fire. Was there a bullet wound, or anything else?"

"Does it matter now?"

"It does to me."

The other photo was of Rose Braden, high on a mountain with sun and wind and wildflowers in her hair. She wore a wool sweater, and her cheeks were flushed; her eyes were green—turquoise green. Ada had not known her eyes were green. But it was the girl's laugh that broke her heart. It was a laugh on the tip of her tongue ready to be shared; barely the sweet promise of a laugh left forever unfinished by the click of the shutter.

She packed the articles into her car and took the lonely way back to Camas, via Mill Creek Pass—desolate and dark on a Sunday night. The moon rose full over the treetops, and it kept her company most of the way, reflecting broad ribbons of silver in the rapids where the Yankee Fork and the road twisted together.

Corey had left the letters for her—let her see them after all. But why? He could have taken them with him to his grave. He'd left no confession letter, no allocution of the crime. But he'd known something—maybe everything. Why would he not at least give her a clue? And he made no other mention of Rose, although he still loved her. He just gave up her letters, the letters that broke his heart, then went home and lit a fire.

She drove slowly up the pass with the window down and the Buick's tires plinking and plunking through the gravel. There was no one left to hurry for. Everyone who had depended on her—depended on the person behind the badge—was gone.

Just before the summit she pulled off the main road and drove along a two-track through scrub aspen standing twisted and ghostly in the moonlight. She parked in a penstemon-laced meadow between volcanic bluffs. The place was quiet, but for crickets and the breeze in the aspen leaves, and hidden from all the world. She spread a blanket in the grass and sat with her thermos and the sandwich she had ignored all day.

She sipped from the coffee, which was tepid, but still couldn't touch the sandwich. She lit a smoke, and watched for a long time as the moon rose out of the branches of the aspens. Bugs darted in and out of the soft light.

The cigarette burned her finger, startling her, and she flipped it down and it smoldered in the grass and died. She lay down on the blanket, pulled her service jacket over her, and closed her eyes. An owl hooted in the trees above her.

She woke to a cold cerulean eastern sky, and a big pink moon hanging above the far Sawtooth peaks. The last of the coffee was cold, but she drank it down and finished the sandwich, then drove down the pass into Camas.

CHAPTER TWENTY-ONE

16 July – 4:15 a.m., Rose Braden was
pulled from the water two weeks ago.

AND SHE'D HAD TO PULL LONNIE BARR FROM THE ICE, and now Corey Braden from the ashes. With the moon set and the eastern sky a violent orange, Ada lit a fire in her kitchen range, then sat with a hot coffee and searched the radio frequencies for anything other than static. There was nothing. She laid her head in her arms and closed her eyes again. The Monday morning sun, when it finally poked over the Pahsimeroi Hills, lit afire her unwashed kitchen window, jarring her from her second slumber. She took up, tasted, then put down the cold coffee, and re-started the fire in the range.

The small stack of hand-written letters and their respective envelopes covered the Formica table, and she cleared her head enough to shift and switch them around to get them into a chronological order. Within the stack, an extra envelope addressed to Fitzwilliam Darcy was marked with the Sunbeam return address. That envelope contained no letter. But the penmanship on the empty envelope was the same as she'd seen composing the poems in Rose's carriage house, with metered heights and open, girlish loops.

Each letter from Aaron began, *My Wilde Yankee Rose*, and each was signed, *Your Mr. Darcy*. In mid-April, Aaron wrote,

> *. . . and it was perfect, wasn't it?—with the apple trees blushing almost as much as you, and new grass greening the hillsides. You should see the Berkeley hills now. They're so brown and dry it hurts my eyes to walk through them. I need you walking with me, lying with me. You make flowers bloom.*

ADA SHUDDERED. THIS WAS WORSE than seeing the girl naked on the examination table. Then, the flesh had been cold and there was no life to offend; no feelings to burglarize. Here, though, the flesh was still warm. She could hear the two of them laughing together, see them lying together, dreaming together.

She poured herself a second cup of coffee and picked up another letter. In May, he'd written,

> *Dear Wilde Rose . . . Darling I haven't heard from you in two weeks. I know you're trying to get your travelling money together, and yes it would make a nice start for us. But don't you have enough . . . ?*

WHAT MONEY? FROM WHERE? ADA SKIMMED a third letter. This one was chatty as the others had been, but a little nervous sounding as well. She discovered why:

> *. . . I'm worried about the other thing. Do you think he's really following you? On purpose? Please, Rose, you have what you need. Just come to me; I've found us a place . . .*

GOOD GOD, THE GIRL KNEW she was being stalked! Rose's last weeks had to have been awful, even without her private letters being stolen. What kept her there when Aaron was begging her to come to him? *Just go!* Ada thought. *It never gets better!*

The empty envelope, the one addressed from Rose to Aaron, had a date of June 22 on the back. The letters had to have been taken no more than a week before Rose died.

Ada closed her eyes and sat with her chin in her hand until her coffee went cold again and the sun rose well above the hills. She cried a little, although it wasn't professional, and she threw her cup at one point, smashing it against the wall and letting the coffee trickle in amber beads down the floral print, although that wasn't professional either. It was just that Rose Braden must have lived her last days feeling scared and all alone. And that only reminded Ada how alone she was, and how false her life had been. And too, Rose had to have been desperate in the end. God, to have all her dreams and deeds spread out in front of her husband like that? It was no wonder the girl had packed to go.

But then she hadn't gone. Why? The letters were not—they still were not—a reason to go onto the dredge that night. It was all enough to ruin the girl's life, but not enough to take her life. She dropped the stack of letters onto the table with the empty one, the one addressed by Rose to Aaron, lying atop the others.

And what money were they talking about? Was Lonnie Barr right about the medallions? She dialed the long-distance operator, and within a minute had the Idaho City assayist on the line. His report, she hoped, would answer one question at least. But when she got it, heard the numbers, it just opened a slew of new questions.

9:30 a.m. – Gold! Whose was it? How did she come by it?
Office work and the motor shop. Then back to Custer
to follow up with Mrs. Li.

THE MORNING WAS HALF GONE BY the time Ada found the strength to go into the office. She walked up from her house with the expectation that her pickup would be repaired and delivered that afternoon. She locked the door behind her and left the lights off, hoping to get some of her damned paperwork done in the meantime.

A tap on her office window just before noon startled her. She tried to ignore it, but it wouldn't go away. After a couple more taps, Mayor Applegate cleared his throat and said, "Your truck is here, Ada. We need to talk, honey." She dried her eyes and straightened herself a little, and let him in. He was followed through the door by pinch-faced Larry Marsh of the County Board of Trustees, and Dee Mansfield. They entered like a posse—or a lynch mob.

The men hung their hats on the rack but seemed undecided as to jackets. They glanced at one another and moved forward to the center of the office, backing Ada to her desk. Applegate spoke: "Pleased to find you here, Ada. I couldn't find you all yesterday."

Ada looked from one gentleman to the other. "I was at . . . I was looking into more evidence regarding the Yankee Fork investigation."

Mansfield pursed his lips. "I believe that case is now closed."

The coldness of the statement left her speechless. She took a deep breath expecting to feel the old ache in her chest. It wasn't there, nor were her hands shaking. She leaned back on the edge of her desk. "The case is closed when I close it," she said.

The three men moved forward, and as she tried to step around toward the coffee table, Marsh shifted, effectively hemming her in. "Are you asking me to dance, Larry?"

"Huh?"

"Give me a little room here, please." She pushed around him, then let the men wait while she filled the pot with water and the basket with grounds. Still her hands didn't shake.

"Why are you talking to the old China woman, Li?" Mansfield asked. He leaned on the sill and stared out the window. "You've been up Jordan Creek as well. Have I not explained to you the dangers up there?"

"You've been watching me closely, Dee." She set the full pot on the hot plate to perk. "Don't you have a company to run?"

"As a member of the Board, I have a county to run too." He turned to the others and nodded. "Ada, we all like you, but you are just getting yourself into dangerous situations. Hell, you say you've been shot at, and Ephraim tells me now your brake line was cut. I had no idea. You're up visiting that psychopath's mine . . ."

"Some risk is part of the job. It would be the same with anyone in the position."

Applegate hitched up his belt and breathed out long and slow, waited for a nod from Marsh, and said, "Ada, hon, we've decided. We're going to insist you resign your duties as acting sheriff. I don't think I need to go into details of why. You're well aware of the conflicts that have come up in the course of your unnecessary . . . let's call it an over-zealous investigation of the Brady girl's death."

"Braden. Rose Braden." She cleaned three coffee cups at the sink and dried them with a towel, then waited for Mansfield and the mayor to part so she could make her way over to the reading stand.

She said, "Is it overzealous, Mayor, to try to find Rose's killer?"

The men shifted their feet. She took her time paging through the book of statutes, screwed up her lips at last, and shook her head. To Applegate she said, "You saw last week it couldn't have been a blow from Corey Braden that killed his wife. You saw the photos."

"Well, hon, that isn't exactly the point right now. Mr. Mansfield has brought up some over-arching considerations."

"Mayor, I've told you, too, what made the tracks by the pond. They were not made by Sergeant Braden's wheelchair." All three men looked uncomfortable. Ada turned the pages and ran her finger through the County laws.

Mansfield was sitting casually on the edge of her desk wearing the same amused smile he'd worn in his own office. She'd known that face for years: Montgomery's best friend. He sat calmly, self-assured and in charge as ever.

Except he wasn't, quite. It's easy enough to know when a man is sneaking looks, and Dee had been. At her. But they were not looks of admiration, they were furtive, even nervous glances. "Dee," she asked, "did you buy the roadhouse from Corey Braden, and pay cash?"

His reaction was barely more than a raised brow. "Is that a crime in your county?" he asked evenly.

"It's not a crime, but your cash could not have come at a worse time for the kid, could it? It was your cash that bailed him out so he could end his own life."

Applegate and Marsh sucked in their breath and stood speechless. Ada was a bit shocked herself, but she breathed just fine.

Mansfield said, "I have been very patient, but I will not . . ."

"Any jackass would know better!"

"That's enough!" He jumped up with his arm stretched toward her. "You are through, you troublemaking little . . . Larry and I are on the County Board, and we agree your employment with Yellowpine County"—He could barely spit out the words—"You are hereby terminated!"

And heaven above, wouldn't that make it easy? It would free her of all the work and worry, the snubs and sneers, and the constant doubting. It would put an end to the lonely days and empty evenings. But . . . with a sigh and a glance around her drab, mossgreen office she said, "No, I'm afraid I am not."

Mansfield scoffed. Ada slammed the book closed, making the other gentlemen jump. "*A sworn-in law officer can be terminated for cause by his direct supervisor, or by an action of the Board,*" she quoted.

"Which we have just shown you."

"No, Mr. Councilman. A recall action requires a quorum. Title Fourteen, Section Five, Part b. Looks to me like it's just you and Councilman Marsh. You need a third."

"Mayor Applegate is at every meeting."

"As a non-voting observer for the Town of Camas."

There was a silent moment when Mansfield's face tightened and turned red. "Goddamn you! There's no quorum available, and you know it. Russel is east on business; Ibarra and Noxon are with their herds in summer pasture."

Ada grabbed her service jacket from the rack, then stepped back to turn off the hot plate. "Let the grounds settle for a minute, Uncle Eph." She winked. "The sugar's in the cupboard."

She took her time belting on her holster, then shrugged and said as she crossed the room, "Better send for Noxon or Ibarra, gentlemen. You're going to need that quorum." It had been a long time since she'd smiled. She dared just a small grin as she walked, badge first, out the door.

But she had nowhere to go with her badge. Promising—insisting now—she would not quit was one thing but knowing where to take the investigation was quite another. And now, boy, her hands were shaking. She could barely steer the truck. Her breathing quickened as she gassed up at the motor shop, and she had to wait a moment before pulling out into traffic. But then she wasn't sure which way to steer when she got to Main Street. She only knew she had to get out of town. She had to figure things out quickly, too, because she sure as hell would be terminated. She grimaced thinking of Mansfield's parting glare then laughed. *Terminated one way or the other.*

CHAPTER TWENTY-TWO

1:30 p.m. – Back to the scene of the crime.
On my own and running out of time.

THE SCRAPED AND DENTED SHERIFF'S TRUCK ran just fine, and it carried her up and over Mill Creek summit and down the upper Yankee Fork valley into Custer. She parked half a block from the jailhouse, and for a quarter hour sat in the truck with her head resting on the back of the seat, still not sure she could face the memories inside. In the end, she left the truck where it sat and walked out of town. She walked west, past the damp, sour ashes of the roadhouse toward the Bottoms and Mrs. Li's house.

The gold dredge was not operating, although the diesel engines were smoking. The engineers were winching the barge around in its pond, lining it up for its final cut. Mrs. Li's parlor, taking advantage of the lull, was bright and warm with the drapes tied back and the window sash thrown open. But for an occasional waft of black diesel smoke, the summer morning was pleasant and relatively quiet. Ada and Li settled down on dark red upholstered furniture with a myrtle wood tea table between them. The yin-yang plaque hung on the wall, gleaming in unaccustomed sunlight.

"Lonnie Barr had it in his room. I didn't know how to fill out the evidence forms for this sort of thing, and then I wasn't sure if I would have to charge him with a crime if I did. So, it's been sitting in my office next to the Folgers. Anyway, I thought you could use it. For medicine, I mean." She handed the jar of cannabis to Mrs. Li.

Li opened the lid and smelled the contents. "It is dàmá. How much . . . I mean, should I pay you for it?"

"No. Gosh, no! That would make me a whatever, a narcotic dealer, wouldn't it?"

"I guess it would. Let's leave it you are a bringer of medicinal herbs." She took a pinch of the dried leaves and stuffed it into her pipe. "How then can I show my appreciation?"

"You don't have to. You don't owe me anything." Ada stood, then sat back on the arm of the chair. "I know how Rose died. I just want to know why she died. What was she doing with Pearen and the others?"

"Cuss? They were young men once, you know, with all the dreams of the young."

"Rose was wearing a heavy belt of medallions."

Li lit the pipe from a wooden match, closed her eyes, and exhaled slowly. She said, "The medallions, yes; her dreams, her many albatrosses." She coughed softly and turned her head to stare out the window.

"Do you know where the gold came from? The assay lab tells me the medallions contain a fair amount."

Li said, "Not this assay lab."

"The one in Idaho City."

"Yes, they are a little more honest. The medallions contain about seven to eight percent gold, on average."

As they talked, the room filled with the sweet, rancid smoke. Li said, "You could say Rose died for gold, I suppose. But remember, *the allure of gold is not for gold, but for the means of freedom and benefit.*" She rubbed her forehead and rested her eyes a moment.

Ada asked, "Confucius?"

"Actually, Ralph Waldo Emerson—paraphrased, I suppose."

"The means of benefit, sure. But freedom? Really, her means of freedom was not gold."

"You are going to say love?"

Ada folded her arms and stared down at the floor. She said, "You know her husband was mean to her; he hit her sometimes. Corey hated himself for it, and it made Rose hate herself too. And day by day, working and waiting and worrying over his return . . ."

Li nodded and smiled, though sadly.

Ada got up and examined a row of photographs. She said, "And then, you know, suddenly someone else was there; someone nice came along and treated her decently, and it was like a burden was taken from her." Li's eyes followed her to the open window where she lifted the edge of the lace. Birds chattered in the plum tree just outside. Ada said, "Rose felt a breeze through a window she never expected to open for her again."

"I suppose that part is true," Li said. "But Rose was more than just half of a love affair." She re-lit her pipe and inhaled. As the smoke escaped, she said, "So are you."

"I don't know what you mean." Ada quickly sat. "It has nothing at all to do with me."

"Forgive my impertinence."

Ada gave it a moment. "Rose was leaving. She was packed and had a little cash and a plan. What else was so important; what brought her back to the pond?" She waved away the fumes. "There were letters, from her young man. It must have been devastating for her when they were found."

Li drew from the pipe, leaned back into the chair, and blew a slow stream of smoke.

Ada said, "And there was another letter. One she'd written to him. But I could only find the envelope; the pages are missing. Could Rose have gone onto the dredge to find another, a damning letter?"

There was silence for a moment. Li looked up and said, "She was smarter than that. She would not have risked it all to retrieve a letter. A letter would already have been read; its damage already done."

"Yes, I guess you're right."

"Yes." Li nodded.

Ada knew Mrs. Li would be helpful for only a few minutes more. "Where did she get the medallions?" she asked. "They were each stamped with your *Taijitu* symbol. Do you know anything about them?"

"How easily it can all be taken from us."

"She stole them from you?"

Li laughed until she coughed. "Heavens no, she . . ." Her head lolled side to side on the chair back, and whatever thought she might have had wove itself into reverie. Ada settled into the chair and crossed her legs. The old woman sighed, and very quietly said, "The waste of this world is all the likes of us are left to dream on. The trash, the cast-off and scorned."

Ada looked up and smiled. "*The junk and jetsam, the dreams and rust.*"

"Exactly so." She nodded and picked up her pipe. "*Lay up not your treasures upon the earth, where rust doth corrupt, and where thieves break through and steal.*"

"That isn't Confucius either."

"No, it's biblical I'm pretty sure."

"I need to know what it means, Mrs. Li."

"Please: Maggie."

"What does it mean, Maggie?"

She puffed the embers up and held the smoke in, then exhaled slowly. "*It is not only in the rose . . .*" She coughed and laughed at the same time and had to wipe her eyes with a handkerchief because she was crying, too. "*. . . not only in the rose, but in the mud and scum of things—there always, always something sings.*"

"That's not Scripture."

"Sort of Emerson, as I said."

3:00 p.m. - Working a hunch - Up the hill and down the draw

The conversation slowed until Ada understood the old woman had fallen asleep. She left the house quietly, picking her way through the piles of incinerated trash and crushed cans, through the neat garden to the fence recently white-washed. The diesel engines rumbled deep inside the dredge, and as she moved along the edge of the pond the beltline and trommel started up. The sudden banging caused her to jump and to worry about Mrs. Li's—Maggie's rest. But then, the last resident of the Bottoms would have learned by then to sleep through any noise.

At the intersection where the roadhouse should have stood she came upon Dar Colemaker and another worker from the dredge with their backs turned, peering into the back yard through blackened honeysuckle and seared lilacs. The two men did not hear her because of the dredge, and she was able to approach very near before they saw her. A startled Colemaker stammered, "What can I do for you, ma'am, uhh . . . Sheriff, ma'am?"

Ada started to edge through the charred tangle to where they stood, but the second worker, a thick man with a bucket of a head, held up his hand and said, "It's private property. Nobody enters."

"Mr. Colemaker, I need to access this property in order to complete my investigation."

"Sorry ma'am. We were told 'no' on that score in particular," Colemaker replied.

"Do you understand a young man died here?" Ada moved again to enter.

Colemaker and the thick guy squared themselves. "Mr. Mansfield called us on the telephone just an hour ago. He said Munson and the fire chief already sifted through the ashes, and you can see what you need to see from the public roadway, ma'am, or you can get a warrant."

That hadn't taken long. She didn't argue further, but left the two men standing in the soot and bramble and headed into town.

Main Street was nearly deserted in the afternoon heat. The north-side boardwalk smelled of old wood and tarpaper baking in the sun as Ada strode the worn timbers with her hands locked behind her back. She looked in at doors and windows to maybe catch the eye of a citizen or two. Few met her gaze with more than a glance, and those who did seemed more flustered by the sudden social connection than concerned for anything beyond their immediate business.

The next block was much the same: a few shoppers absently marked her progress through the bargain-painted windows of the IGA, and a few more through the double doors of the dry-goods store where it smelled of sorghum, leather, and liniment. Old men smoked and seemed not to notice her at all from a bench in front of the pawn shop. Three had died in their midst, and a look of dull bewilderment was the most she could draw from anyone. These folks and the two minions guarding the roadhouse were the very people who had worn out their tongues disparaging Rose Braden, and it was consoling, in a way, to know that Rose would not have given a tinker's damn for the lot of them.

She angled over to her truck and fished an old rucksack from behind the seat: Montgomery's army issue field pack. After a moment's hesitation, she reached in the jockey box for her holstered gun and stashed it in the rucksack. Again, she did not stop at the jailhouse but followed Second Street in a twisting climb up Dickens Hill, past mine dumps and loading chutes of weathered timber jutting between the residential shacks. A few dogs barked at her passing, and one young woman hanging clothes on a line showed an open-eyed curiosity, but otherwise she climbed alone.

At the top of High Street, the sun still hung a good two hands above distant Red Mountain. She stopped a minute to catch her breath, then cut up through a vacant lot into the shadowed crook of the ridge, where she entered a small remnant of pine forest. It was easier climbing in the trees, with pine duff to give her footholds, so she clambered through the trees to the top of the ridge and came out atop an outcrop of volcanic rock in sunlight now beginning to soften.

Going down the other side was not as easy as climbing had been because there were few trees on the west-facing slope, and the white, acid-leached soil was thin and hard-packed and gave her no foothold. She boot-skied parts of it, grabbing for roots and branches to check her descent and falling here and there and sliding on her behind.

Mine cuts and abandoned tunnels pocked the hillside, and the workings were littered with barrels and rail ties, and streaked with iron oxides bleeding from sulfide veins. At mine level after mine level she found prints of a woman's work shoe pressed into the soft earth leading into the mines. Red-umber solutions oozed from the portals and trickled over the wasterock dumps, coating rocks and rails and beer cans with orange limonitic slime.

Ada followed the seeps down as they coalesced into rills, and the rills into gullies. Shadows filled the steep-walled gulch by the time she reached the bottom, although the sky above still held some daylight. Gullies joined to become a small acid stream, and the stream led to a barbed wire fence. Beyond the fence, the solutions flowed through piles of grey stone, and through the ruined orchard in the back lot of what once had been a roadhouse and a home, where Rose Braden had labored and schemed. As she'd expected, Colemaker and his partner had done their job keeping her out, and had gone. She ducked through the fence.

The stream was littered with tin cans as Ada had seen before but had not really noticed before. She found a long stick, and with it fished a can out of the slurry. She wiped the muck from the can, and in the dying light of the day it glowed brightly metallic where it had been submerged: a bronze color. "*Even in the mud and scum of things . . .*" she whispered. She stuck the can in her rucksack and fished out more, wiping them clean and stowing them until the pack was full.

Night was fully upon her by the time she slogged through the ashes of the roadhouse to stand at the intersection of roads. A light shined through the bars of the jailhouse a quarter-mile distant, but there was a Cadillac parked in front, which she recognized even in the moonlight to be Mansfield's. She left her sheriff's truck where it was parked and walked the other way, toward Margaret Li's house.

WHEN LI ANSWERED HER KNOCK, Ada held up one of the metal-plated cans. It gleamed in the light of the doorway. Li nodded. "Come in," she said.

"Is this how Rose got the metal for the medallions? Is there gold in this coating?" Ada asked.

Li led her shuffling into the kitchen. "Yes, she plated-out the metals from the acid solutions, and we melted it down. Yes, there is gold; about seven percent by weight. Let me see it." She took the can and under the kitchen light scraped the edge of a knife against it. A foil of reddish-yellow metal peeled away. "This one is ready. How many do you have, just the one can?"

"About twenty."

"Then I can show you how, if you wish."

Ada brought the rucksack and followed Li to the backyard, to where a shed roof connected the back of the house to a brick furnace. The old woman tossed pottery and baskets aside and indicated a heavy iron cauldron, which Ada hefted onto a hook to suspend it over an opening in the furnace. "I'll start the fire," Li said. "You make tea, please. It will be a long night."

MARGARET LI FED STICKS INTO THE FIRE for an hour as she nodded in and out of sleep. When the bright flames died down to coals, she added charcoal from a burlap bag, and showed Ada how to work a set of bellows. As the coals glowed brighter, she flattened the cans and arranged them in the cauldron, then opened a plate in the furnace and lowered the cauldron on its chain through the opening and onto the glowing coals.

Ada stepped in to watch, but the heat from the opening knocked her back. "How hot does the fire have to be?" she asked.

"It depends on the alloy, of course," Li said. "Seventeen hundred and fifty Fahrenheit for the metals from behind the roadhouse. The platings from Jubal's War Eagle contain a little more silver, so just sixteen hundred and fifty is hot enough."

"Jubal's? You did other mine discharges?"

"Oh, yes. Rose tested them all over the many months. Eighteen hundred degrees for the alloy from the Sunnyside. The solutions carry more copper there, you see, and less zinc. But all contain significant gold."

"The Sunnyside? The Pirate's Gold, too?"

"Yes, and others as well."

The cans began to ping after an hour. Ada stood on a box and craned to see into the furnace, holding a hand in front of her face against the intense heat. The cauldron sat among white-hot coals, and the cans inside glowed faintly. "So, what was the limestone all about, the piles of rocks in the stream? I assume it was limestone. Rose drove a long way to get it."

Li added more sticks of charcoal through the front door of the furnace, then sat back heavily. "You've done well, Ada Reed. Limestone buffers the acidity so the metals will plate out. A little heavier on the bellows, I think."

"Did you learn all this at the School of Mines?"

"No, good heavens—from my grandfather." She rubbed her knees and looked slyly at Ada. "So, you investigated me after all? Yes, I studied at Butte, Montana. It seems like a hundred years ago."

Ada worked the bellows steadily, sending sparks twirling into the night sky. Li said, "When I graduated, I worked for mining companies all over the west, usually as assistant in the assay lab." She coughed and spat. "Never as chief metallurgist, of course. Always I was too Asian and too female. But when the war came, all that changed. Then my knowledge was worth something, and I got the head job at Anaconda Company. It was worth all the frustration, all the offense. Finally, I was worthy." She coughed again. "Of course, it changed again when the war ended. My job was given to a man who had fought for his country. And so, I came home, as you see."

A high-country breeze blew down from Jordan Creek. Ada left her bellows for a minute and stepped out from beneath the shed roof to watch the sparks against the cobalt sky. "Do not trust the shoreline," Li called to her. The moon was high in the sky, and the dredge pond rippled in the breeze. "I had to warn Rose too. She loved to watch the sparks fly and was never careful." The old woman sighed. "She loved the fireworks and the stars. 'A poor girl's festival,' she would call it."

Ada returned and took up the bellows again. "Your grandfather produced metals like this?"

"It was the only way he could feed his family. Chinese were not allowed to own mining claims, you know."

"I did not know."

A night wind blew from the West Fork and banged through sheets of corrugated metal somewhere across the Bottoms. Ada settled in under the shed roof out of the breeze, staying warm next to the old brick furnace. The water of the pond rippled against the metal hull of the dredge, and the huffing of the coals rose like a restless dragon as Ada worked her bellows. When the moon slipped behind a cloud all went dark but for slivers of firelight through the bricks shining randomly on roots and cuttings, on carved sticks, and on baskets and potteries. "Rose was happy here," Ada said—to herself mostly, but loud enough for Li to hear.

The old woman's jaundiced face glowed in the scattered light of the furnace. She folded her arms and leaned back into the chair. "It was a couple of years ago," she said. "Rose helped me to get my groceries home one rainy day. I couldn't pull the cart through the mud. I felt old and helpless. She saw from her window and hurried down. She got soaking wet, of course, and muddy. I made her an herbal tea, and we talked into the night. You would have liked Rose. She would have grown up much like you, I think."

"She felt safe here, and strong. She was strong here."

"Yes."

For another hour they fed the coals, until at last Mrs. Li held up her hand. She showed Ada how to work the chains and let the younger and taller woman bring up the cauldron. The cans inside glowed a deep red, and Ada had to shield her face from the heat. Li donned a visor and heavy gloves, and with iron tongs picked the cans out one by one, dropping them smoking and whistling into a dust bin.

With a heavy handle, then, she tipped the cauldron on its chain, and a trickle of bright orange metal poured from the lip of the cauldron into a ceramic mold. There was enough molten metal to make a fat, dollar-size coin. "Not much," Li said. "We usually roasted four dozen cans to make an eight-ounce medallion."

Li let the mold cool for just a minute before upending it and dropping out the glowing disc. The metal dimmed from scarlet to crimson to burgundy, and left a black circle on the wooden table next to dozens of other black circles.

Ada poured a cup of water over it and waited for it to stop spitting and steaming before flipping it over. A yin-yang symbol was cast into the back of the coin. She hefted it and admired it in the moonlight before putting the shiny thing, still warm, into her pocket.

The moon was nearly down, and a cool breeze was rising out of the south. "I will smoke a bit and sleep here tonight," the old woman said. She collapsed into her chair. "I don't hear the breeze enough these days, nor the crickets, and the furnace will keep my bones warm until dawn." She put a brand into the coals, and when it flared, lit her pipe. "You should stay on the davenport," she told Ada. "There is a blanket already, and you are not so tall that you will be uncomfortable. Rose was nearly as tall as you, I think, and she slept well there."

CHAPTER TWENTY-THREE

17 July. Tuesday, I guess – Staying in Custer till I work things out. Finally with something in my pocket!

ADA WOKE TO THE FAINT GLOW from the dial of a radio. It was a fancy Philco, and she smiled to think Margaret Li would have one or two frivolous things like that in her Zen life. She pulled on her boots, found her jacket, and crept out to the backyard. A blanket had fallen from the still-sleeping Mrs. Li, and Ada tucked it back up, being careful not to disturb her.

The moon was nearly gone, and the sun was still an hour away. Beyond the picket fence it was just light enough to see the dew glowing on the tips of the grasses. A mist lay low on the water where she skirted the pond, and the mist draped in tattered wisps as she climbed the hill above the road. She found a rock where she could sit and watch the day come on, knowing that it would be a telling day, perhaps her last as sheriff. She pulled her jacket close and lit a smoke. There were no lights on in any of the houses or businesses across the valley; all was dark but for moonlight catching on the sentinel chimneys of the roadhouse. Below her, the Yankee Fork slid by in its channel. She could just see a hint of purple waves reflecting the eastern sky and hear the waters spilling from culverts farther below. Except for that and the distant calls of birds in the mist, the valley lay quiet.

She dug the shiny new medallion from her pocket and held it in the faint glow of the eastern sky. Rose had been smarter than the whole lot of them, and that part made her smile. "But then, why weren't you smart enough to get away?" she whispered. "What kept you here a day too long?" She put the coin back in her pocket and watched for the dawn.

6:05 a.m. – Custer, Idaho with Police Chief Kellen Munson

THE NUGGET CAFE ON MAIN STREET BUZZED with the clatter of plates, table talk, and shouted orders to the cook. Someone in the next booth smoked a cigarette, and the nicotine swirled with bacon smoke in the morning's first shaft of sunlight. Ada waved at the smoke and squinted into the light. "A deer jumped onto the highway on my way home the other night," she said. "I jerked the wheel and nearly put the Buick in the river." She shoveled in a forkful of hotcakes and took a swallow of coffee. "I didn't feel scared, although I should have. I just got the wheels going the right way and kept driving. It didn't used to be like that."

Chief Munson had spied her walking up from the Bottoms and called to her as she was getting into her truck. She joined him in a booth near the back. He said "God dang, Ada. I know you've had a rough go, but you have got to give up this crusade or you're going to get someone killed." He didn't say 'someone *else* killed,' but when he followed with, "More than likely yourself this time," it was clear that was what he meant. He took a can of snuff from his shirt pocket, packed it on the ball of his hand, but then put it back. He said, "Corey Braden most likely killed his wife, and that's true no matter how much we don't want it to be. His wheelchair tracks were down by the scene of the crime."

"They weren't . . ." She stopped short of explaining the grocery cart. She wasn't sure why.

"Ada, listen." He caught the waitress's eye and held up his empty cup. "I spoke with Mansfield yesterday."

"I know you did."

"They can have Dave Wickers take the Sheriff's job till God-willing Montgomery gets back, or until the November election."

They were keeping their voices low amid the sounds of the breakfast crowd. She said, "Corey's blow didn't kill his wife; you've seen that. The tracks by the pond were made by Mrs. Li's grocery cart."

"They were?"

"Uh-huh. And Corey sure as hell didn't . . ." She balked again, not telling him about the crescent marks on the girl's hands. It made her queasy, this time, to hold information from him.

For a minute he said nothing, and there was just clinking and clattering, and four old men arguing at a table by the window. "Well, if Corey didn't do it," Munson asked, "then why would he do what he did? Why would he kill himself like that?"

She waited while the waitress freshened their coffees. "His heart was broken, Kel. The letters Corey kept with him?—they were written to Rose from Aaron Niedermeyer. They were love letters."

Munson nodded. "I 'spected maybe so. You think that's why he did it?"

"They were filled with young silliness and plans for all the things they wanted to do and the places they wanted to go. Rose wanted to go to Italy, Kel, to see Florence and walk where Michelangelo walked. Aaron wrote of going to England and sitting where John Donne sat. There were poems." Ada pulled a napkin from the dispenser and wiped her eyes and nose. "She was just a kid with so many dreams. But they were dreams with Aaron, not with Corey."

Munson turned his head away. "The letters," Ada said, "were taken from her room. They're right here." She pulled the bundle from her jacket pocket. "Look at them. You can see for yourself Rose was not stepping out with a lover. The boy she loved was in California."

Munson pulled out a letter, read a bit of it, then pulled out several more. "She shouldn't have loved someone else," he said at last.

"But she did, Kel. One of the envelopes is empty." She held up a menu to shield the sun from her eyes. "Do you know anything about that?"

"What do you mean?"

"You got the letters from Corey before I got them. The missing letter is one she must still have been writing to Aaron. I was just wondering what happened to it." She put the menu down.

He shrugged and shook his head.

"Okay," she told him. And it was okay. Kellen Munson was a good man, and honest as he understood honest to be. He was going to see things as he'd always heard they should be seen, and she wouldn't change him in that and didn't want to.

She paid both their checks, then sat in her truck for twenty minutes with her head down on the steering wheel. Rose, with the laughing eyes and the wind in her hair was dead. And poor, sweet Lonnie. And now Corey, too. But Rose Braden was at the crux of it all. The logical approach would be to start back where things had begun to fall apart for Rose. And that meant back to the old mine: the Sunnyside, where her killer had stalked her, and where she and Ada had both panicked.

11:15 a.m. – Cuss Pearen's Sunnyside Mine.
I have to go back underground.

THE SUN-BLEACHED BOWL WAS AS BRIGHT and hot as the last time she'd dropped down over the ridge into the Sunnyside, and the road just as rocky and rutted. Ada parked by the toolshed and, crouching by her truck, scanned the surrounding hills and woods with binoculars.

The air was calm, and the log buildings and tarpaper shacks of the minesite baked in the mid-morning sun. The equipment yard, as she stole through, smelled of warm rubber tires, old grease, and rusting iron.

The hills showed no movement, so she dashed up the haul road, stopping only on the flat mine dump to catch her breath. The air wafting from the portal was cool and tangy with clays and sulfate minerals. For a minute longer she sat on an old timber, not ready yet to re-enter the dark hole. She threw a stone, which clattered down the side of the mine dump dislodging other stones that dislodged others until dust rose from a minor landslide below her. It had all started here, or hereabouts, but how, she wondered, had it ended in the deaths of three young people? She kicked another cobble off the edge, took up her binoculars, and scanned the hills all around. There was nothing; no movement, no threatening dust. She glanced around a last time, then entered the darkness.

It was not difficult to find the footprints again, and she followed them beyond where she'd stopped before, deeper into the mine. At two hundred yards into the mountain the iron rails turned left on another drift, but in the narrow beam of her flashlight the man's and woman's footprints continued straight. They led into a heading of the mine that had seen little traffic. The workings there were less maintained; wallrocks bled orange through fractures and bolt holes, and timbers were thrown up to brace the roof every ten feet or so. Pipes and electrical wires hung between the wooden square sets, dripping with orange slime.

The darkness was all-enveloping, suffocating. She swept her flashlight side to side to ward off the unnatural dread of the place. Puddles of water reflected the light eerily onto the rock walls. There was no sound but the suck of her own boots in the mud and faint drips of water in the distant drifts. Still the footprints led deeper.

She had no way to guess how far she'd come when, at a turn in the drift, she found a scattering of footprints and dozens of beer cans strewn in shallow minewater pools. These would have been what Rose had come for, what had brought her into the gloom and peril.

"Okay, Rose, you have it," Ada whispered. "Gather it up and get out!" But the footprints didn't turn back. From the acid pools, Rose's prints continued on, now deeper cast and at a greater spacing. She was running! Ada traced the tracks twenty yards to a crosscut where they paused and turned and then took off widespaced again. The crescent-heeled bootprints followed, now also at a run. The chase turned again at another crosscut a hundred feet farther in, and then again two hundred feet beyond that.

Ada stopped and swept her light side to side and all around. She had no idea where she was, and the condition of the workings had badly deteriorated. The walls were crumbling, and rusty solutions oozed from cracks everywhere. There were far fewer timber supports, and slabs of rock hung over head or had fallen so that she had to scramble over piles of sluff. The footprints continued between the rubble, though, so she was hopeful she could follow them back out.

When she stopped again to catch her breath, another factor presented itself—something troubling that she'd been ignoring. In a smooth, clayey stretch where all the prints could be seen together, the woman's tracks were there, leading in, whereas the man's footprints followed but also returned. The woman's footprints only went in; they did not come out. She began to dread what she might find around each turn. Had Rose died here, in the mine? Had her body then been carried out by her killer?

Within minutes the tracks led her to a dead heading: a turn of the tunnel that went in about fifty feet and stopped. The man's bootprints exited the chamber, but the woman's did not. Ada followed her narrow flashlight beam to the end, to the face of the drift, and there the chase apparently ended. An empty rucksack lay on the floor of the tunnel, with a few shiny, metal-coated cans scattered around.

But there was no sign of a scuffle of any sort. In one corner of the dead heading, though, a wooden ladder led up into darkness. The girl's footprints ended at the ladder.

Ada had to take her own rucksack off her back in order to fit up the ladder chase. Swinging the sack over her left arm, she could just hold the flashlight between the thumb and forefinger of her right hand as she climbed. Twenty feet up, though, her foot slipped off a loose rung and she barely caught herself from falling. She banged heavily into the rock wall, scraping her face; the rucksack and flashlight tumbled to the bottom. Going down for her gear was even trickier than going up. But she gathered her things, threw the sack this time over her right arm, and started up again.

The ladder was vertical, not inclined like a construction ladder, so her arms ached as she climbed. The first ladder flight took her up maybe forty feet, where the woman's tracks led her across a landing to a second ladder. She climbed that another forty feet to an open drift.

She could barely lift her arms by the time she stepped off into the drift. She checked the roof above, then checked the clayey floor for Rose's footprints. The beam of her flashlight was starting to yellow, and she needed to turn around if she hoped to follow the footprints out to daylight. But Rose's footprints, coming back and forth now, led on, so she followed them a little farther as hurriedly as she dared. She hadn't gone fifty yards, though, when she caught a slight glimmer from the corner of her eye; just a sylph dancing for a moment on a wet surface.

She pressed hard against the wall of the drift, switched off her light, and tried desperately to listen over her own breathing. There was another glimmer, and then a faint glow on the wallrocks. She held her breath. A boot scraped on gravel, and then an explosion of light as a bright cap lamp pointed right at her. She raised her arm against the light. A man stood in silhouette, and he carried . . . It might have been a gun.

"Madam Sheriff," Cuss Pearen said, "I wondered if you were done poking around up here." He came right up to her then, and Ada flinched when he leaned his cap lamp in close. She was smeared with white clays and orange oxides from the timbers and from the wallrocks, and her breathing was irregular and shallow. It wasn't a gun he carried but it was deadly enough. He gripped a sharp-pointed rock hammer like a tomahawk in his left hand. "Kind of hazardous to be roaming around alone down here," he said.

"I'm following up some leads Mr. Pearen," she said. She had to catch her breath. "And are you here working with your Sunnyside partners?"

"My partners? We're shut down for maintenance. But in point of fact, you're not in the Sunnyside anymore." He grinned. "You've crossed over to Mason's War Eagle."

"Is Jubal okay?"

"Far as I know. We're all part owners, now, of all these worthless holes in the ground."

They faced each other for a moment in the glare of his light. "You looking for a way out?" he asked.

She paused, but then nodded. She had little choice; there was nothing but uncharted darkness ahead, and she wasn't sure her arms would hold out if she tried to escape back down the two ladder runs. Besides, Rose's footprints continued in the direction Pearen had turned, so she caught her breath and followed behind when he started away. She switched her flashlight off to save the batteries and followed in the dancing light cast ahead by his cap lamp.

The floor of the tunnel became rocky, and with her feet moving in darkness she stumbled here and there. She didn't know if the rocky floor would show footprints anymore, so she tried to memorize the route, but the turns were too fast and too many. "But it's not worthless is it?" she asked, hoping to slow him down. "Your mine. It's not a worthless hole. You know for a fact there's gold here." Her voice echoed off the walls and she couldn't be sure Pearen had even heard her.

But he stopped. "You figured that much out, did you?" His boots scraped the floor as he stepped back to where she waited. "The mines are worthless because we got no money to develop them, and no mill anymore where we can make some money. How come you haven't figured that part out?"

She flicked on her flashlight for just a moment. In the amber light, he wasn't wearing heavy-lugged miner's boots, but western boots.

He spit into the side ditch. "It's not like nuggets are just waiting to be plucked out with a knife." He took a deep breath and considered a minute, then indicated the wall of the tunnel with a nod of his cap lamp. The rock of the wall was bleached and marbled; he gouged it with the point of his rock pick. It was soft. Up close, tiny quartz veinlets cut through in a boxwork pattern. "The main veins played out a long time ago," he explained, "but the country rock here carries a low concentration of gold. Not enough to make it worth mining underground; you'd have to come at it with steam shovels and big trucks."

He started down the drift again with Ada following close, relying on his light. Over his shoulder he said, "I got no money for steam shovels and trucks. We went into partnership, the boys and me, to keep it out of Mansfield's hands. You mine this in a big pit like Bingham or Butte, you'd be a very rich man."

Ada said, "Worth killing for, I guess."

Pearen turned, letting his lamp beam blind her for a second. "To some, maybe. To some worth dying for."

"And to you?"

He nodded ahead twenty feet to another ladder leading up. "No one ever knows himself for sure, does he? No one knows how the gold fever's gonna act on a person."

She let him get a few steps ahead. "Rose Braden was here at the mine, wasn't she? The day she died."

"I guess that makes me your prime suspect, don't it?"

"It doesn't make you Snow White."

He reached the ladder and shined his light up the chase. She clicked the flashlight on, drew her service revolver out of her rucksack, and levelled it at his cap lamp. "Drop the rock pick, Cuss."

He stopped when she cocked the hammer, his hand on a ladder rung. He didn't turn, but said, "Are you crazy? If you shoot me down in these workings, how are you going to find your way out?"

"I'll follow the footprints back."

"Good luck with that, and your flashlight's almost dead."

"If I shoot you, you won't be needing your lamp."

He nodded. "That's a point." He tossed the pick down. "Do you want to go up the ladder first, or follow me up?"

She hadn't considered that. "You, uhm, you lead. I don't want to drop my gun on your head."

Pearen shrugged and started up the ladder. Ada put the rock pick in her rucksack and stuck the dying flashlight in her breast pocket so it shined straight up, half blinding her. She slung the rucksack over her left shoulder and held the gun in her right hand. She let him get ten feet up the shaft before starting up after him. Pearen climbed slowly, and Ada nearly caught up to him a couple of times. His lamp gave her some light, but it was shadowy and shifting, and the rock walls absorbed most of it.

It was too late, Ada realized when she'd climbed thirty feet, to worry that Rose Braden might well have had her hands stomped on just like this: going up a damned ladder. And then fell, maybe, and hit her head—her unconscious body carried out and dumped in the dredge pond.

She climbed too fast and nearly caught Pearen again, his boots were just at forehead level, and the heels of his boots right there in her face.

Pearen stepped off into an open drift and waited. "Give me a little room please," Ada said. When his light didn't move, she shouted, "Back on down the drift. Now!" The ladder shaft darkened, and the light patterns on the walls shifted as Pearen's cap lamp turned away and moved down the tunnel. She climbed the last few steps and jumped onto the landing. "You had one more partner: Rose Braden. What happened to her?" she called to him.

Pearen stopped twenty paces ahead. He turned and looked her over in the light of his cap lamp; she was bent forward with hands on knees, resting her back and catching her breath. He took a few steps toward her. She couldn't see his eyes for the bright beam from his cap lamp. He said, "Is that what you think? Because Rose was a partner?"

"Something here scared her."

The beam of light swept the floor as he shook his head. "That young lady . . . No one ever treated me as fair as she did." He took a few more steps. "She was a partner, sure. We were all partners; we all thought we could make a go of it if we hung together." He stopped and wiped his hand over his face, then scanned the roof above, having to hold his words for a minute. "We all loved Rose. Hell, we wouldn't have even thought to look for the low-grade gold if she hadn't showed us with those damned cans of hers. But then she couldn't let it go."

"What do you mean, let it go?"

"Rose could never stop thinking about that gold once the fever took hold of her."

"No, that part I don't believe," Ada said. "Gold was the key for Rose, not the chain." She straightened her back but then stopped and sighed. Her *chain!* Rose could never manage to get away. Even after her letters were pilfered; even with her lover writing to her, begging her to come, she couldn't give it up. What did Maggie Li call her chain of medallions? Her damned *albatross.*

Pearen said, "She wanted to buy in, to own a share, and what could we say? We owed her that much. But then we all told her to get out; we'd watch after her interest. She just needed to leave town and start over somewhere." He shook his head. "But she never had quite enough money for the trip."

Ada stared a long moment past Pearen into the perfect darkness behind his caplamp. "She was here, wasn't she? Did you see her?"

He nodded. "She was here that day. Her face was banged up; she'd lost her footing in one of the shafts." He took a deep breath and wiped his face on his sleeve. "Her light was nearly dead like yours, but she wouldn't come out with me. She borrowed a cap and lamp and went back in, back down the ladders."

Ada stared at her boots for a moment and nodded. "Yes. She had dropped something. She'd dropped her rucksack when she fell."

"She came out an hour later in tears." Pearen turned, and Ada noticed a dim, distant light beyond him. He wiped his eyes on his arms. "'He took everything!' is what she told me, and she was mad as hell."

Ada swung her rucksack down and tossed the rock pick to Pearen. She put away her gun. "What's this?" he asked. "I'm no longer your prime suspect?"

She sighed and threw the rucksack over her shoulder. "Let's get out of here, Cuss. You're not a suspect. For one thing, your bootheels are worn down to the nails."

"Bootheels?"

They walked toward the light, not talking. The running and climbing, and the weight of uncertainty caught up to her, and her own boots scraped heavily over the rocks.

CHAPTER TWENTY-FOUR

5:40 p.m. – Sunnyside, back where I started.
Somehow I've come a complete circle.

PEAREN SAT WITH ADA ON THE PORCH for half an hour with the afternoon sun baking the pine needles and the grease-caked equipment in the yard. He mopped his face with a bandana and waited for her to stop writing. "There were letters," Ada said, "stolen from her. I think that would have . . ." She looked up and Pearen was still carrying his rifle. He'd grabbed it as they exited the War Eagle portal and carried it as they hiked and boot-skied and tumbled back down to the Sunnyside. He still had it across his knees.

He saw where her eyes went and said, "There's a mountain lion hanging around. Best I keep this rifle close while we're outside." He tipped his hat back and squinted into the sun.

She said, "A mountain lion? You know, I thought I saw . . ."

"Yeah. I had a good shot at it last week till someone honked her damned horn." He turned and grinned—a wider grin than she'd have thought he could muster. "Mansfield do that to your head?" he asked.

"Which?"

"Over your eye."

"No, that one was the preacher's wife. You and Jubal talk a lot about Dee Mansfield. Why does his name keep coming up? What interest does he have in all this?"

"Everything. Him and his geologists know about the low-grade gold, too. Maybe they even knew it first. He isn't interested in the dredging ground anymore; to hell with that. He's trying to tie up the entire hard-rock district."

"Helping out the old codgers."

"Helping them out of their life's work." Pearen laid the rifle down and leaned forward, resting his elbows on his knees. "Rose showed us we could incorporate, get bank loans, and make a go of it without his money. So, I expect they weren't good friends on that account."

A warm piney breeze swirled through the mine site. The underground had chilled her more than she realized, and it felt good to sit awhile in the sun. Some of the puzzle was beginning to come together, and that felt good, too. Rose had learned to plate out gold from the acid-mine effluent all around the district. And if she had in that way discovered a hidden potential of the district and was telling others about it—others whom someone would rather keep ignorant—then maybe that was enough to get her killed. But why Lonnie? They had to be connected, the two of them, but Ada could see no point in the killing of Lonnie Barr. Lonnie had sold the medallions for Rose but knew nothing of their making. The miners never spoke of him, and Maggie Li never mentioned his name.

"Did you know a kid named Lonnie Barr?" she asked.

"Heard the name maybe, but that's all."

"He was a good kid." She put down her notes, and with binoculars scanned the hills. Nothing. But then, looking off to the southeast, she paused at a cone-shaped mountain standing prominently in her field of view. She looked without the binoculars. The mountain was maybe three miles distant, forested to two-thirds of its height then grey and rocky to the top. A tiny nub sat at the crest. "Is that Greylock?" she asked.

"That'd be it."

With the binoculars, the nub was definitely the fire lookout. But it was too far away. Even with her binoculars, she was sure, no one could watch the comings and goings all the way down here. *But if he had a twenty-power theodolite!* She stared across the shadowy ridges between the lookout and the mine and, "By God, but it makes sense," she said.

"How's that?"

"Sorry, never mind." It was as simple as that: Rose had learned too much, and Lonnie Barr must have seen too much! Lonnie had to have seen who was stalking Rose—who wore the crescent-heeled boots.

And hell yes, Ada knew what was written in the missing letter. Her hands shook as she flipped through her notebook. There was something in one of her interviews with Corey, it was . . . Yes: *If I passed a letter on to a friend, gave him a heads-up, why shouldn't I?*

"A friend!" She jumped up and stowed the binoculars.

Pearen was haloed in golden afternoon light, his face in shadow. He said, "Can you prove who killed Rose, ya think?"

"I think I can, but not from here." She threw the rucksack over her shoulder but then walked to her truck, there being no real hurry.

8:45 p.m. – Down in The Bottoms

"THEY NO LONGER LOOK FOR TIMES TO IMPROVE, but vaguely wonder when times might end." From her knees, old Mrs. Li lifted and tossed a spade of soil, breathed heavily, and leaned on the shovel handle. "Still, no one—not one, I'm sure—has packed a suitcase."

"And have you packed a suitcase, Maggie?"

"Only metaphorically, I'm afraid."

The dredge had long shut down for the night, but the sky still glowed amber and green beyond the cone of Red Mountain. Ada leaned on the edge of a wheelbarrow and watched Li work. She said, "Rose packed a suitcase but did not leave. She had every reason to, but I think she became ensnared by a gold fever; seduced by it. She lost the meaning."

"Yes. I fear I may have helped her to that end."

"It wasn't your fault. You gave Rose the means of freedom. It was up to her to use it." A moon was working its way through the pine trees of the east ridge. Ada said, "Rose got caught up in the conflict, too, and the treachery."

"Yes, that as well. She could not let it go. She'd come too far to give in." Li looked up from her work. "You've come a long way yourself, Ada Reed. Don't repeat Rose's mistake."

Ada started to speak, but Li held up her hand and nodded to the south edge of her yard just as the ancient cherry tree finished its slow, arcuate plunge into the pond. Li turned, picked up a cherry sapling, and set its root ball gently into the hole she had dug.

"Do you think this one will fare any better in the long run?" Ada asked.

"Perhaps who follows me will know the answer. I can only do what I do and have faith that the sun will not burn out." With bare hands she pulled dirt into the hole, separated the roots of the small tree, and packed the dirt around. She asked, "What brings you here tonight, Ada? What are you planning to do?"

"I have to go onto the dredge tonight."

"Yes, I feared so. I wish you would not."

"I think I know who killed Rose and why Lonnie had to die too. But I have nothing yet to take to a grand jury; nothing to show. I have to go where Rose went. I have to see what she saw."

Li did not answer at once but stood with Ada's help and moved back toward the house. She wiped her hands on a garden apron and said, *"The fire you kindle for your enemy often burns you more than him."*

They paused for Li to catch her breath. "What does that mean?" Ada asked.

"I don't know, there are so many of the damned things."

Ada stared, and Li burst with laughter. Ada laughed until she cried. She asked, "Are you smoking dàmá?"

"Not tonight. I wish you would not go there. Rose is dead, you cannot bring her back." She closed her eyes and winced.

Ada dried her eyes and got serious. "Lonnie said you are sick. I think you're being poisoned."

"I've been poisoned. It has happened; there is nothing to do about it."

"Who poisoned you?"

"It is in the blood. My kidneys are dying—you can see my skin color. And the bones. It gets into the joints and hurts terribly." She sighed. "It is not what you think. Forty years in the assay labs did this to me. The fumes from heated ore samples often contain lead. I breathed in the fumes and the lead slowly accumulated. I will die from it now, if I don't drown first."

Ada picked up the lantern and helped Maggie into the house and onto the stuffed chair in the parlor. "Well, we can do something," she said. "We can get the companies to pay."

The old woman's head drooped, and her eyes barely reflected the lamplight. "I killed myself, Ada."

Ada started to speak a couple of times, but waited, and the two women sat quietly for a few minutes. "Margaret," she asked at last, "why did you say you were a whore? The first time we met you told me that."

Li looked away and rubbed her knees. When she turned back her eyes were clear and dry. She said, "Not every whore lies on her back. I gave to the mines and the mills all my integrity. I wanted to be wanted, and I was willing to do anything they asked." She looked up and smiled. "Do me a favor, Ada Reed."

"Of course."

"You will be sheriff."

"But I am the sheriff."

"When you are sheriff in your own heart, be no one's whore."

Chapter twenty-five

11:45 p.m. – The dredge

Aᴅᴀ Rᴇᴇᴅ ꜱᴋɪʀᴛᴇᴅ ᴛʜᴇ ᴘᴏɴᴅ, sᴛᴀʏɪɴɢ away from the sluffing edges. By starlight she found the bridge gate, but the pontoon gangplank was pulled hard in against the hull of the dredge, and the ropes and pulleys were locked up so she couldn't swing it over to shore. There was only one other way onto the barge, but it would be tricky. She made her way back along the grassy shore to where the bucket line was left in its last cut of the day. The waning gibbous moon had climbed above the eastern ridges, and in its glow the lip of the first bucket jutted just six feet from the edge of the grassy bank. She put her gun and flashlight into the rucksack and tossed the sack across.

Finding a solid foothold and marking it with her eye, she got a running start and leapt the open water. She caught one foot on the bucket edge but banged her other knee and her ribs as she landed. But she was aboard, sort of, and dry but for one leg.

In the midnight stillness, then, she climbed the line of empty buckets hand over hand, tossing the rucksack ahead, then leaping, swinging free, and pulling herself up and over the lip of each one. The moon lit her way, flooding the hills and forests above her with a soft silver light. But the climb was exhausting, with over twenty buckets to scale, and as she neared the top her arms and back ached, and she barely could swing a leg over the lip and drag herself into the next bucket. Still, she managed somehow to get to the top, and there she stared down into the black iron and timber maw of the dredge workings. Once inside, the moon would be of no further help.

With the rucksack on her back, she lowered herself over the edge of the bucket truss, feeling blindly for a knob or a rail to land a foot on. There was a trommel chute somewhere—how in hell did it all fit together? If she fell into the trommel she would be unable to get out on her own and would have to stay till morning and hope the workers found her before the boulders did. Her legs flailed in search of footholds, but eventually she was able to lower herself down onto Dar Colemaker's station platform. There she dared to pull out her flashlight, but wrapped a sock around the end of it to keep the beam low.

She would have to find the way through the factory by trial and error. A catwalk led her around the inclined trommel, and from there she felt her way between gear wheels and massive cable drums, rubbing against timbers in the dark and getting grease on her uniform—just as Rose must have done.

Would Rose have taken this same wandering path, or did she know the dredge? Had she learned the route? After what seemed forever, tripping and bumping, Ada found the stairs and ramps leading to the control room—the route she had followed out when she left in such humiliation on her last visit. Mansfield's office door was closed when she got to it, but it took just a second to jimmy the latch with her pocketknife.

The office was dark but for the moon streaming through the starboard windows. Ada checked all the dark corners and peeked into Mansfield's sleeping quarters. She was alone.

Inside the sleeping quarters a row of file cabinets stood along one wall, but she doubted what she was looking for would be filed. She dared to sweep the light around the room. The place looked different from when she'd first seen it. It was neat now. Shirts were hung properly with the right slacks and the right jackets; shoes were matched and lined up neatly where before they'd been heaped into the closet. Repairs had been made to a footlocker. It was as though the room had earlier been searched, and it had only been thrown back together—not really cleaned—when she'd seen it on her first visit.

And now that, too, made sense. Rose must have been there, and she had searched Mansfield's room. Ada clicked off her light and stood quietly in the darkness. Clearly, Rose had found what she was looking for. She could not have carried the medallions aboard. She could not have made the leap and then the climb up the bucket line wearing such a heavy belt. But she was wearing the belt when she went into the water. So, she had to have come looking for her chain of gold—the medallions she'd dropped when she was chased through the mine. And she'd found it.

Ada hurried to the window and peeked outside. All was as she'd left it. She held her ear to the bulkhead and listened. Water dripped, just faintly, from pipes and tanks on the production deck, and ripples licked against the steel hull. There was no other sound.

At the mahogany desk the top side drawer contained business files: receipts and bills, and letters to and from suppliers. The drawer below contained assay results from a dozen different properties, including Jubal Mason's, Cuss Pearen's, and the small mines above the roadhouse. She sat down in Mansfield's swivel chair for a moment and caught her breath, then pried the lock on the broad, flat desk drawer.

She found what she was looking for in the far back of the drawer. It was Lonnie Barr's journal, which she'd given back to him in Sunbeam, and which she'd not found at the lookout. Stuffed inside were three pages of a letter, crushed and wadded up, then smoothed again and folded. In the letter she read:

Dear Mr. Darcy . . . There's gold in them hills! It's so exciting,

*Aaron. But don't worry, I'm on my way. I should have my
travelling money soon now.*

Ada skimmed the lines; the letter was full of light heartedness,
but it got serious as well:

*. . . Lonnie says he saw Mansfield following me again, not an
hour after I left the Gold Coin. Just like at the Pirate's Gold,
Mansfield goes in while Colemaker stays out watching. . . .
Lonnie is keeping track of it, making a note now every time
he sees Mansfield following me.*

It was as she'd suspected, and as Rose must have feared. The
stalker had seen the letter mentioning Lonnie's sightings. She
fanned the pages of Lonnie's journal in the white light of the moon.
The last entries were in blue ink.

But this was not the place to sit and think things through. She
was on the enemy's turf now, and in as much danger as Rose had
been. She crept back to the starboard window, looked out, and
nearly cried aloud. The pontoon bridge, which had been hard in
against the hull, was now pulled over to the shore, and the gangway
gate stood open. She held her ear to the bulkhead again and heard
drips and ripples . . . and maybe the faintest steps.

She clicked off her flashlight, then stumbled back to the desk
and struggled to push the desk drawer back into its slides. With
her heart racing and her breath hardly able to keep up, she put the
letter and the book into her rucksack and hurried out of the office
and through the engineering room. She stopped again in a shadowed stairwell and held her ear to the iron wall. The steps were
real. They were not hesitant or furtive; he was coming straight on.
Just one person, she believed.

In the blackness but for shafts of moonlight, she made her
way back into the mechanical maze. Retreating slowly at first,

she backed over a catwalk and descended wooden steps, half the time having to feel her way through. But in her panic, she missed Colemaker's station and her bucket-line exit, and ended up dropping down all the way to the main deck. With no idea how to get back now, she crept forward between iron struts and massive timbers crisscrossing in the shadows like great traps and snares.

The enormity of the machinery and the broken half-light and darkness confused her, but she kept the moonlit windows to her right. That moved her generally toward the bow, she was sure, and toward the pontoon gangplank, her only remaining escape. A wet, greasy walkway barely gleaming in the light from sooted windows led her between massive piston pumps, still warm from the day's work, tilted shaker tables, and foul-smelling flotation tanks. Her breathing was loud in her ears, and she had to stop every few paces to hold her breath and listen for steps.

A breeze blew up the valley, tilting the deck and splashing ripples against the port-side hull. But it also blew a cloud across the moon, leaving her blind. She crawled under a shaker table still dripping with water and tripped over coil after coil of rubber hose as she slowly worked her way forward.

Just as she reached the open deck, a metal gate clanged shut like a rifle shot. She cried out, then quickly ducked into a deep shadow, pressed her ear to a beam, and held her breath to listen. The steps sounded clearer and closer, then stopped.

She dropped to a knee and fumbled for her service revolver. The moonlight had returned, but it lit only a small portion of the bow; most remained in darkness and half-shadow. A slight movement caught the corner of her eye, and a dim figure stopped in the shadows behind the bow gantry pillar. The man was barely silhouetted against the night sky, waiting just a dozen steps from her, between her and the gangplank.

From one knee she pointed the gun. "Move into the light please," she said. The loudness of her own voice startled her. The silhouette didn't move. She aimed her gun at the shadow. "Don't make me fire a warning shot when I can't see you clearly. You might not like the outcome."

The man stepped casually to the edge of the moonlight, his hands clasped behind his back. Ada stood slowly and stepped from the shadows as well. "Mr. Mansfield," she said, "what are you doing on the dredge so late at night?"

"I might ask the same of you, Ada. I was having a drink in town—business, you know—when I heard there might be a prowler moving about on my property."

She waved her gun at his hands behind his back, and he grinned and dropped them to his side. "Why would I be armed?" he asked.

"Dee, I'd like you to move over into the moonlight, please."

"Silliness. So much silliness. But Charlie Ibarra will be in town tomorrow morning. We'll have a quorum, and your amusing little adventure will be over."

She raised the revolver and pointed it at his chest. He laughed but raised his hands theatrically and took four paces to his left. His heels clicked across the iron deck. They made a metallic sound that made Ada's head snap around and her breath escape almost in a laugh. "Turn around and raise your right foot for me" she said. "Just bend at the knee."

"What the hell is this about, Ada."

"I just want to see for myself."

He faced away from her and bent his leg, raising his boot until the moon glinted on a crescent of metal, about two inches across. "You wear taps on your heels," she said as evenly as she could.

"Of course, they're . . ." He paused and leaned his hand against a slender pole. "They're hundred-dollar boots. Certainly, I want to protect them."

"You stomped on her hands, you son-of a bitch!" Ada shuffled her feet and sniffed. She could feel the old ache rising in her chest and her eyes beginning to tear up. "Turn and face me, goddamn you!"

"I don't know what you're talking about." He turned, still smiling, and leaned on the pole with his other hand.

"Did you push Rose Braden into the water, or did she fall trying to get away from you?" Ada backed a step, still holding the gun on him. "It doesn't matter. Mr. Mansfield, you're under arrest for the murders of Rose Braden and Lonnie Barr."

He whistled. "Anyone else you want to add in the mix?"

"I wish I could hang you for Corey Braden, too." She backed another step.

"Stop and hear how silly you sound, Ada."

"Killing Rose wasn't even planned, was it? But the little trouble-maker was right there, trespassing on your dredge, and suddenly she was in the water. Instead of helping her, you stomped your boot down on her hands!" Ada wiped tears from her eyes. "Then what, Dee? Lonnie Barr saw you following her, so you had to get rid of him, too?"

"Interesting plot. It sounds like a Lash Larue adventure." He grinned, squared his shoulders, and stood casually with his hand on the pole.

She took another step back and nearly stumbled.

"A handful of ridiculous charges with not a shred of proof. I guess this is why some jobs are left to the boys." His eyes panned left and right, shifting from the sheriff, who stood now in a half crouch, to the equipment and crates littering the deck. "Are you going to stand in front of a jury and tell them to convict me because I wear taps on my boots?" He sneered. "They'll laugh you out of town; they'll laugh in the papers, in the barber shops. Monty's name—Major Montgomery Reed's name—will be made a laughingstock!"

The long pole he had his hand on shifted, and a heavy iron hook glinted in the moonlight. "Take your hand off the gaff, Dee," she said.

"Or what?"

"Or I'll shoot you."

"Do you even know how to fire that thing Madam Sheriff?"

"I've been practicing."

He shifted his weight to his left foot. "You'll never get a conviction. You must know that. Just a lot of laughter."

"You might be right. I don't know if I can prove you killed Rose."

Mansfield shrugged.

Ada's arm began to tire holding the big revolver, and it drooped slightly in front of her. She said, "Except, I think you made a mistake after all." She forced a smile and saw Mansfield's eyes open just slightly and his grin lose a little of its satisfaction. She said, "I'm going to send Barr's journal out for fingerprints."

"Fingerprints on paper?" He laughed. "Learn your profession, lady."

"The book you gave me, Dee—*Modern Methods of Criminal Investigation?*—I think the FBI can get some prints." A trickle of sweat stung her eye. "Colemaker did that job for you, didn't he? I bet we'll find his prints on the journal, too."

The pole rotated slightly, and again the hook glinted in the moonlight, catching her attention for just a moment. When she glanced back down Mansfield's face had changed. "Be careful, Ada," he said. "You're on tricky footing."

"Your problem is Colemaker's not quite dumb enough to take the rap by himself."

"Take the rap? For God's sake, now we're in a Mickey Spillane novel."

"What's your plan for Colemaker, how's he going to come out of all this?"

Mansfield's poker face failed him completely. Between shallow breaths he said, "I'm going to need Barr's journal. And I expect you have the girl's letter as well."

"The girl's name was Rose."

A cloud crossed over the gibbous moon and the deck went dark. When the moon returned a second later, Mansfield had grasped the pole with both hands and was leaning heavily into it. Ada realized only dreamily a blow was coming meant for her. At the last instant she dodged to her left, but her foot caught against a heavy pulley, and she tumbled into coils of rope just as the gaff crashed down where she'd been standing, smashing her ankle. A sharp pain shot up her leg, and she rolled off the ropes onto the iron deck. The gun jarred from her fingers and slid into the shadows.

She dragged herself behind a stack of wooden cases and struggled to quiet her breathing. The shadows returned, and then quickly moonlight, and then shadows again. She couldn't see Mansfield from her hiding place, but she could hear his bootheels. The clacking and scraping of metal on metal told her he'd moved to his right and pivoted, just a few feet away. She waited a second more, then on one good leg dove across a patch of moonlight and grabbed up her gun.

Mansfield wheeled, and swung the pole. Ada judged the angle and crouched low, letting a wooden crate take most of the blow. Still, it knocked the wind from her. He raised the gaff and swung again. This time, unable to dodge to the side, she dove forward under the crashing pole. From her belly on the iron deck, she raised the revolver with both hands, cocked the hammer, and squeezed.

The flash registered first: Mansfield standing over her lit brightly in stop-action, like an old-time movie poster. Then the explosion reached her ears and a hard kick travelled through her hands and down her arms and shoulders, clacking her teeth together. Powder smoke burned her nose just as she noticed the change in Mansfield. His face turned from hateful to shocked, and in that instant it struck Ada as strange that after all he'd done he could still be shocked.

With the first echo the gaff fell from his hands, and Mansfield stumbled back, arms whipping a backstroke through the air. She hopped up and limped to the edge of the deck in time to see the splash recede and the body resurface. It floated a moment in the undulating moonlight off the starboard bow, arms and legs spread, eyes wide, and bubbles escaping the mouth. She lowered the gun to her side and watched Dee Mansfield sink boots-first into his own dark slough.

CHAPTER TWENTY-SIX

21 August 1951, Custer, Idaho
Wrapping up loose ends in the Yankee Fork case.

"I SAW YOU PLASTERED ALL OVER LADIES' *Home Journal*," Maggie Li said. "It was quite the spread.

"You read *Ladies' Home Journal*?"

"I live alone, Ada. That doesn't make me a hermit."

The two women sat at a round oak table, front and center in the Pinyon Bar on Main Street in Custer. Ada had limped over and jerked the blinds open when they'd first entered the bar, and the sudden light had sent a handful of grizzled old men scurrying to the corners of the room, freeing up the table. The old boys stared out from the shadows saying little, barely touching their beers. Ada sipped a brandy sidecar; Li had sent the bartender scrambling to his cocktail book to prepare a Singapore sling.

Li said, "You're a movie star, you know. The *Home Journal*, like the others, focused more on your feminine characteristics than on the downfall of a captain of industry. 'Men kill every day,' the editor seemed fond of saying, 'but a woman who shoots back is news.'"

Ada rolled her eyes.

"When did you get back to Town?" Li asked.

"I got back Sunday night. The Governor's commission wrapped up sooner than expected." She looked down with a grim smile. "Mansfield's shooting was found to be justified, as expected, as found in all the previous hearings."

Li nodded her approval. "That was fast for a bunch of politicians and doorknob polishers."

"Yes, well . . ." Ada sipped her cocktail and sighed. She had spent the last half of July and most of August with her foot in a cast sitting through closed-door hearings and open-door hearings and the recent showboating in Boise. The hearings had all started with great noise and arm-waving, and all had ended quietly amid whispers of ledgers, and letters, and names found in Mansfield's safe. In between, she'd boiled buckets of coffee for the local criminologists and chinwaggers, and answered hundreds of questions put to her by an army of reporters who descended on unsuspecting Camas, Idaho. She was tired.

"And the deaths of Rose and her young friend, Lonnie?" Li asked. "What of them?"

They'd had to row Rose's coffin across the dredge pond on the day of the funeral because the last isthmus of land had sluffed away, and Li's house sat precariously upon an island. They buried her in Maggie's flower garden. Ada stood through the service on crutches with Ben McGann on one side of her and Kellen Munson on the other. Cuss and Jubal and a few others had cleaned themselves up and crossed the water for Rose, but the rest of the good folks of Custer stayed home. Young Aaron Niedermeyer delivered the sermon even though he was weak from travel and grief. He'd come two days and two nights by bus after Ada's telephone call. He was so handsome and so gentle when Ada finally met him that she cried all over again.

She sat up and, twisting in her seat, looked around the stale, dusty barroom, peering into the dark corners at the timid old men so done with their lives. No one would meet her eyes. Rose had been so full of life—the best of them, the best ever to come from this faded old town. How in God's name could she ever let the girl go? She dropped her eyes and took a deep breath. "The grand jury found both their deaths to be homicide, and Mansfield was confirmed the likely killer. Colemaker testified; he'll serve three years for complicity." She sighed and swirled the ice cubes in her glass. "And that is that."

Li said, "It's best to let it be over."

"Yes, let it be." What else could she do but let it be? Three young people dead, and nothing gained in return for their lives; nothing at all to make up for the beauty and the lost promise. And she, having witnessed it all and having to be the one to remember and make sense of it all, she now had to put her own life back together. Or maybe let that be over, too. Maybe instead, build anew, because there was damned little she could see of her old life worth returning to.

"I got a letter from Montgomery last week," she said. "A short one—Mansfield was his best friend, you know." She squeezed her eyes shut for just a moment, then shrugged. "He signed on to extend his commission. He says he can't leave the boys in the mess they're in."

Li nodded and sipped her cocktail. "I suppose that's for the best, as well."

"I wrote back to him. 'I never go dancing anymore because the music is hollow,' I told him, 'And the movie theater and the country club are dull, and socials don't interest me in the least.' I said I understand why he has to stay, and I pray for his safety."

Li did not answer, but studied the antler chandeliers and the deer trophies on the wall.

"Not a word of it is untrue," Ada said.

"I know. And now what are you going to do, Ada Reed?"

She blew a strand of hair out of her face and chuckled. "I'm going to sleep for a week. And then . . ." She emptied her glass. "Uncle Ephraim and Aunt Corrine won't like it, but Ethel is going to help me with the paperwork. I'm going to file, Maggie. I'm going to stand for sheriff in the November election."

Maggie Li, spotting the sun glinting on fine carvings of the old mahogany bar, smiled and nodded. "I know you are," she said. And after a moment, "She'd have grown up much like you."

Authors Note

WHEN I WORKED IN THE YANKEE FORK forty years ago, I camped with my friends in the old townsite of Custer. From there we hiked out daily to map the geology of the surrounding hills and to work out the mineralogy of the mining district. There were no tourists then, just us and a half dozen old codgers still winning a little pay from the rocks. The Sunbeam store, eight miles downriver, sold cold beer, and you could get a fine steak at Torrey's Hole down on Highway 75. For dancing and over-drinking, we'd head to Stanley and *Casanova Jack's Rod and Gun Club*.

The miles of tailings behind the dredge had not yet been smoothed and re-contoured for fish passage, and the road up the Yankee Fork was not nearly so wide and accommodating. The Yankee Fork dredge floated in its pond, not yet kid-proofed and commissioned as an attraction. It was inaccessible—it might even have been posted *No Trespassing* (I admit nothing). But one evening after a visit to the Sunbeam store, one of our crew bet that he could leap the six feet from shore to the first bucket without getting wet. He couldn't, but I could, and we and a couple others climbed the bucket line to the top, then clambered down into the guts of that river monster.

In dim light through dirt-streaked windows we balanced

along beams, ducked under struts, and climbed onto high cat-walks. Cobbles sat on the beltline and sand lay in the riffles of the shaker table just as they'd been left when the engines shut down and the men walked away a generation earlier. We found boots and slickers and shift report books, and notes scribbled on office walls by long-extinct foremen and engineers. We talked little and took nothing, not even photos. But I've never forgotten the feel or even the smell of that Ozymandian place nor the sense of a world and a time before my own inhabited by fathers and hardy aunts and uncles—tall people with tall tales of how life once was lived.

I've tried to put a little of those feelings and that sense into Ada's story. And it is just that: a story. It is pure fiction, and any resemblance to happenings or to tall people living or dead is pure coincidence.

In this book again I've shown no respect for geography. Custer actually sits a mile farther upstream than I, for convenience, put it; I short-changed Bonanza, and Camas doesn't exist (well, it does, but not by that name). Finally, the main road up the canyon was not designated Highway 75 back in 1951. It was called U.S. 93 until 1977, and the current U.S. 93 was designated Alt-93. But imagine the spitting and fussing if I tried to stick to those historical particulars.

Anyway, that's all just detail. I have been true to the geology, and as ever, that is what matters.

ROGER HOWELL WAS RAISED IN a somewhat migratory family and mostly in a score of houses in Boise, Idaho Falls,
Aberdeen, Cobalt, Butte, La Push, and Baker. There were a couple of wall tents along the way, and a Studebaker for a very short
time. Things settled down eventually, and he attended Boise State
University, U.C. Santa Barbara, Gonzaga University, and Clemson
University. Notwithstanding an international career as a geologist
and environmental engineer, Howell has lived and worked all over
the western U.S. He has walked the two-track roads and danced
and drank and fished the length of the Rockies. Not coincidentally,
his stories tend to be set in small towns in the west, and usually take
place in the mid-century—a time of prosperity and innocence, but
also of paranoia and prejudice. A father of two, he lives in Santa Fe
now with his wife and their second-hand dog.